Enjoy!

DEADMAN'S FURY

(THE DEADMAN BOOK 2)

LINELL JEPPSEN

Linell Jeppsen

WOLFPACK PUBLISHING
— EST 2013 —

Deadman's Fury

Paperback Edition
Copyright © 2019 Linell Jeppsen

Wolfpack Publishing
6032 Wheat Penny Avenue
Las Vegas, NV 89122

wolfpackpublishing.com

Paperback ISBN 978-1-64119-518-8
eBook ISBN 978-1-62918-292-6

DEADMAN'S FURY

AMELIA

AMELIA WINTERS STEPPED OFF THE TRAIN AND GAZED AT the dusty little town with delight. Her adventure had begun and she wanted to twirl around on tiptoe with excitement. She was on her way to live with her Auntie Iris and her family while going to nursing school about twenty miles outside of Spokane. Although Amelia had been helping her father—Dr. Lewis Winters—in his small medical practice in Marysville, Washington since she was twelve years old, he had decided he needed someone to assist in real medical work like surgeries, triage and post-surgical care.

The logical choice for surgical assistant had been Amelia's older brother, James. Indeed, Lewis Winters had groomed his son for the position but James had enlisted in the army four years ago and was subsequently killed in an avalanche along with twelve other Cavalry officers while on assignment.

Although Amelia's heart still stuttered occasionally

with grief at the loss of her handsome older brother, she was thrilled with the prospect of learning her father's skills and possibly becoming a doctor in her own right. After all, it was 1892. A bright new future— a whole new century—was just around the corner and she, for one, was ready to embrace all the possibilities.

Her daydreams were interrupted by the conductor, a wizened old man with an enormous pocket watch in hand, who said, "Miss, you can go into the café with the others for refreshments. And if you need the necessary," he cleared his throat in embarrassment, "it's right behind the building…you can see the corner of it, just there."

He pointed and Amelia saw the edge of an outhouse behind the larger café/post and telegraph office. Even as she watched, a small, dirty pony bearing a small, dirty man tore around the disembarking passengers and pulled to a stop in front of the post office section of the building in a cloud of dust.

"Thank you, sir," she said politely and stepped forward a few paces to join her fellow passengers. Mrs. Dorothy Jones, a widow, had stopped and was impatiently waiting for Amelia to catch up.

"One must not dawdle when traveling alone, young lady," the plump, middle-aged woman admonished.

"I am sorry, Mrs. Jones!" Amelia exclaimed. "The conductor…"

"Never you mind," Mrs. Jones interrupted. "Just stay close by my side. This is a wild place, as are all of these little towns east of the Cascades. My son told me to step sharp and keep an eye out for riff-raff while on my way to his home."

She sniffed, adding, "Since your father saw fit to send his daughter into the wilds all alone, I feel it is my duty to serve as chaperone until you are well met at the train station in Spokane."

It was all Amelia could do to keep from rolling her eyes, but she meekly followed the older woman into the café and sat next to her at a table. The widow Jones was nice, if over-protective, and although she was sure she could navigate her way from the train depot in Marysville to the depot in Spokane, Amelia did not have the heart to be rude or rebuff the woman's good intentions.

Her bladder was starting to protest; although the train was new, the only accommodations were chamber pots hidden behind a canvas curtain for the men and a smelly bench behind another curtain for the womenfolk.

Amelia figured it was the conductor's job to keep the bench—with its hole that gave a clear view of the tracks whizzing by under the train's wheels—clean, but he was so old and frail-looking, she wondered if he was shirking his duties. There were odious brown streaks all over it and the odor was unbelievable.

Besides that, Amelia had wondered how on Earth she was supposed to squat over that horrid hole with her corset, petticoat and heavy layered skirt. She was determined to be as pretty and fresh as possible—not to stink like a chamber pot—when she met her relatives at the train depot.

Pulling a photograph out of her small, beaded handbag, Amelia studied the two people who would be picking her up at the station and whose roof she would share for the next year. Her auntie was beautiful in the black and white image. Amelia remembered Iris well, although she hadn't seen her in a long time.

Iris had long, curly auburn hair much like Amelia's, ginger freckles and merry brown eyes. She always smelled like flowers and her white teeth sparkled often with mirth. In this photograph, Iris held a young child in her arms. The baby wore a white baptismal gown and seemed to be wailing at something or another while his parents grinned in resignation.

Amelia grinned, too. Photographers often told people to sit very still while having their likeness taken and, above all, never smile. Her Auntie and Uncle did not seem to care at all about the rules of photography as their amusement was plainly obvious. Squinting at the dog-eared picture, Amelia acknowledged the only reason she knew the baby was a boy was that Iris had written and told her so. *Chance Jonathon Wilcox* was his name and Amelia could not wait to meet him, although by now that screaming infant was almost five years old.

The young woman traced her finger over the face of Matthew Wilcox, her auntie's husband. As always, two things struck her simultaneously. First, Matthew Wilcox was one of the handsomest men she had ever seen.

Second, he was one of the most frightening men she had ever laid eyes on. She had heard, of course, about the "Granville Stand-off" and she had even read about what her Uncle Matthew had done to stop Top Hat and his gang of thugs six years ago in a penny-dreadful.

Maybe that is what made her see such menace in his handsome countenance but Amelia didn't think so. Although he stood tall and straight and had a fine, strong body, there was something about the look in his eyes and the set of his lips that made her blood run cold. She had no way of knowing what color those wide, pretty eyes were or what made his stare so fierce despite his grin, but there seemed to be a sort of gloom about him... a dark shadow.

Amelia shivered and prayed she never gave him reason to be angry with her; she also prayed that he was not too strict when she moved into his home. But Iris had written and said that she couldn't be happier with her husband so Amelia felt confident that this hard-faced man was kind at heart…at least she hoped so. Still, she jumped a little in her chair as a tray of tea was set down on the table along with some milk, butter and a small plate of muffins.

"Well, it's about time, I say!" Mrs. Jones grumbled. "I was beginning to think the train would leave before we had time to eat lunch." She eagerly plucked a muffin from the plate and grabbed a knife.

Amelia was famished as well but she could ignore her bladder no longer. Regretfully, she pushed her chair back and said, "I *must* use the facilities, Mrs. Jones. I won't be long."

The stout woman glanced her way and muttered, "I will come with you if you like…"

Amelia saw the look of frustrated hunger in her companion's eyes as she held her butter-laden knife in the air and she shook her head. "No, that's alright, ma'am. I'll only be a minute."

Stepping outside, Amelia moved down the board-walk toward the outhouse. She plucked at the lace of her shirtwaist as sweat sprang up on her skin and trickled between her breasts. *It is the middle of September and still hot as blazes,* she thought and then stifled a gasp as a man came around the corner of the building and bumped into her, causing her to back up a step.

The tall, barrel-chested man grabbed her by the upper arm and said, "Pardon me, miss…didn't see you standing there."

Amelia tried looking up into his face but the sun was directly behind him so his features were silhou-etted in darkness.

Yet there was no harm done and she *really* needed to relieve herself, so she smiled up at the stranger and said, "That's quite all right, sir. Excuse me, please."

He released her arm and she stepped off the side-walk onto a dirt path and into the outhouse that she observed with approval. Unlike the train, this building seemed spanking clean with a private stall, a deep basin sink sitting next to a water barrel with its own hand pump, and a cracked but serviceable mirror.

Amelia stepped into the cubicle, heaved up her skirt, unbuttoned the lower part of her corset, pulled down her petticoat and sighed with relief. Watching an industrious spider spin a web by the ceiling, she heard the door to the outhouse open and then water being drawn into the sink.

"I'll be done in just a moment!" she called.

A woman replied, "Take your time, m'dear. I'm just fetching some water."

The voice sounded foreign, perhaps Irish, and Amelia hastened to finish her business and get back to a couple of those muffins before Mrs. Jones ate them all. Corset buttoned, petticoat and skirt back in order, she stepped out of the stall and saw a very tall older lady standing by the sink.

The woman might once have been pretty but now she looked hot, dusty, and tired. She had black hair liberally streaked with gray and slightly-slanted blue eyes; however, whatever beauty she might have once possessed was obscured by crow's feet and bitter, downturned lips.

There were a number of canteens and water receptacles lined up on a narrow shelf above the sink. Although Amelia wanted to wash her hands, she hesitated to disturb the woman's task. As though sensing the girl's discomfort, the woman—whose name was Margaret Donnelly—stepped away and said, "Please, help yourself."

Smiling, Amelia replied, "Thank you," and pumped the lever for more water, washing her hands with a sliver of harsh lye soap from the shelf. Two rumpled towels hung from wooden nails by the sink and, as she stepped toward them, she glanced into the cracked mirror and saw the lady suddenly come up behind her.

At five feet six inches, Amelia was tall for a seventeen-year-old girl. But as Margaret grabbed her from behind and wrapped her left arm around her chest, Amelia realized that the woman was huge...maybe six feet and frightfully strong.

She squealed in alarm but Margaret placed a wet, smelly rag over her mouth. Panting in fear, Amelia locked eyes in the mirror with her captor; the older woman gazed back and smiled as the girl's eyes grew dim and then closed.

Placing her "catch" on the floor, Margaret stepped quickly to the door and hissed, "You there, Patrick?"

"I am," her brother answered. "You got her ready?"

"Just about...hurry up, now!"

Margaret Donnelly tied Amelia's hands together and tucked the little bitch's fancy reticule into her own carpetbag along with the water bottles. She heard the surrey pull around to the front of the building and then a quick two-tap on the wooden door. Unlatching the hook from the door, she let Patrick inside and watched as he grabbed the girl's limp body from the floor and placed her in the back of their closed carriage.

Margaret looked around, making sure that nothing of hers was left behind. Then she climbed into the back of the carriage with the girl. All the heavy canvas drapes were tied down so neither she nor her captive were visible. She felt Patrick step up onto the front bench and then heard him snap his whip above the rumps of the horses.

Within moments, Patrick and Margaret Donnelly—along with their latest victim—were trotting down the dusty road. Taking her Da's pocket watch out of her coat, Margaret checked the time. Eight minutes...a record!

Of course, the brother and sister team had done this many times before and as Da always said, "Practice makes perfect."

2

MATTHEW AND IRIS

"But, Mama, I really want to go with you!" Abigail wailed.

Iris stared out the kitchen window, willing herself to be patient with her thirteen-year-old daughter...especially now that the girl had started her menses. Every little obstacle, every single frustration was amplified in her daughter's mind lately and Abigail was not afraid to share her malcontent with everyone in the house.

Turning to her red-cheeked offspring, Iris said, "Abby dear, you *know* that someone has to teach school today and that someone is you! Your father and I had planned on going to the train station alone to meet your cousin Amelia. The only reason your brother is going is to pick up the oats that are arriving on the train!"

"Well, Sam *always* gets to go places while I'm stuck here at home!" Abby cried. The girl's red curls were tousled and her pretty hazel eyes awash with tears.

Still, she was a real beauty with a normally sweet disposition. Iris took two steps forward and wrapped her arms around her weeping daughter.

"Please don't cry so much, honey. You'll make your eyes all puffy. Don't you want Amelia to see you at your best? She will be so proud that you can run a classroom all by yourself but upset, I think, if she sees how much you resent it."

Abby stepped back a pace and angrily swiped the tears from her cheeks. "I do NOT resent teaching the children, Mother! I just...just...oh! Never mind!" She turned and ran down the hallway.

A few moments later, Iris heard the sound of splashing water and knew that, for now, another teenage crisis had been averted. Walking back toward the kitchen window and the dish-filled sink underneath it, she sighed. Grabbing a washcloth, Iris thought about the day ahead.

It was only a five-mile trek into town and the train station. Amelia would need a few minutes to freshen up and then she and Matthew would take her to Minnie's Restaurant for luncheon, while fifteen-year-old Samuel and her ranch foreman Lenny Michaels, loaded the wagon with oats.

Iris made a mental note to buy extra meat pies for Lenny and Samuel to eat on the way back home, and to visit the mercantile to see if the book she had ordered for Abby—"Mary Midthorn"—had arrived yet. She smiled. With its romance and derring-do, that novel would wipe the frown from her daughter's face.

Finishing the breakfast dishes, Iris opened the cold cellar and double-checked tonight's supper preparations: German potato salad, pickled beets (Matthew's favorite), fresh-baked dinner rolls and a succulent ham were all ready to serve. Iris knew that her good friend Louise Smithers was bringing a chocolate cake by for dessert and she nodded her head in satisfaction.

Everything is as ready as it can be, except for me! She thought. The only clothing she wore now was her union suit, an ankle-length canvas milking skirt and apron. She started to step back when two large, warm hands cupped her breasts. Iris gasped at the familiar, warm flutter of passion that throbbed in her belly.

"Is this how you're going to greet your niece, wife?" Matthew's soft voice tickled her right ear as his thumbs caressed her nipples, causing them to stand at attention like soldiers at the ready. She groaned and spun around, rising on her toes to meet his smiling lips with her own.

Iris and Matthew had been married for almost five years and her body still trembled with desire at his slightest touch. He had just taken a bath and shaved for the special trip into town and she rubbed her cheek against his.

"You smell delicious, husband. Is this the cologne I bought you?"

Matthew smiled. "I was worried that I smelled like a fancy boy in a parlor house but this stuff is okay. I can bear it if you can."

Iris had purchased it from the barbershop in town.

The owner claimed it was the newest men's fragrance out of Paris but she didn't know, or care, about French fashion. She only knew that she loved the cologne's earthy smell of bergamot and musk and had made the purchase on the spot.

Now, she wanted to eat her beautiful, young husband alive but she sighed and stepped back from his reach. "We must be going soon and I really do need to get dressed," she said.

Matthew grinned and let her go, unmolested. "May I have a rain check, Mrs. Wilcox?"

Iris laughed. "You can count on it, Mr. Wilcox."

Then the silence was shattered by the jubilant shouts of her youngest son, Chance. "Mama! Mama! Look what Papa found!"

Her chubby five-year-old had run into the kitchen and plunked a tin cup on the table. He stared up at her with excitement shining in his beautiful green eyes. His hair, as always, stood up in strawberry-blonde cowlicks and his nose was black with mud.

Grabbing a washcloth, Iris bent over and scrubbed the dirt off her son's nose. Then she peeked into the cup that was teeming with polliwogs and exclaimed, "Ooooh, they're lovely! Now you must put them back in the pond and get ready for school."

"Oh, Mama. I don't wanna go to school!" he cried.

Matthew said, "Maybe not, but you will go anyway. Don't you want to grow up smart like your brother and sister?"

Besides his parents, the two people in the world

Chance loved and admired above all were his older siblings. Frowning thoughtfully, his shoulders slumped. "Okay, I'll go," he grumbled.

Matthew was almost ready to leave; he wore his suit pants and dress boots. The only thing he needed to put on was his shirt and tie. Iris, on the other hand, wasn't ready at all and she needed to hurry if they were to be on time for the train's arrival.

"Mattie, will you help Chance clean up a little and make sure he makes it to class?" she pleaded.

"Of course," he answered. "You better hurry, though. You have a date to keep...two dates, actually," he added, winking.

Iris hurried away to get dressed and Matthew washed his son's face with a soapy cloth. Then, checking for mud stains on the boy's clothes, he shrugged and led Chance out the back door and about two-hundred feet to the little one-room schoolhouse he had had built for the farm kids in the area.

Abby was already there, and she smiled as her step-father and little brother stepped inside. Three other children were also in attendance and Chance ran to meet them, hollering, "Look what Papa let me bring for Show and Tell!"

Matthew could see more children approaching from the south end of the ranch and he moved close to his stepdaughter. "We'll be back soon...no later than three-o-clock, I think. Will you be okay by yourself?"

The girl frowned for a second, then grinned and

said, "Of course, Papa! I want Cousin Amelia to be proud of me when she comes."

Matthew started to say, "Of course she'll be proud…" but Abby had walked away and was placing schoolbooks on the desks.

———

Two hours later, Matthew, Iris, Samuel, Lenny Michaels, and an old wolf named Bandit arrived at the train station in a buckboard. Iris stared at the tiny, gold watch-necklace Matthew had bought her last year for Christmas and said, "I can hardly believe we made it on time!"

"Oh ye of little faith." Matthew laughed, to which Iris arched an eyebrow.

"You really shouldn't mock the pastor, Matthew. I have a hard enough time convincing the children to attend church on Sundays without you making fun of the sermons."

Matthew nodded, but turned away with a grin. Gesturing to his stepson he said, "Samuel, since the train hasn't arrived yet, why don't you head over to the confectioner's shop?" Handing a few coins over, he added, "Pick up a pound of buttercreams…no, a pound and a half. You and Lenny can share the half pound. We'll make the pound a welcome gift to your cousin."

Samuel, a tall and gangly youth with a gap-toothed grin and light brown eyes and hair, smiled broadly and said, "Yes, sir!" Turning to the ranch foreman, he said, "Come on, Mr. Michaels, before Ma says no!"

Iris smiled and said, "Go ahead, but don't tarry. The train should be here any minute." She watched fondly as her oldest son scampered off down the road and her hired man limped after him. Then she turned to her husband and looped her arm through his.

"You are a kind and generous man, Matthew. Thank you."

Sheriff Wilcox gazed down at his wife's face and thanked *his* lucky stars. Iris wore a spotless white blouse and a new skirt - a yellow concoction with tiny black and red bouquets scattered on the background like wildflowers in an autumn pasture. Her red hair was plaited down her back and she wore a straw boater-style hat. At thirty-four years old, Iris could still pass for a young girl.

Bandit whined and leaned his weight against Matthew's legs. His beloved wolf had grown old and sometimes suffered the effects of arthritis or too much heat. Leading Iris and Bandit up onto the boardwalk of the train station, Matthew said, "Looks like the train is running late again. We might as well sit in the shade while we wait."

Knowing that her husband worried over his pet, she gladly sat on one of the benches and rubbed Bandit's ears as he sat down with a groan between the two humans he loved. She also worried about the old wolf and dreaded the day when they might find him curled up under his favorite tamarack tree, dead.

Twenty minutes had passed when Sam and Lenny returned. Surprisingly, her son had not eaten all the chocolates and offered what remained in the bag to his parents. They made small talk for a little while and then Matthew rose and said, "I'll go in and see what the delay is."

Stepping inside the depot, he saw Trevor Maddock shake his head. "I don't know why the train is late, Sheriff. Until we get that telegraph we were promised during the last election, I can't find out unless someone goes down the street and sees for themself."

Maddock had been a sourpuss for as long as Matthew could remember and age had not mellowed his flavor one bit. He cleared his throat and said, "Would you like me to head down to the telegraph office?"

Maddock glared. "No! Train is only a half hour behind. And I heard the wood chute in Ellensburg has been acting up lately. More broken promises..."

Matthew tipped his hat and backed out the door. It was true that state funding was sporadic and some of the bigger oaths sworn by the rail companies were nothing more than a ploy to buy land on the cheap for their trains. Still, things did happen. Wood for the fuel needed to raise steam sometimes came up missing or the wood-chutes malfunctioned. Sometimes, especially during the heat of summer, wells ran dry which caused a shortage of water for the trains to function properly.

He sent Samuel to the mercantile to fetch a book and some victuals for lunch, and then settled by Iris's side to wait. And wait...for another hour and a half. Finally, they heard a distant whistle and saw the smoke rising out of a train about a mile to the east.

They all stood up in preparation for the train's arrival, but then Matthew saw his deputy and best friend Roy Smithers trotting quickly down Main Street toward them. Staring up into Roy's face, Matthew didn't like what he saw.

Excusing himself, he stepped off the boardwalk and approached the deputy who clutched a yellow piece of paper in his hand. Roy's long, bony face and mild blue eyes were set in a familiar expression—a look Matthew knew all too well, although he had not seen it for many years.

"What's wrong, Roy?" he asked as his deputy slid down off his horse.

Roy looked down at his boots for a moment and then he handed the telegraph to the sheriff. "Looks like someone nabbed your niece, boss."

3

THE DONNELLY'S

In the year of our Lord 1848, twins—Patrick and Margaret—were born unto Sean and Moira O'Donnell in a small hamlet just outside of Kilkenny, Ireland. Their first years of life were blessed with love and plenty. Then the great potato blight devastated the green island, bringing both low- and high-born to their knees in starvation and desperation.

At first, Sean O' Donnell thought that he and his family would weather the storm. He was not a potato farmer—he didn't even care for spuds—but a fisherman by trade and had been successful in his endeavors with two small but sturdy boats and a busy stall in the market square just a stone's throw away from the great St. Canice Cathedral.

What he did not count on were the long-term effects of the diseased crops and the toll it would take on his friends and neighbors. His best customers had no money because they had nothing of value to sell.

This meant they could not afford to supplement their meager food stores with fresh fish.

Day after day, Sean's boats brought fresh salmon, haddock and trout to the docks, only to have the seafood spoil and rot on the oilskin-covered tables in Moira's stall. One by one, the other stalls at the market closed; the tinsmith, the flower-seller, the apothecary and the baker left and never came back until the only stall left open was Patrick's fishery.

He dismissed the crew of his largest boat and put it into dry-dock. Then, he let the men that piloted his other boat go. After that, Sean and his son took the smaller vessel and fished the river Rone for trout or river salmon. He knew those fish would bring no profit. At this point, he fished simply because it was the only thing he could think of to do.

Whatever bounty he brought in from the river at night he now gave to the starving people...his friends and neighbors who wandered about the market with hollow, terror-stricken eyes. For months, Sean and his family helped ease the pang of hunger from their fellow citizen's bellies until one night he caught sight of his young wife bent over her table, scrubbing oil, scales and fish guts off the surface with harsh lye soap.

Moira was a pretty cailin, almost as tall as he was, with rich black hair and bright blue eyes. She had always been a little stout but now Sean saw that she had become a shadow of herself. Her skin hung off her bones and her eyes were ringed in shadow. Wearing her shawl although the evening was warm, he watched as she shivered with chill.

"Wife, what ails ye?" he asked.

"Oh, it's nothing, Sean. Just purely tired is all," she answered.

He called to his children who were floating bits of wood on a nearby stream like boats. Then he told his wife to sit for a spell while he finished cleaning. A few minutes later, the small family trooped home in the lavender dusk. They ate crab and salt-bread, although Moira only picked at her food and stared into the flames of their stone fireplace with listless eyes.

The next day, she could not get out of bed...a week and a half later, she died of cholera. Sean knew that he had to get what remained of his family out of Ireland before they all perished so he telegraphed his older sister, offering his two boats and his house to her and her husband for half their value.

His sister Lizzy had married a gowl tool by the name of Joseph Licket. They lived in northern England and ran a successful grocer's store in Yorkshire. When the Irish famine first struck, Lizzy sent letters of sympathy and offers of help but as the conditions in Ireland worsened her letters grew more distant and the tone of those missives most chilly.

Apparently, Licket was a great supporter of the devil Charles Trevelyan, a British dignitary who pronounced the Irish lazy, incompetent and victims of their own foolhardy actions. Up until recently, Britain had tried to help their ailing neighbors to the west with

shipments of food, maize seed and medicines but
Trevelyan had important friends in Parliament. And
relief from Britain meant more taxes from its citizens.

As the Irish famine wore on, more and more
English citizens were feeling the pinch of charity in
their pocketbooks and the resentment that inevitably
follows throwing "good money after bad." Now, relief
was no longer forthcoming. Instead, the British set up
workhouses for starving Irish families who could
barely stand upright much less work for the meager
rations offered in return for backbreaking labor.

Apparently, Lizzy's husband felt the pinch more
than most although he lived in a fancy house and his
waistline grew more corpulent by the year. Two whole
weeks passed before a telegram finally arrived,
informing Sean that the Lickets would purchase the
property but only if the price was again reduced
by half.

Desperate to escape the fate of millions of his fellow
countrymen, Sean swallowed his rage and accepted his
brother-in-law's offer. The money finally arrived,
along with three men who would sail his boats across
the channel to Northern England. After giving the
Englishman ten pounds, Sean begged passage on the
larger of the boats and—with his children—left his
homeland forever.

They booked sail on a steamer from London to
New York and the passage was horrible. Although
there were calm days when the ocean seemed to be

made of glass and porpoises leapt from the waves like children at play, most of the voyage was beset with one squall after another.

If Sean had received the money from his property that he'd asked for, he and his children might have been able to afford second-class accommodations: their own cabin, fresh water, fruit and the same food the captain ate every day. Instead, he and his family rode steerage and were treated no better than the animals penned in the back of the hull. The flux had walked aboard the boat in London and, within days of leaving harbor, the straw that littered the floor of the ship was sour with diarrhea and vomit.

They finally arrived in North America just as winter embraced the northeastern coastline in its icy arms. A harried customs agent at Ellis Island promptly changed Sean's last name to Donnelly. Affronted, Sean wanted to argue that he was proud to carry his Da's name but a strange, frightening tickle had developed in his lungs, a heavy itch that no amount of coughing could ease.

He had heard many stories of people turned away from North America by these same agents at the first sign of sickness and Sean could ill afford to fail now. Passage to this country had depleted most of his purse but he still had enough left to start anew if he was careful. So he swallowed his pride and herded his children ahead of him, down the gangplank, and into the city of New York.

Two years passed and, at first, Sean thought that his "American Dream" might come true. Luckily, within minutes of arriving in America, Sean heard the Gaelic being spoken around the corner of a dilapidated warehouse that stunk of creosote and fish.

Approaching cautiously, Sean saw two men arguing loudly by a pile of nets on the boardwalk in front of the building. "I'll not have ye coming in late fer work, Donovan, ye hear me?" The older of the two men hollered.

Indeed, it looked like the younger man was in his cups because he gave as good as he got. "And I'll not have ye pushing me around, ye old sot!" He hiccupped, grinning.

"Alrighty then," the older man exclaimed. "Off wit ye! You are fired!" Then another man who had been lingering by the building's big sliding doors came rushing up behind the young drunk, seized him by the back of his shirt and the seat of his pants, and heaved him off the pier into the water below.

A chorus of hoarse shouts filled the air as the men who worked in the warehouse saw what happened and cheered. Seizing the moment, Sean stepped up to the older man, extended his hand and begged for a job.

"Fresh off the boat, are ye?" the man, whose name was Danny O'Malley, asked.

Sean nodded and then stated his credentials, his

birthplace, and the names of his two children. O'Malley studied the man's wind-burned face and the calluses on his palms, all of which bespoke a lifetime of experience on the sea.

Remembering his own humble beginning in this wild and formidable country, O'Malley's heart went out to the young family. "Okay then. You start tomorrow at 6:00 am, sharp. Use the rest of this day to find accommodations. I recommend Mrs. Pratt's Boarding House. She tolerates the Irish and keeps a clean larder. Remember! 6:00 am, sharp!"

Sean led his children away and up the street to the boarding house, trying to ignore the heaviness in his lungs and the persistent tickle that tormented the back of his throat.

A YEAR AND A HALF LATER, Sean knew that he was seriously ill. It became harder and harder to get out of bed every morning and he knew that he wasn't doing as well at the fish house as O'Malley demanded. Strangely, the old man remained as kind as ever and moved Sean into the accounting office rather than out on the processing floor.

Patrick and Maggie did what they could to help. They were tall for their age and looked much older than their seven years so Patrick helped one of his friends—a young tough named Quinn Sully—either hawk newspapers or deliver them to the businesses and homes in the area.

Maggie sometimes helped Mrs. Pratt with laundry and stitch work. She also emptied the boarding house's many chamber pots for $2 a month off the rent. Life went on and, some days, Sean fooled himself into thinking that everything would be all right.

He had put off his own care for too long, however. One day, after a particularly fierce bout of coughing nearly brought him to his knees, Mr. O'Malley entered the accounting office, dismissed Sean's fellow clerk, and closed the door.

He sat down on one of the wooden chairs and pulled his cap off his bald head with a sigh. "I hate to, boyo, but I have to let you go."

Sean had barely gotten himself under control and, when he heard his boss's words, he burst into another coughing fit. Wiping tears from his eyes, he sat down, trembling, on the other chair.

"I want to thank ye, sir, for all you done fer me and mine," he whispered.

O'Malley reached in his pocket and pulled out an envelope. "This here is yer wages. There's a bit more tucked away besides, Sean. I want ye to go see the doc and I won't hear no argument from ye, neither."

The old man stared out the window for a moment. Then he looked at Sean, adding, "Someone turned ye inta the authorities, son. That's why I am forced to let ye go, see. They think you got the consumption and I suspect it's so. Here in this country, if you walk around with a disease and don't have a doctor's say-so, they put you away. So you go on in and get yerself checked out." He smiled. "Who knows? Maybe it's just a passing thing and it'll be gone along with the last of the winter's snow."

Spring did not thaw the sickness in Sean's lungs, however. He never went to see the doctor, choosing instead to use the precious extra coin for room and board. Unfortunately, as tuberculosis ate away at the lining of Sean's lungs and it became more difficult to breathe, Mrs. Pratt and the other boarders in her house became concerned.

They were concerned for the young family but, in truth, more worried about their own health. It was obvious that a "lunger" was gasping his life away upstairs and they wanted no part of it, either from the dying man or the possibility of contracting the illness. Finally, although she cherished young Maggie's help, Mrs. Pratt was forced to evict the Irish family.

They were almost out of money by then and Sean reluctantly moved his two children into an attic of a tenement house. By now, summer sent heat from the dusty streets in fly-shot waves high into the air and the extremely hot air seemed to culminate in the Donnelly's garret room. Sean spent his days either sweltering like a pig in his own sweat or—despite the heat—shivering against death's bony embrace.

Maggie did what she could to help her Da although he gasped and choked like a fish on dry land. She cleaned their room and fetched water from the downstairs well, trudging up six flights of steps to the attic. She cooked rice and beans and sometimes traded stitch work for a ham hock or a beef knuckle. She did this while thinking that eventually her Da would get better, sit up in bed with a smile and tell more stories about their homeland...the sweet, green island of his youth.

Instead, Sean grew frailer every day and the flesh seemed to melt from his bones. Now, the only thing he was able to stomach was thin gruel and the occasional piece of moistened bread. Maggie gave up doing any piecework as most of her time was spent holding her dying father in her arms or helping him to the privy pot.

Meanwhile, since Patrick had moved too far away to profit from his friendship with young Quinn, he met a new group of boys who called themselves Ike's Spikes. He did not know it at first but the Spikes were runners and roustabouts for one of the most notorious gangsters in New York, Ike Banyon.

4

MATTHEW

Iris, Samuel, Lenny and Bandit headed home after finding out Amelia was not on the train nor would she be arriving any time soon. Upon hearing the news, Iris stared up into Matthew's eyes with fear, sorrow and anger. She knew he would be going after the girl come hell or high water, a fact that made her feel proud and terrified at the same time for both her niece's *and* her husband's safety.

"Will you be coming home before you go?" she asked.

Nodding, he replied, "Yes. I've already spoken to Maddock. The next train back to Ellensburg leaves at 6:30 this evening. I plan to get a quick start but I still need to pack some things before I leave."

"Okay, I better get going then. I'll try to have some things packed for you by the time you get home." She kissed him on the cheek and climbed up into the

wagon where Lenny snapped the reins and
yelled, "Ha!"

Matthew and Roy were in the sheriff's office,
staring at a map of Ellensburg and the surrounding
area. As with much of Washington state, there were
vast tracts of unoccupied land. Many towns had sprung
up almost overnight as tracks were laid for the SLS&E
—Seattle, Lake Shore and Eastern Railway—and had
just as quickly been abandoned when the rail-line ultimately went out of business, giving way for the
Northern Pacific to re-route the eastern lines to the
Tri-Cities.

One of the spurs still stopped just outside of Ellensburg where Amelia had been kidnapped. The good
news for Matthew was that the town was much closer
to Granville than the Tri-Cities. The bad news was,
despite a fairly new and active train station, the rest of
the surrounding landscape was a vast network of
private farms, ranches and very little commerce. Thus,
a shortage of eyes on the situation so Amelia and her
kidnappers could be anywhere.

Staring down at the map on his desk, Matthew felt
his heart sink. *It will be like finding a very small needle in
a very large haystack*, he thought.

"It won't take long for the deputies to arrive,
Matthew," Roy murmured. "If I push it, they can be
here by tonight."

Matthew had told Roy to follow him to Ellensburg
the next day. Ever since the ordeal with the Mad

Hatters nearly six years ago, he felt uncomfortable leaving the people in his town alone. Now though, after studying the map, he was starting to change his mind. He would need another hand, maybe even two, if he were to have a hope of finding his wife's niece in that high, wild country. After all, he had been there before...lost, injured and alone in a winter blizzard in the Cascades.

"Okay, I agree. Go ahead and telegraph the Spokane sheriff's office and ask for two deputies. If I can have an assurance that they will be here by tonight, you, me and Abner will catch the westbound at 6:30."

Roy immediately strode out the door and up the street to the telegraph office. Exiting his private office, Matthew stepped outside, walked up the boardwalk a few steps and entered the jailhouse. Two deputies were inside, Abner Smalley and Tom "Bean" Tolson. Bean was holding a rifle in his arms, keeping careful watch as Abner led a handcuffed prisoner out the back door to the privy.

Matthew sat down at his desk and started listing a few things the Spokane deputies would need to do and watch out for in Granville while Matthew and his men were away. A few minutes later, Abner, Bean and a prisoner named Beetle came back inside.

"When you're finished there, come on over and sit down" Matthew called out.

A few minutes later, Bean and Abner sat in the chairs in front of the sheriff's desk.

"I assume you two have heard about my wife's

niece?" Seeing both men nod, Matthew continued, "Well, Roy and I are going after her and, Abner, I want you to come with us. What do you think? Can your ma spare you for a week or two?"

Abner, a young man of nineteen, took care of his aging mother when he was not working as a deputy. He was an enormous man, at least six foot five and over 250 pounds, but gentle as a kitten. Some people thought he was a little simple, but Matthew thought it was more than that. Although Abner was no intellectual, he had a good feel for life—and who was on the wrong side of it. He was a deliberate man who thought everything out before he acted.

He was calm and careful, another deliberation on his part as he had once dislocated his little sister's shoulder when he was only eleven years old. The incident was not intentional...he was just so strong he had pulled the girl's arm out of its socket as they were playing. Nevertheless, he still remembered the horror of what he had done and took great care now with his staggering strength.

"Yes, sir," he said. "I'll get my sister Minnie to look after Ma."

"Okay, good." Matthew replied. "Go on and get packed. Once you get back, I want you to have three of our fastest horses geared up and ready to go. Get old Sam ready to haul while you're at it. I know he's mean as a snake but that mule is the best and the fastest hauler we've got once he gets the kinks out of his system."

Grinning, Matthew watched the color leave Abner's face. "Yessir, but I sure hope I don't have to punch that old bastard again like the last time I saddled him..."

"I hope not either, son. But just in case, stand back and let him get the vinegar out of his blood before you put the pack saddle on him. Be ready to leave by six o'clock."

Abner got up and left, and Matthew spent a few minutes explaining his lists and priorities to Bean. Finally, Roy walked back in with another telegraph paper in his hand. He placed the message on the sheriff's desk and said, "Spence and Davey are leaving Spokane right now, by buggy. They should be here within a couple of hours."

Relieved, Matthew stood up and pulled his watch from his vest. "Good, but I better get a move on if we're going to make that train. Roy, pack your bags for a couple of weeks and if Abner needs some help getting the horses and mule loaded, give him a hand, alright?"

"Sure thing, boss." Roy nodded and walked outside again.

Studying their one and only prisoner, Matthew asked, "You think you can handle this on your own for a couple of hours, Bean?"

Bean looked affronted. "Well, of course, Sheriff! It's just old Beetle and he's still as drunk as a fiddler's clerk. My guess is he'll just sleep through the rest of the night."

Matthew grinned in agreement. "Still, you keep a sharp eye out. Chances are the Spokane deputies will be here before we even leave but if there's any problem, you skedaddle down to the telegraph office and send for the Spokane County Marshal, okay?"

"You got it, Matthew," Bean said, adding, "Good luck finding Iris's niece, sir."

A few minutes later, Matthew trotted out of town towards home. He needed to pick up a few things and say goodbye to his family.

His leather valise was packed by the time he arrived, which Matthew appreciated. The only things he needed now were a couple of extra guns, more ammunition and some spending cash. He kept glancing at his watch...time was wasting. If he didn't get a move on he would miss the train although Matthew had no doubt that Roy would hold the locomotive in the name of the law. Still, the sheriff didn't want that sort of headache on top of everything else so he hastily removed his dress clothes, exchanging them for his favorite old denim shirt, jeans and his most comfortable boots.

Finally, he was ready to leave. Moving down the staircase, Matthew looked lovingly at his family standing by the front door. They were all dressed nicely, even young Samuel, and Abby had tears in her eyes.

"Papa, I wanna come!" young Chance yelled, running up to cling to Matthew's leg.

A sudden chill ran up and down the sheriff's spine. There was no question in his mind that he would go to look for his wife's missing niece, but this was the first time he had ever left his family alone. Remembering his last mission out of town and the series of mishaps on that trip, Matthew's eyes grew sharp as he memorized every feature of his loved one's faces.

He hugged his stepdaughter and shook his stepson's hand, even as his littlest rode his papa's leg like a horse. Then he bent and placed his lips on Iris's mouth. At this point, Chance screamed, "Ewww, Ma! Pa! Stoppit!"

The kiss continued for another moment and then Matthew stepped back with a smile. "I'll be back before you know it. As soon as I hear word about Amelia's whereabouts, I'll send a telegraph."

Turning to Samuel, he said, "You are the man of the house, son. Take care of these ladies and your little brother while I'm away, won't you?"

Nodding, Samuel answered, "Yes, sir. I will."

Looking down at his son, Matthew saw that Chance was starting to worry. Jewel-like tears were in his large green eyes and his lower lip started to quiver with anxiety. Bending down, he said, "Come here and give your Pa a hug!"

The little boy leapt into Matthew's arms and burst into tears. "Now, now...I'll only be gone for a little while. I want you to help your big brother watch out for the ladyfolk around here, alright?"

Puffing up slightly with the gravity of his task, Chance knuckled the tears away from his face and said, "Okay, Pa."

Putting the boy into his mother's arms, Matthew stepped out the door, strode down the porch steps and tied his satchel to the saddlehorn. Then he strapped two rifles to the bedroll. He heard Iris running up behind him.

"Mattie!" She cried and he turned to take her in his arms once more. They kissed again and he could feel her body trembling. He wanted to comfort her and tell her it was going to be okay but he couldn't. Mounting his horse, he just smiled as she finally stepped away from his embrace.

"I'll be home soon, wife. I love you." Matthew tipped his hat and urged his horse into a brisk trot.

The train was just pulling into the station as Matthew rode up. He saw three horses nibbling at a small mound of hay and one cantankerous old mule pulling at the rope in Roy's hands.

There was a pile of luggage close to his deputy's feet and a large sack of grain as well. Matthew sighed in relief...at least they weren't too far behind the kidnappers. Looking down the road, he saw a sleek, black buggy pulled by two horses round the corner and come his way.

It carried the deputies he had called in from Spokane and they waved at him, grinning with pride. Walking up, he said, "Well, I hope you two didn't wear your ponies out getting here so fast."

"No, sir!" Davey stammered, nervously. "It's this new racing buggy we got. It's faster 'n greased lightnin'!"

Matthew grinned. "Well, that's a load off my mind." Turning serious, he added, "We're headed out now but I tried to make a list of the things you might need to do while I'm gone. It's been pretty quiet around here lately and I hope it stays that way. But if you have a problem, any problem at all, you telegraph the marshal. Got it?"

"Yes, sir!" both young men responded as one.

"Well, then...Let's head on over to the jail. I'll give you a quick run-down before we take off."

Tipping their hats, the deputies nodded. Matthew followed and gave last minute instructions to Bean and the fill-in lawmen while Roy and Abner loaded their gear and livestock up onto the flatbed of the train. Twenty minutes later, they headed west.

5

MARGARET

MARGARET STARED AT THE GIRL WITH TIRED, GRITTY eyes. The young woman—Amelia Winters, according to the diary she kept in her purse—had come close to dying over the last few hours and Margaret knew it was her fault. She ran her tongue over the swollen, bloody cut that graced her bottom lip and winced; Patrick had been furious and showed his displeasure by punching her in the face before storming off into the night.

She sighed. When had her brother begun to hate her so? Was it just recently, as her value as a prostitute began to diminish? Or had his scorn for her started when he was only a boy? Margaret had once been a raving beauty, renowned for her prowess in bed. She and the girls in her stable had made her brother wealthy and powerful—one of the kings of both the New Orleans and San Francisco underworlds. Now he treated her like a dirty, broken doll...

a piece of rubbish fit only to be thrown on the trash pile.

Knowing that their latest victim was finally out of the woods, medically speaking, Margaret lay her head down on her pillow and closed her eyes. She had done wrong and she knew it. Her addiction to opium had started long ago and, although God knew she tried to control it, Margaret always sought ways to attain the only inner peace she ever felt within the warm embrace of the poppy.

It was one thing to lie on satin sheets in her beautiful, gold-gilded bedroom back in San Francisco. When she sucked the opulent fumes from her hookah, her dreams were vivid and bright, her shame submerged within foggy hallucinations of power and glory. It was quite another here in this godforsaken country where the only opium she could find was in the form of small, sticky balls of sap, obtained on the sly and at great cost from Chinese workers on the rail-lines.

Patrick had destroyed Margaret's pipe when they fled New Orleans but she knew all the tricks that an opium addict needed to survive. She made laudanum—rubbing alcohol with balls of opium melted in the liquid—and learned to roll tiny amounts of the resin into balls which she inserted into the back of her cheek for a minor but long-lasting high.

She purchased Green Fairy juice—which was absinthe—and supplemented her waking dreams in alcoholic bliss. She occasionally bought small squares of hashish as well but it held a distinct odor that her brother could easily detect so Margaret tried to curtail her use of that product. Yet she was just barely able to keep her addiction and recent withdrawal pangs under control.

A week ago, however, she bought two rather large and lumpy wads of opium from a doctor in Seattle's Chinatown while her brother visited the local hospital to purchase a few bottles of ether. She noticed later that night that this batch of opium seemed stronger than what she was accustomed to but, like many addicts, she promptly threw caution to the wind and decided to enjoy the drug's extra potency.

Forgetting that she might be asked to perform her part in Patrick's latest 'get rich quick' scheme, Margaret spent a few days floating on a pink, soft-edged cloud of narcotic euphoria, her brother none the wiser. Then Patrick said they would leave the following morning to search for another batch of girls to sell.

While in Seattle, he had learned that an Arabian sultan was in need of ten new girls for his harem. The man had heard that American women were highly sexed and far less constrained in bed than their European counterparts. When Patrick found out that the sultan would pay up to a thousand dollars a head for the right batch of women, he grew excited. Knowing his competitors would be wasting no time in fulfilling the Arabian's order, he commanded his sister to sober up and help him or he would give her a beating she would not soon forget.

Lying in her bed now, Margaret sighed again. She

had tried to get sober but apparently her mind was still opium-fogged when she kidnapped the girl as she had radically misjudged the amount of ether on the cloth she put over Amelia's mouth. When the girl fell into a coma, Patrick was enraged.

After smacking his sister around, he went through her things, found what was left of her opium and threw it into the woodstove. Margaret had wept as she bled on the floor but rejoiced as well. She still had a half bottle of laudanum that she had placed in her corset and two full bottles of the precious Green Fairy juice.

She winced once more as a trickle of saliva seeped over her split lip and then she fell into a light, dream-filled slumber. Her dreams roamed like translucent spirits, traveling far into the past, back into the present —and frighteningly—into the future as the last of the opium dissipated from her bloodstream and dampened her pillow.

The Donnelly family went completely broke at almost the same moment Sean died of tuberculosis. At first, Patrick mourned the loss of his Da and huddled tearfully by his sister's side. There was still some food left in the larder and another ten days before the land-lord—a fat, smelly man who leered at Margaret behind her brother's back—expected to be paid for next month's rent.

Still, they had to pay to bury their Da in Potter's Field which left them with only a few dollars and some copper pennies to their name. Neither one of them knew what to do or where they would live when their meager funds ran out. The ten-year-old twins stayed in their hot, garret room like forgotten ghosts...lost and silent.

A few days later, there was a knock on the door. Patrick got up to answer and saw three of his newfound friends, members of Ike's Spikes gang, standing in the hall outside their room. An older man who Patrick had never met but had heard tales of, spoken in fearful whispers like a spook tale, accompanied them. His name was Syrus Monk and he was Ike Banyan's right-hand man.

Monk was in charge of new hires. It was his job to see that the newest members of Ike's gang had the right training for whatever tasks were assigned to them. Young Patrick had already shown some talent in pick-pocketing which was a good thing in itself. But Monk was more interested in the boy's uncanny size; the ten-year-old was already almost five and a half feet tall, as was his sister.

The thing his boss needed most right now was more strong-arm men. The Italians were spilling from the trans-Atlantic steamers in droves and Ike Banyan required willing and able men to deal with the spaghetti-eating upstarts that dared cut in on his territory.

It will take some time yet, Monk thought, but this boy will do nicely with a little training.

In truth though, Monk's real interest lay in the girl. Margaret was already a beauty, with long black ringlets and clear blue eyes. She was also just as big as her brother Patrick. Knowing she was only a child did not deter Monk from measuring her weight in gold. *She can work as a cleaning girl for the time it takes to reach her maturity*, he decided, *and then I will put her out to the highest bidder.*

Monk was a personable and handsome man with fancy clothes and a wide, sunny smile. When he asked the Donnelly twins if they would like to come to work for his boss, Ike Banyan, it seemed like a wish come true. Within days, Patrick and Margaret found themselves ensconced in a four-story brownstone in Brooklyn, dressed in worn but clean clothes, and filled up with good food in their bellies.

Three years passed in relative ease. Patrick enjoyed his work as a pickpocket and general runabout, and Margaret did housework as well as some cooking and sewing for the prostitutes that lived on the second floor of the building. Whenever clients came to call, every day from 2:00 pm until midnight, Margaret was sent upstairs out of harm's way and away from prying eyes.

Then one day she became ill. Blood flowed from between her legs and her stomach cramped with nausea. She talked to her supervisor, a dour woman by the name of Mrs. Coyne, who said, "Its yer time, girl. Go and have a lie down. Today only, mind ye, and I'll talk to Mr. Monk about yer condition."

Little did Margaret know that Monk had been waiting patiently for this day to arrive. He immediately gave orders for one of the whore's rooms to be cleaned and made ready for a new occupant. He did not care that Margaret was only thirteen years old. He only knew that she would bring in an enormous amount of money from some of their wealthier clients.

The girl was given a reprieve from work and her head swam with all of the sudden attention she received from Madame Winslow and some of the other women in the brothel. A seamstress came as well and took Margaret's measurements for new frocks, dresses, underclothes and nightgowns. Parasols, umbrellas, feathered hats and button-up kid boots were delivered to her new bedroom—a fancy place with lavender walls, a large four-poster bed, gilded paintings and mirrors on the walls and ceiling.

Over the last three years, Margaret had remained mostly innocent of what went on downstairs, although she was no fool and had heard some whisperings about the beautiful, painted ladies on the second floor who made a living "on their backs."

She had an idea what that meant and, to her way of thinking, that didn't sound so hard. After all, what could be so hard about looking pretty and lying on your back all of the time? She did not fully comprehend the mechanics involved in lying on her back for paying customers. Margaret had been kept mostly ignorant by design; Monk knew that in order to train a prize filly, one should not strap her into the traces too early in her career lest she turn "gate-shy" or mean.

A week later, Madame Winslow came to her room. She had ordered a bathtub filled to the brim with warm, sudsy water and helped Margaret wash her hair and scrub her body until it tingled. Then she helped the girl put on a gown in the deepest shade of purple so that her eyes gleamed like amethysts in the candlelight.

The woman rubbed oil on the top of Margaret's breasts so they glowed and dabbed spots of rouge high on the girl's cheeks and lips. Finally, with help from one of the scullery maids, Winslow wove Margaret's glossy black locks into a waterfall cascade of ringlets that fell over her small bosom and down her back.

Margaret gazed at herself in the mirror and thought she looked like a fairy princess. She turned to the woman and tried to hug her in thanks but Winslow stepped away from the girl's embrace, her expression cold and remote.

The first fluttering of fear tickled Margaret's innards. What is wrong? she wondered. All I have to do is lie on my back and look pretty. Is there something else I need to do?

It was too late for answers and, before she knew it, Margaret was walking down the hallway dressed in her new finery. There were many men standing there, including her brother, who stared at her with dead eyes.

Her heart was beating fast now in dread and worry. Something intangible had changed and she felt that everyone, except herself, was sharing a secret. She panicked and tried to turn around but Madame Winslow barred her path, blocking her escape. Winslow grasped Margaret's upper arm and her long, painted nails sunk into the tender flesh like talons.

"You move forward now!" the older woman hissed. "You do yer duty or you and yer brother will be out on yer asses by sunup tomorrow."

Giving the girl a little shove, she saw Margaret stop for moment, square her shoulders and step into the main parlor.

Margaret hesitated at the threshold of the room and stared in amazement at the twenty or thirty men who stood and sat around the parlor's exterior. As far as she could tell, they were all gents dressed in fine, black suits, cravats and silk vests. They stared at her with bright eyes and wide, grinning lips. A strange sort of communication started when she entered the room… men raised their fingers, hissed at each other in derision and sneered in triumph.

Winslow led the confused and frightened girl up onto a raised dais where one piece of clothing after another was removed and taken away until the only thing left on her body were her kid boots. Margaret tried to cover her breasts but the madam glared at her with such venom, she let her arms drop. Trying to stop the tears of shame that sprang up into her eyes,

Margaret stared across the room at her benefactor, Syrus Monk.

He was grinning with pride and excitement. This little girl is fetching the best price this house has ever seen, he thought. Mr. Banyan will be most pleased.

He did not see the look of betrayed trust in Margaret's eyes nor the smoldering resentment in his best runner's gaze. Monk did not realize it but his ultimate fate had just been sealed.

Margaret awoke with a start when she heard a soft voice whisper, "Hel...hello? Is anybody there?"

The girl was awake and it was time for Margaret to go to work. She picked up a canteen of water and a small plate of yesterday's biscuits. She had no doubt that Amelia was famished and probably still somewhat ill from the overdose of ether she'd been given. Margaret walked over to the hay-filled stall where the girl was handcuffed to the wall and opened the wooden gate.

"Shhh. I am here with some food and water. I expect you're not feeling so fine but, if you behave, I will bring you a powder."

She stared down at the rumpled young woman who stared back at her with wide brown eyes.

"Oh," the girl whispered. "Are you ever going to be sorry for taking me against my will!"

Margaret heard the young woman's words but she just smiled. She and Patrick had done this countless times and were well past getting rich from the endeavor so Amelia's words rang with false bravado.

Still, there was a certainty in the girl's voice that gave the older woman pause. What was so different about *this* particular young woman that she would speak with such certainty?

Staring out at the large barn with its fifteen stalls, eight of which were occupied by girls of every race, creed and color, Margaret replied, "Maybe so. But, for now, you better keep a civil tongue in yer mouth because yer ass is mine."

6

MATTHEW AND HIS DEPUTIES

MATTHEW AND HIS DEPUTIES STEPPED OFF THE TRAIN IN Ellensburg at 8:42 pm. Except for a few departing passengers and one old man slowly loading sacks of flour onto the back of a wagon, the station was deserted. Looking past the depot building, Matthew noticed a woman sweeping the boardwalk in front of a café/post office about sixty feet away.

According to eyewitnesses, that was where Amelia had vanished. Picking up his rucksack, Matthew turned to his deputies and said, "Go ahead and unload the livestock. I'll go see if that woman knows anything about Amelia's disappearance and if there's a place to stay the night around here."

Roy and Abner walked toward the back of the train where they could hear old Sam kicking the sideboards in equine frustration. While they led the mule and horses down the ramp and let them take some water out of a nearby trough, Matthew walked up to the woman who was sweeping mud and fallen leaves.

Displaying the sheriff's badge on his vest, Matthew tipped his hat and said, "Good evening, Ma'am. I wonder if you heard anything about the kidnapping of the young girl who was here earlier today."

The woman was as thin as a hickory switch and her careworn features arranged themselves into a defensive frown. "I am done being questioned by the law, young man. I don't care whether you're a sheriff or not! My man and I had nothin' to do with that girl's kidnapping."

Matthew set his valise down on the ground and smiled. He thought the woman protested too much and wondered what she "and her man" *were* guilty of, but he doubted that their crimes were related to his niece's abduction. They were probably just skinflinting their paying customers for everything from hay to coffee as, from the look of things, they were running a monopoly.

"I was not accusing you, Ma'am," he said politely. "I just wondered whether you might have some information to help me and my deputies in our search. That girl is my niece."

The woman stopped sweeping and for the first time her hard expression softened. "Oh...I am sorry to hear that, Sheriff."

The train started chugging down the tracks with a toot and a puff of sooty smoke just as Roy and Abner walked up with their mounts and tied them to a rail.

The old man and his wagon were heading toward the restaurant as well. One of the flour sacks must have torn open as his face and arms were as white as snow and he was swearing under his breath.

"Dangit, them bags are gettin' flimsier by the minute," he muttered. The stern-faced woman stared at her husband and then broke into a genuine smile. "Hank, you look like a haint!" she chortled.

The old man waved one arm at her in disgust and trudged around the back of the building with his horse and cart. Looking amused, the woman said, "We're closed, but you boys look tuckered out. Why don't you step inside? I made a fresh pot of coffee since this is a late night for us on account of the flour delivery. There's even a bit of rhubarb cobbler left..."

Placing her broom against the doorjamb, she stepped inside. The lawmen followed and noticed Hank carrying the sacks through the back door. Matthew and his men pitched in and made short work of the task which brought a grateful smile from the old man and his wife.

Finally, they all sat down at one of the tables with steaming cups of black coffee and a square of rhubarb cobbler each. Hank had washed most of the flour from his face and arms. After wolfing down the dessert and taking a few sips of coffee, he looked up from his plate and said, "We really don't know nuthin' about what happened to the girl but the wife and I have been hearing some strange rumors lately."

"What kind of rumors?" Matthew asked.

Hank sat back and rubbed the gray whiskers on his cheeks. "Been hearing that a lot of girls have gone missing, not just this one...did you say she's your niece?"

At Matthew's nod, he added, "Well, I am surely sorry about that, Sheriff."

Hank stared up at the ceiling, then said, "It seems to me there have been at least a half a dozen girls disappeared the last few months." Glancing at the sheriff and his deputies, he added, "Not from here, of course...just around this general area. A number of men have come in asking after their daughters, sisters, what have you. It's like those girls just went up in a puff of smoke."

The old woman glared. "That's why I forgot my manners earlier, Sheriff. You're not the first lawman to come to us asking for information *and* treating us like we're criminals to boot."

Hank patted his wife's hand and murmured, "Now, Elmira, no need to get all puffed up over spilt milk."

The woman nodded. "I just didn't want these men to think I don't have a heart, that's all."

Matthew thought for a moment and said, "Do you remember which direction these men come in from? Maybe, if we knew that, we would have a better idea of where to search."

Hank closed his eyes in concentration. Then he sat up in his chair, eyes wide with recollection. "By God, son, that's a good idea! I *do* remember that a couple of those men came in from the Wenatchee area, places like Leavenworth and Cashmere...so, from the north." Scratching at his chin, he grimaced in frustration, adding, "On the other hand, one man and his sons came through here looking for a lost girl about a month ago. They claimed they was from the Othello area and that's southeast."

Glancing at his deputy and best friend, Matthew asked, "Did you bring that map in?"

Roy stood up and walked over to his leather valise. Rummaging around, he pulled out a state map of Washington and placed it on the table in front of the sheriff. Matthew pulled a pencil out of his vest pocket and commenced to drawing lines from Ellensburg to Leavenworth and from Odessa to Waterville. Finally, he sat back in his chair with a grunt.

Three large triangles now marked an area encompassing over three hundred square miles. The worst part: train tracks interspersed all three sections, assuring the kidnappers many avenues of escape. Matthew's head suddenly throbbed with tension. Iris's niece could be anywhere in that huge area of wild territory. Or she could be long gone by now...lost in the city of Seattle, on her way to Portland, Oregon or even San Francisco.

Roy muttered, "Well, if those rascals *do* catch the train every time they nab a girl, they must have a lot of cash." Looking into Matthew's eyes, he added, "Train tickets are expensive, Matthew. At least for most folks. I think whoever is kidnapping those girls has a hidey-hole somewhere in this general vicinity so I would be willing to bet they don't use the rails to transport their victims."

Matthew smiled. If he had a character flaw as a sheriff, it was impatience. He liked to cut to the heart of a matter and follow a straight path to an outlaw and his lair. Roy, as usual, had circumvented Matthew's frustration. Taking a circular path, the deputy had arrived at the correct conclusion.

Nodding, Matthew replied, "You're right. Their operation must be around here somewhere...but where?"

Bending over, he drew a large, charcoal circle around the three triangles on the map. Then he stabbed his pencil in the middle and the point marked the Palisades area, east of Wenatchee. Looking up at his two deputy's faces, Matthew shrugged and asked, "What do you think?"

Abner put his hands in the air, clearly reluctant to weigh in on the matter, but Roy agreed. "Yeah, I don't like it any more than you do, boss. Though I think their hideout will be within a day's ride of wherever they do their mischief."

"I think you're right. Which means we wasted time coming here. No offense, Ma'am," he said. "That rhubarb pie was worth the trip."

Hank said, "The northbound gets here tomorrow at 7:00 am, boys. Elmira and I have an old bunkhouse out back; we lived in it while this place was built. Why don't you stay there for the night and then you can head out. Only takes about an hour to get to Wenatchee by train. You can start the real chase tomorrow when you're fresh."

Matthew agreed and laid a couple of silvers under his napkin for the old woman to find. Then he and his deputies followed Hank out the door to a clean but chilly shack behind the outhouse.

Early the next morning, Matthew and his deputies got up from their bunks and dressed for the coming day. It was still dark so Matthew grabbed a lantern to light his way to the outhouse.

Once inside, he hung the light up on a wooden dowel. He used the necessary and then pumped the handle for some fresh, cold water. Something about the way the shadows flickered on the walls and floor caused the sheriff to look down. He saw a strange shape behind the sink and bent down to take a look.

A small bottle butted up against the wallboard. Plucking it from the floor, Matthew held it up to the lantern. There was no label so he removed the cork and sniffed. Immediately, his eyes began to water and he knew he held homemade laudanum in his hand. The smell was unmistakable as were the small bits and coils of opium that swirled in the bottom.

He placed the vial in his vest pocket and felt the

thrill of the chase. Of course, the laudanum could belong to anyone but he knew, deep in his gut, that he had just found a clue…and, more importantly, a weakness in his quarry's character.

Three and a half hours later, Matthew and his deputies arrived at the train depot in Wenatchee, Washington. After offloading and stabling their livestock, the lawmen walked to the closest hotel.

It was a three-story affair with a café, a laundry, and a telegraph office in the lobby. Matthew paid for a large room and ordered a cot brought up for either Roy or Abner to sleep on.

He realized that this wasn't going to be a straightforward apprehension. Somehow, a group of kidnappers had settled into the area and commenced to snatching young women right out from under people's noses. This meant they were either well-equipped and fast as greased lightning or operating undercover.

Knowing he and his deputies could not just ride off and expect to stumble across the kidnapper's lair— there was simply too much uncharted territory—they needed to do some interviews. Ask questions and try to uncover the subterfuge that had so far confounded the frustrated and grieving families. It would take a lot longer and Matthew could hardly bear the thought of what young Amelia might be going through. But it would do no good to run off on a wild goose chase out of sheer frustration.

Sheriff Wilcox swallowed his impatience and settled in to do some detective work.

7

PATRICK

PATRICK SAT AT HIS CUSTOMARY TABLE TOWARD THE BACK of the Shamrock Saloon. His two henchmen, Dan O'Reilly and Frederick "The Bullet" Marston, sat by his side in wary silence. Patrick had been in a foul mood since last night when he'd found their latest acquisition near death's door and his sister Margaret in a state of calamitous stupor.

Both men knew how easy it was to provoke Patrick into a rage when he was sullen like this so they prudently waited for their boss to speak and give orders for the day ahead. Both of them, at one time or another over the last twenty-four years, had been on the receiving end of the man's meaty fists and neither wanted that treatment this morning.

How many times, Patrick fumed to himself, *have I told that woman I will not stand for her addle-brained, opium addiction?* He glared at nothing and sucked at the abrasion on his knuckle. *Still, I shouldn't have hit her quite so hard...*He grimaced and took a drink of the whiskey in front of him.

A city council member approached, hat in hand, but stopped when he saw a waitress bring Donnelly's lunch on a large, steaming platter. The politician wanted to ask Donnelly if he still planned to widen the road from town out to the new cemetery before the snow flew but everybody knew Patrick did not like to be disturbed while dining.

Sitting back down at his own table, the councilman gazed at the saloon-owner/undertaker. Patrick Donnelly—a middle-aged man—was huge at 6 feet, 6 inches tall and two hundred and fifty pounds of solid muscle. He was handsome in a rough way with long black hair, just starting to go gray, and brilliant blue eyes. He wore fine, fancy suits and polished, button-up boots. In every aspect, the man seemed a gentleman. And yet there was something about him...a coarseness that made the wealthy patron seem like more of a road agent than a proper mortician and business owner.

Patrick had noticed that little worm, Clyde Dixon, approach and then slump back to his table in defeat and he couldn't help but grin. Money spoke volumes, especially in these small frontier towns out west. When he and Margaret had first settled in the Wenatchee area three years ago and bought twenty acres of farmland just outside of town with the stated intention of building a fancy new cemetery, the high and mighty had come crawling out of the city's woodwork like termites.

The Donnellys moved into the large, abandoned house on the property, completely remodeled the interior, painted the clapboards white and replaced all the old window glass with new, modern panes. They fixed up the barn, the bunkhouses and the outbuildings. Then Patrick, his business associates and a small army of well-paid men around the area, leveled five acres of land around the property.

They cut down trees and pulled stumps from the ground. They hauled in topsoil and planted the acreage with Kentucky bluegrass. They brought in statuary and built a large mausoleum. They built high, wrought-iron fencing and, finally, they disinterred many old bones from the existing cemetery close to town and replanted them in new gravesites in Donnelly's cemetery.

A few months later, Patrick opened up the town's first florist shop and bought an expensive corner lot in the city center. A year and four months later, the doors opened to The Shamrock Saloon and Eatery.

Patrick and, to a lesser degree, Margaret became an overnight success story. No one wanted to bury a loved one without Patrick Donnelly's help. The Donnelly Funeral Parlor with its fancy black carriages, matching plumed horses and exotic purple lilies became the stamp of a high-society funeral.

Even the saloon carried a lofty and elevated air in such a rough and tumble locale. Painted kelly green with bright gold letters, the establishment boasted a chef from San Francisco who served high tea at 4:00 pm for the ladies in town and Angus steaks shipped in from the Spokane area. Folks around town dressed for a night out on the town if they wanted to visit The Shamrock. Malingerers and drunkards were *not* welcome and neither were whores or card sharks. It was a first-class operation run by a first-class entrepreneur.

Patrick finished his beef stew and dinner rolls. Wiping his mouth and mustache with a fine, linen napkin, he said, "I want you two to load up six caskets for delivery to our warehouse in Seattle. You will leave first thing in the morning."

Both men knew this meant that six of their captives would be shipping out and they had best hurry. Standing up, Dan said, "Right away, sir."

Patrick responded, "I won't be far behind you. I just want to finish my drink in peace."

Tipping their hats, his long-time lackeys left the saloon and hurried to do their boss's bidding. Patrick gestured to the waitress, pointing to his office and the woman nodded, pouring her employer another whiskey.

He smiled at the customers in his saloon and walked into his office, closing the door behind him. A moment later, one of his best girls—young Sandra Williams—brought him his drink and asked if he needed anything else. Knowing what she offered, he considered for a moment and then declined. She nodded politely and left.

Patrick sighed and untied the bow around his neck. Six girls would be hauled to their warehouse in Seattle tomorrow. Once there, his female employees would fatten them up a little, clean their bodies and make them ready for the auction to be held October 1st, only three weeks away.

There would be two girls remaining here at home and both of them were sick. Their latest victim had come close to dying from the nearly lethal overdose of ether Margaret had delivered and the other girl, an Indian squaw of about fifteen years, had refused to eat since her capture two weeks earlier. Although Margaret and the boys had done everything besides hog-tie the teenager, anything put in her mouth was either spat out or vomited back up.

Patrick was ready to give up on that one. The easiest thing to do would be to put her out of her misery, bury the body and look for four more girls. Time was running out, though, and he gritted his teeth in rage. Taking another sip of whiskey, he sat back in his chair and stared up at the ceiling.

A few minutes later, Patrick's snores filled the room and he dreamed of a time when he was just a boy. He did not know it then, but hard times and circumstance had molded his character with the deft, artful fingers of a master of the macabre.

After Patrick's father died, at first it was a relief to be part of Ike Banyan's gang. He felt like he had a family of sorts, an income and a purpose in life. He no longer needed to worry about what would become of him and his sister, his belly was always full, and his bosses treated him with respect and gruff affection.

The first few years of their new life seemed wonderful. The work was fun—mainly running up and down the streets of Brooklyn, passing messages, delivering or retrieving cash money from grocers, brothels, and saloons and making sure that Ike Banyan's fine suits and shirts were cleaned to perfection by the Chinese laundry he frequented.

Then things changed. He underwent a rapid growth spurt and his handler, Syrus Monk, told him to start working out at one of Banyan's many boxing rings. As he gained weight, height and muscle, he was put up against men who were far taller and bigger than he was and he was often beaten to a bloody pulp. At first, Patrick was afraid to fight back. He worried about reprisal and did not want to make enemies out of boys and men he thought were his friends. But it was that or risk the wrath of his boss. So one day he came up from the bloody mat and beat his opponent, an eighteen-year-old boy named Danny O'Reilly, almost to death.

He knocked out most of the teen's front teeth and hammered so mercilessly at the boy's kidneys he pissed blood for nearly a month. Still, Danny was under orders to take that beating and, as he stared through rapidly swelling eyes, he grinned with relief when Patrick apologized and asked to remain friends.

After that, the word was out and Patrick found himself fighting for money—and usually winning— every other night. When he wasn't in the ring, he helped a man named Floyd Turcel dress and bury the dead. Most of the men Patrick helped bury were Ike Banyan's enemies and no great effort was wasted on those men. These deaths occurred in the shadows and the victims' final resting places resided in shadow, as well.

Yet Ike needed an air of legitimacy to appease the ever-growing constabulary in the city, so Banyan's Mortuary was founded. Patrick ran the front parlor and learned the mortician's craft. He dressed in fine clothes and learned to treat regular, law-abiding citizens with kindness and sensitivity. He begged Mr. Turcel to bring in highly-scented flowers, an extravagance but well worth the cost, to mask death's distinctive odor and used his own money to purchase plumes for their draft horses.

Patrick was filled with pride and, perhaps, happy for the first time in his life. Then one night he was ordered to one of Banyan's brothels to serve guard duty for a big to-do. He showed up on time and waited in the hallway for a chance to say hello to his twin sister who also seemed to be thriving under Banyan's care.

That was the night he realized he and his sister were working for the devil himself. He watched, helplessly, as Margaret was stripped down to her boots and auctioned off to the highest bidder despite the fact she was only thirteen years old. He watched as her eyes searched his for help and knew that he was powerless to stop what was going to happen.

He saw Syrus Monk glance his way a number of times as if gauging his reaction. Patrick didn't have much money yet, and was still too young and weak to rear against the traces that bound his life. But as he stood against the wall and watched his twin sister shiver in mortified fear, he swore vengeance.

It took three years but, one day, during a snowstorm that brought the city to a halt, Patrick snuck into the bedroom of Monk's home. The boss was sleeping off too much whiskey from the night before and most of Syrus's lackeys were in the parlor playing cards close to the fireplace.

Placing an ether-soaked rag over Monk's nose and mouth, he watched as the man's eyes opened in alarm and closed again almost immediately. Then he walked over to the chiffonier and rifled through the bottom drawer where he found over four thousand dollars buried under a mound of undergarments. Over the past few days, Patrick had done the same thing to a number of hiding places and bolt holes all over the city; not too much in any one place, just enough to give him and his sister a head start. Counting in his head, Patrick smiled. He now had nearly six thousand dollars with which to make himself and Margaret a new life.

He stood over Monk's bed, giving considerable thought to taking his knife and putting an end to the man's life but stayed his hand. For now, he was only guilty of stealing from a thief. He doubted whether Monk would even want to share news of his misfortune as Patrick knew that much of the man's ill-gotten gains had come straight from Mr. Banyan's pockets.

Although the man had much to account for, Patrick knew if he gave in to his desire for revenge, no place in the world would be safe from Banyan's reach or that of any number of New York sheriffs. He settled, instead, for screwing his lips into a bitter grimace and spitting in Monk's face before leaving the room.

Outside in the parlor, he tipped his hat. "I gotta go and help Floyd now. See ya later, gents."

"You go get 'em, Undertaker!" Many of Banyan's men had taken to calling Patrick that since he seemed to take to the job so well and held no qualms about handling dead bodies.

"I will," he answered as he walked out the door.

Six hours later, Patrick, Margaret, and Danny were on a stagecoach heading for New Orleans. Patrick was both nervous and elated. He didn't think Banyan's goons would be able to follow as he had paid well for the driver's silence. Freddie Marston was paid so well, in fact, that he and Danny followed the twins to New

Orleans, on into Kansas City and, later, to San Francisco.

Patrick sponsored his sister and his friends with money and muscle. By the time he and Margaret were thirty-eight years old, they were wealthy. Patrick was content...Margaret, however, had never been the same since her world was torn asunder by the cruel and greedy hands of fate.

8

MATTHEW

BY THE TIME MATTHEW AND HIS DEPUTIES WERE finished moving in to the hotel room and stabling their livestock, it was late afternoon. Matthew's frustration grew. The trail to Iris's missing niece was growing colder by the minute but there was nothing to be done this late in the day except grab some chow and see if they could glean information from the locals.

The men used the washbasin to clean up a bit and changed into fresh clothes. Then they headed downstairs and asked the clerk where a good meal might be found. The man behind the counter studied them and their clothing for a moment and said, "Well, there's a dress code at the Shamrock. No offense, gents, but you might do better at Callie's Cafe. She's got good food and her nose ain't so far up in the air she can't see her boots walkin'. Her little restaurant is just two doors down from here on the right."

As Matthew loathed snobbery in any form, he thanked the fellow for his scruples and walked through the front door onto the dusty street. Looking right and left, he spied a gaudy green building with large gold-gilt letters embellishing the front...The Shamrock Saloon and Eatery.

He looked down at his clean shirt and vest. *They must really have some high standards,* he thought. His shirt was snowy white, made of the best cotton and ironed to stern stiffness by Iris's own hand. His vest was new as well; a silk paisley in muted shades of gray and green.

Glancing at his two deputies, Matthew saw that Abner was a bit more threadbare but also as clean as a whistle. Roy, a bit of a peacock by nature, had dressed in his Sunday best with a long, black duster, new boots and brand new hat.

"Guess we're not good enough for that place," Roy muttered angrily.

"Does it matter, Roy? We could head on over there if you really want to."

He knew that Roy was offended. However, Matthew could afford to be cavalier about it as both he and Iris had come from money and were considered "high salt" by many people in the Spokane area.

Roy, on the other hand, came from poor folk. He had worked himself and his family into a comfortable lifestyle through sheer guts and determination. He was also one of the most honorable men Matthew had ever known and worth three times as much as some of the landed gentry in Spokane.

"Nah, let's go to Callie's Cafe. Something smells pretty good," his deputy said.

They walked about fifty feet and entered a boisterous little restaurant with yellow gingham curtains and a number of small round tables. Families, buckaroos and shopkeepers were sitting at the tables while two busy, red-cheeked waitresses scurried here and there with plates, cups and glasses.

"Sit anywhere you like, fellas!" a matronly woman called out. She was moving rapidly from one cook stove to another, three in all, where an assortment of big black kettles sent up plumes of fragrant steam.

The lawmen sat down and studied the chalkboard that advertised "Today's Specials". Chili and cornbread or baked chicken and dumplings were on the menu. The waitress came and took their orders after serving each of them stout, black coffee. An old man sat at another table. After the waitress left, he hailed, "Howdy! You boys serving a warrant in these parts?"

Matthew smiled. Often, law-abiding citizens showed curiosity when star-bearing law officers showed up. Much of that interest stemmed from self-preservation; they wanted to know if they had a personal reason for alarm. Some of it, though, was morbid curiosity. Matthew was appalled at how many people found a hanging to be high entertainment. He had seen whole families come into town, bearing food baskets and blankets for a picnic, in order to observe death warrants meted out.

He nodded, "Yes sir. We are investigating a series of kidnappings that have taken place in this general area the last few months. Have you heard anything?"

The oldster nodded. "Yeah, now and again. Young girls mainly, right?"

Matthew agreed. "What's your name, sir?"

The portly fellow struggled to his feet and extended his gnarled paw in greeting. "My name is Yorkie, Yorkie Smith. I have a small apple orchard east of here about five miles. Mind if I join you?"

Gesturing to the fourth chair at the table, Matthew said, "Please, have a seat."

Smith sat down and wiped his forehead with a large red kerchief. "Those girls that was absconded, I don't know nuthin' about. None of them was local, see. But my buddies and I have a few theories."

The man's little brown eyes were alight with excitement and Matthew cautioned himself to take the man's words with a grain of salt. All too often, rumors became grist for the mill in a small town. Unsubstantiated gossip became truth whether the whispered words were true or false. Leaning forward, Matthew asked, "Can you fill us in, Mr. Smith?"

Sitting back in his chair, Yorkie surprised the sheriff by saying, "I think most of what I say here is just someone's fancy...words uttered with spiteful intent, if you catch my drift. But there are a couple of strange things I have seen with my own two eyes. Don't know if they connect with those girls' disappearance but it don't hurt to fill you in, I reckon."

The waitress brought their meals and Yorkie asked for another cup of coffee. Then he leaned forward while the other men ate dinner and spoke about the oddness of some of his neighbors' behavior. "First off," he said, "there's a bunch of witches down the road from me."

Observing Matthew's raised eyebrow, Yorkie added, "That's bona fide, Sheriff. You can ask my buddies!" Matthew made a mental note to talk to Smith's "buddies" as soon as possible.

Wiping his mouth, he said, "So, these 'witches'... have you seen them do something illegal?"

Yorkie shook his head. "Nah, not really. They actually seem to be good girls. They attend to some of the birthin' around here and grow herbs and spices on their farm. It's just that..." Yorkie turned red. "Well, a few times when I was out late harvesting my apples, I would look over at their property and seen a big fire burning in the dusk."

He swiped his kerchief across his forehead again. "I know my eyesight ain't what it used to be but I swear those girls was dancing around the fire just as nekked as the day is long!"

"Now," he continued, "I would hate to get those gals in any trouble. Like I said before, they seem like good people, just a little strange. On the other hand, there's a house down the road from me. I don't like them folks at all. They are new to the area." Putting his two hands in the air, he glared. "But don't go thinking I hate new arrivals to town because it ain't so."

Gazing at the mild expression on the lawman's faces, Yorkie's shoulders slumped. "Some folks around here seem to think I ain't nuthin' but a gossip but it ain't true. There are some great folks who just came here. Like the Donnelly's who started up the new cemetery and The Shamrock, and that reporter in from Chicago who opened the Wenatchee Telegraph."

Leaning forward, Yorkie almost whispered, "And the reason I don't like the Owens—those neighbors that moved in last year—is that they be a mite hinky whenever I show my face to them. He's some sort of holy-roller preacher but..." Yorkie squirmed a little in his seat. "There be something wrong with their children. I can't put my finger on it but those young 'uns don't act normal."

Matthew and his deputies had finished their meal by this time and sat back in their chairs. "Have you reported any of this to your local sheriff, sir?" Roy asked, and the old man flushed red.

"Ack! That old crook!" he spat. "Yes, godammit, I have but Winslow just looks at me like I'm teched in the head."

Matthew put his napkin down on the table. "Well, Mr. Smith, I happen to think you have good instincts. I think my deputies and I will go and check on your neighbors tomorrow."

Yorkie smiled and then worry etched his brow. "Now, like I said, I hope that you don't hurt them witch girls any. They seem to be sweet even if they are a little odd. Do whatever you like to that other bunch though. I think they are up to no good. And pay special attention to those kids, okay?" The old man winked, then added, "You just head east about five miles...you'll see my apple trees. Come on in and I'll point out where those neighbors are."

"We will, Mr. Smith, and thank you." Matthew paused for a moment, thinking of killing two birds with one stone. "Listen, our search might take us in a different direction entirely but, if we are in town tomorrow evening, why don't you and your buddies meet up with us here for dinner? My treat. I would like to hear what they have to say, too."

Yorkie's eyes gleamed with gratitude. When he was a younger man, he had commanded respect. By God, he *still* held the rights to one of the best and most profitable orchards in the region. Yet age and frailty had taken their toll and, nowadays, the young bucks in town viewed him and his cronies with contempt more often than not. So, promising to bring his friends, Yorkie agreed to meet up with the lawmen tomorrow evening for dinner. Then he put on his hat and walked out the door.

Turning to his deputies, Matthew said, "It's early still. Why don't we head on over to the Shamrock for a drink?"

Roy looked startled. "I thought we weren't going to, Matthew."

The sheriff glowered. "I'd like to see them try to stop us."

Grinning, the two deputies followed Matthew out the door.

They crossed the street and started walking down the boardwalk toward the bright green saloon. At one point, Matthew stopped when a fragrance, both sweet and cloying, assaulted his nostrils. Transported back in time by that smell, he was reminded of the day his Uncle Jon was buried—along with Jon's wife and so many other members of his hometown—after Top Hat and his gang laid waste to Granville.

The sharp olfactory memory caused him to pause and look in the window of a small flower shop. He could see some purple blooms lined up on a low shelf and knew that they were some kind of fancy lily. Gazing at a small sign by the front door, he read, DONNELLY'S FLOWERS AND FUNERAL SERVICES, in small gold letters.

This Donnelly fellow has a finger in a lot of pies, Matthew thought. Shaking off the sad memories, he muttered, "Come on, fellas. Let's go beard the goat."

Abner looked bewildered but Roy smirked as they followed Matthew into The Shamrock Saloon.

Fred Marston watched from the back of the large dining room as three lawmen stepped in the door and walked up to the bar. He grinned slightly as the bartender gave each of the men a once-over and then shrugged at their forbidding expressions as he poured them a whiskey.

Of course, they would have been welcome. For one thing, they were obviously lawmen; for another, they were dressed nicely and would have easily passed the dress code restrictions. So the real question was, *why are they here?* They were clearly from out of town as Fred knew all the local authorities.

Staring across the room, he decided to get as close as he could to the three strangers. He would find out what they were doing here, what their business was, or if they were simply passing through. If nothing else, he would tell Patrick about the men's presence. Fred knew that, for the most part, the Wenatchee authorities had taken up permanent residence in the boss's pockets. But these newcomers were obviously not in thrall to Patrick Donnelly. He picked up his cup of coffee and moved about six stools away from where the men sat talking to the bartender.

"Can I get you something, boss?" Arnie called.

"Nah, just finishing up my coffee before I head on home," Fred replied.

Arnie picked up a glass and polished it as a tall, blonde-haired man—a sheriff according to the badge that gleamed on his vest—asked a question. "We're here looking into a series of disappearances in the area.

Mainly, young girls. So I wondered...have you heard anything about it?"

Fred's heart started beating hard in his chest and he struggled to keep his alarm from showing. One man, a deputy sitting next to the sheriff, was gazing around the room with bright, suspicious eyes. Fred had felt those eyes land on him once already. Schooling his features into nonchalant stillness, he listened to Arnie's response.

"Yeah, I have heard a little. It's hard not to hear things from behind this bar." He studied the men's badges and asked, "Where you boys from, anyway?"

"Spokane," the sheriff answered. "Tell me, where is your sheriff's office? We mean to go have a chat with him but we just got here and haven't had a chance yet."

Arnie set down a polished glass and said, "Well, you go down the street...north, about a quarter-mile. You'll see the jailhouse. Sheriff Winslow's office is there. If you went now, you'd probably run into one of the deputies, I'm sure. Meanwhile, I could tell you a little about what I know. Oh, excuse me," he said and went to serve a well-dressed customer who had just sat down at the far end of the bar.

Fred had heard enough. These men were scratching in Patrick's hen yard and the boss needed to know. Not to mention the fact that six girls were trussed up together in one stall waiting to be loaded into the largest of their coaches, only a few hours away from transport to their "warehouse" in Seattle.

He set his cup down on the bar, put on his hat and

called out, "I'm headin' home, Arnie. See you next week."

"Bye now, Fred," Arnie replied.

Patrick's henchman strolled out the door, walked down the boardwalk and mounted his horse. Forcing himself to go slow and steady, Fred rounded the corner, checked to make sure no one was watching, and then spurred the animal into a frantic gallop.

9

A CHANGE OF PLANS

MARGARET WAS ILL AND SHAKING BY THE TIME FRED Marston rode his horse into the barn, joining Patrick and Dan at the front of the stall that held the six hostages. She thought there was still a vial of laudanum tucked into her corset but a frantic search informed her that it was gone and she silently fretted that maybe she'd lost it during Amelia's kidnapping.

She would not, could not, admit her fears to her brother. He was already angry with her and hearing that she might have left evidence behind that could incriminate them would only enrage him further. Margaret would never admit that she was suffering from withdrawal pangs either; Patrick would have no sympathy for her plight. So she feigned a headache and quietly went about preparing their hostages for transport.

Fred had told his boss that a keen set of lawmen were hot on their trail although he didn't think they realized it yet. Patrick paced back and forth in front of the stall's entrance, frowning in ire.

"What did you say their names were?" he asked Fred.

"I didn't hear, boss. But I did hear the sheriff say they were from Spokane County. They were asking about girls gone missing from the area and where Winslow's office is located."

Patrick spat in disgust. "Well, Winslow doesn't know anything about this end of our business, thank God. I swear he's as loose as a goose. If anyone with real balls asked him what he knew, he'd spill like a cracked egg." He stopped pacing and gazed down at the girls sitting chained together in the straw.

"I hate to do this but I think you two had better get a move on. If you leave now, you could be in Seattle in three days, well ahead of anybody snooping around our personal business. Also, although they're not quite ready, you'd better take the Indian and the new girl. I want this place as clean as possible in case that sheriff decides to pay a visit." Fred and Dan nodded.

"Margaret!" he yelled as he spun in place. "Get these girls dressed for the trip." Standing right behind him, Patrick handed his sister a small bottle of laudanum, one of many he kept under lock and key in order to keep the captives compliant. "Give them each a small sip so they sleep most of the way," he said, looking her in the eye. "And I better not catch you drinking at that trough, either," he added.

She lowered her eyes and went to fetch some old

coats and mufflers. Most of the girls had been dressed lightly when they were abducted but the weather had turned chilly the last couple of days. As the men would be taking the overland pass into Seattle where the temperatures might drop below freezing, it would not do to have their captives grow sick and die from exposure en route.

As Margaret scurried about grabbing the coats and shawls for the drug-addled girls, Patrick turned to Fred once again. "So," he said. "You don't think that sheriff is on to us?"

Fred shook his head. "Nah, I really don't. They could be trouble, though. I'm with you on cleaning this place up, pronto."

Patrick agreed and walked out of the barn, then into the house. He gathered some cash, a couple more bottles of laudanum and a few firearms while his men harnessed four of their biggest draft horses onto a large, covered freight-wagon. By the time he got back to the barn, the girls were being carried out. Each of them was gagged before they were chained together on the floorboards.

Patrick handed the cash, drugs and weapons to Fred and wished the two men good speed. "Once you get to the halfway house, change these horses out, let the girls rest for the night and then head on in to the warehouse."

The 'warehouse' was actually one of Patrick's brothels but the madam in charge, Polly Cumberlain, would do her best to make the new arrivals appear healthy and pretty. Some of them, though—due to the circumstances of their abduction—would be easier to work with than others.

Staring in at Amelia Winters, Patrick told his sister, "That one still looks pretty sick. Maybe we should just do her right now."

Margaret, trying to mask her sudden exhilaration from the large dose of laudanum she had swallowed rather than waste it on the squaw, looked at Patrick and said, "She'll be fine, brother. She just needs a little more time."

A few moments later, the wagon headed out of the barnyard and down the road.

Patrick turned to his sister. "I would have you stay in the house tonight. There is a chance that the sheriff and his deputies will come to call within the next couple of days. We both need a good night's sleep and then, first thing in the morning, we will clean this barn from top to bottom."

Margaret nodded and followed her brother. She clutched the scant amount of laudanum remaining in the vial in her fist and, before mounting the porch steps, tucked it into a hidden pocket of her skirt.

Deputy Richard "Dicky" McNulty sat at the desk in the Kittitas County sheriff's office, staring out the window at the brilliant blue skies of late September. Red and gold leaves fell like rain from maple trees across the street in the little municipal park that used to house the dead until the Donnelly's dug them up and transported the bones to the new graveyard.

He sighed in frustration. Dicky had spent the better part of his youth daydreaming about being a "lawman." He wanted to do right and be recognized as a man of honor, integrity and principal. He was one step up the ladder to fulfilling his dreams but feared that was as far as he was liable to get.

For one thing, he was a runt. His size seemed normal enough to him when he was a youngster. Although his pa—Joseph McNulty—was short at only 5 feet, 4 inches, he was as wide as a tree stump and bigger than life itself to his starstruck son. He used to say, "Size is not the measure of strength, laddie. Strength comes from in here." Joseph would then pound his red-furred chest for emphasis and declare, "The McNultys were always a wee clan, but known verra well for their fierceness in battle!"

Unfortunately, Dicky took after his mother's side of the family, so he was not only short in stature but slight in frame as well. At twenty-two years old, Dicky stood only 5'5" and weighed in at 129 pounds sopping wet.

Worse yet, when a falling tree later killed his pa, Dicky developed a stutter. The doctor told his mother that the boy was in a state of shock from seeing his pa killed in front of his eyes. He assured her that eventually the shock would pass and Dicky would regain his former tongue but, so far, that had not happened.

He couldn't even mutter "Good morning" without the words backing up in his throat like a clogged pipe. "Gu,gu,gu...od mmmmorning!" he had barely managed to utter earlier when Sheriff Winslow walked into the office. The shifty old coot had stared at him with ugly eyes and said, "Try not to talk unless you have to, Dicky...got it?"

Dicky turned as red as a beet with mortification and bowed his head in shame at the smirks he saw in his fellow deputies' eyes.

Winslow and the other men had left soon after, heading to the train depot to meet up with some bigwigs who were coming to town to sign documents detailing the changes involved in turning their area from Kittitas County into Chelan County. The sheriff wore his best seersucker suit and a new derby in order to woo the legislators. Even so, he looked like a portly, puffed up Banty rooster.

Dicky knew the sheriff was resolved toward politics and making money. Ever since the Great Northern Railway had come to the area, real estate was selling like hotcakes. Winslow didn't give a fig about keeping law and order; the only thing he wanted to do was line his pockets with all the new cash coming in by the trainload every day.

Although the young man suspected he was twice as smart as his boss and three times the man, he burned with frustration knowing that his impediment would keep him on the bottom rung of society while fat, crooked, cruel men like Winslow would rise to the top like clots of cream in a pitcher of milk.

A flurry of activity caught Dicky's eye and he focused his attention out the window as one of Donnelly's carriages whizzed by. He stood up and walked outside, staring south as the shiny new contrivance stopped in front of the flower shop/funeral parlor.

Mr. Donnelly sat on the driver's bench, accompanied by his sister Margaret. She was dressed in a fine gown of gray brocade with purple piping and wore a matching velvet hat with a long plume of lavender feathers covering half her face that Dicky figured was, as usual, pale and wan as a ghost. He shuddered. There was something about those two that he did not like or trust. It wasn't anything he could put his finger on...just a feeling of goose bumps that tickled his neck whenever he was in their company.

Being the youngest and newest deputy on Winslow's staff meant that he was often called upon to work late, early, or on weekends while his fellow officers idled in bed or took picnics with their families on Sunday afternoons.

At first, Dicky thought it was a fluke. But often, while working the darkest hours of night, the young deputy had seen the Donnelly's black carriage and matching horses sail down the street—the canvas window openings closed—and Donnelly's men sitting armed and ominous on the front bench.

Initially, he reasoned that someone had died and the funeral home was picking up the body and hauling it back to Donnelly's home for burial preparations. Yet something deep inside scoffed at that idea. *Why would they feel compelled to pick up a body in the very "dead" of night?* he wondered.

Just a couple of nights ago, standing outside on the boardwalk smoking his pa's old pipe and listening to the first trills of morning birds in the thickets, he heard the sound of hoof beats approaching up the street. It was still quite dark and Dicky could not tell who was there until Donnelly's coach was almost upon him.

The lantern light on the front porch of the sheriff's office illuminated the driver's face and Dicky saw Mr. Donnelly and his sister staring over at him with cold, hostile eyes. He skedaddled inside, his heart pounding like an Indian war drum and waited for his boss and fellow deputies to arrive. Later, when he mentioned the Donnelly's nocturnal activities, Winslow told him to shut up and mind his own business.

Now, hearing footsteps coming up from behind him, the deputy turned around and saw three men approaching. His small, brown eyes got big and his mouth sagged open in awe as the epitome of law and justice walked toward him.

Tall and lean, handsome and clean, a sheriff and two deputies strode up the boardwalk with eyes open wide and smiles wreathing their striking features. The man with the sheriff's star on his vest held out his hand and said, "How do you do?"

Oh, Dicky thought, if only I worked with such men as these.

Matthew saw the little deputy with bright, ginger hair and rusty freckles gape at him and his men as they walked up. Grinning, he shook each of their hands and nodded at their introductions but turned an unfortunate beet color when he tried to introduce himself. Stuttering and squirming as his unruly tongue mangled the words, he finally shrugged in silent mortification.

Matthew had met a few stutterers in his life and felt sorry for their predicament. Often, their lack of communication hid stunning intelligence and he decided to test that theory now.

Reaching into his vest pocket, Matthew took out a sheaf of notepaper pinned at the top edge with one of Iris's sewing needles. Then he asked, "Can you write?"

The young man's shoulders sagged with relief and he smiled. "Ye.. yeah!"

"Well, let's head on inside. Maybe you can write your answers to a couple of questions me and my men have, okay?"

Dicky sighed with relief. He had literally begged his boss to let him communicate in this manner but Winslow had turned mean and hissed, "You will talk like a man or be out on yer ass, hear me?"

Now Dicky followed his new hero, Sheriff Matthew Wilcox, and his deputies into the office and wrote the answer to every question asked of him in a fine and flowing hand.

It had never occurred to Dicky that Sheriff Winslow barely knew how to read or write himself, or that the man was a coward deep in his heart, any more than it occurred to Winslow that Dicky was an educated man—a measurable genius—and the best shot in the county. Nor did Winslow realize that Dicky's diminutive frame housed the heart of a lion and the blood of one of the fiercest, fighting clans in Scotland.

10

CHOMPING AT THE BIT

MATTHEW OFTEN WISHED HE DIDN'T WEAR A STAR ON HIS vest. Along with the power to serve arrest warrants and mete out the occasional justice in his hometown, he was also compelled to follow the rules whether he liked it or not. This was one of those occasions as he needed permission from the local authorities to conduct his search or run the risk of being jailed himself while the affronted party examined his credentials.

The answers to the questions he asked young Dicky were well written and concise, but maddening in the extreme.

"Where is your boss?" he asked. *"Meeting up with some politicos out of Olympia at the courthouse,"* was the answer. *"When will he return?" "Sorry, not until later this afternoon,"* Dicky wrote.

The sheriff gritted his teeth. The young deputy

stared up at his gloomy countenance and scribbled another question. "*Is there something I can help you with?*"

Matthew shook his head. "No, I don't think so. My deputies and I are searching for some missing girls...my niece in particular. It seems like the trail either starts or ends in this area. But, in order to operate here, I need written authority from the sheriff or closest marshal. Is there a marshal around these parts?"

Dicky shook his head and wrote, "That is why those legislators are here, Sheriff. They brought papers turning this into a new county, Chelan County. When that happens, we will have a lot more resources but it has not happened yet. Sheriff Winslow is the top hand right now."

Matthew thought for a moment and said, "Dicky, do you think your boss would mind if we showed up at the courthouse and asked him if we might proceed with our search?"

The deputy blushed and his fiery red brows drew together in a frown. He stared into space for a second and then wrote, "*Sir, my boss is an angry sort of man. He has ambitions.*" Dicky glanced up at Matthew's face as though considering whether his words were wise or not. Then he shrugged and continued scribbling. "*You could try, sir, but he will not thank you for it. In fact, he might say no to your request just to be spiteful.*"

Matthew nodded. He had run into quite a few petty despots since he first picked up his star. Men who liked the power and prestige that came with the office but had no feeling or affection for the people they had sworn to protect. Matthew thought that some of the sheriffs he had met over the years were worse than many criminals, not to mention in a position to do terrible damage to their towns and constituents.

"Okay, Dicky." He sighed. "We'll come back later this afternoon and talk to your sheriff then. Will you let him know we're here?"

Dicky nodded. Matthew looked into the kid's bright eyes and asked, "How about you? Have you seen anything strange around here lately or heard about girls gone missing from the area?"

The deputy stared up at the sheriff and wondered whether or not he should voice his suspicions about the Donnelly's behavior. A moment passed, then another, while Matthew watched the young man's face with keen interest.

Finally, Dicky shook his head and wrote, "Most of us have heard about abductions in the area but I do not have any particular knowledge. And none of the girls that I know of are locals. Sorry!"

Matthew stared at him. For the first time since entering the office, he felt that the deputy was either lying or holding back information. Filing his feelings away for the time being, he tipped his hat and said, "Thanks for your help, son. Please inform your sheriff that we will be calling on him later this afternoon."

Dicky blushed. He did not miss how the man's green eyes studied his nor the tense attention of the two deputies who accompanied him. He wanted to confide his fears but he had been told all too often by Sheriff Winslow that he did not know what he was talking about and to mind his own business.

Now he'd lost Sheriff Wilcox's trust and, in doing so, lost even more of his own self-confidence. Getting to his feet, he blurted, "Ththth..ank you, sir. I'll tutu, tell him."

The lawmen waved goodbye and walked away down the boardwalk as young Dicky McNulty wrung his hat in his hands and wished he were not such a hopeless coward.

MATTHEW ASKED, "DID YOU SEE THAT?"

He and his deputies were saddling their horses, getting ready to head out to Yorkie Smith's house to check out the man's strange neighbors.

Matthew knew he and his men walked a fine line as, after all, they were going to investigate some of Sheriff Winslow's own citizens without the man's authority. Still, Matthew reasoned, they were invited to visit by the old man himself. If they saw something out of place or illegal, he had no doubt that Yorkie would speak to that fact, one which should appease any circuit judge should the need arise.

"Dicky's face? Yeah, he's hiding something...or lying," Roy muttered.

"I think he was scared, boss," Abner spoke up.

Matthew mounted his horse and stared over at his young deputy. "I think you're right. You have good instincts." Abner blushed with pride.

"I agree, Abner, but don't forget to speak up once in awhile, okay? Matthew and I can't be expected to know everything." Roy's gruff manner hid a tenderness that had helped shape the timid young man into a good deputy.

"Yes, sir!" he said and gave his big plow horse a slight kick. It was an old animal but huge, hearty and—more importantly—stout enough to carry Abner's weight for miles on end.

The sheriff and his deputies rode north down a well-maintained dirt road. It was beautiful country with numerous farms, wheat fields, fruit trees, and a busy human population. Matthew saw clay huts with thatched roofs, temporary living quarters for the people who had settled in the area. Even at this early hour, he could hear the sound of saws and hammers piercing the air as the landowners worked feverishly on new houses and barns in preparation for the coming winter.

A half hour later, the lawmen came upon an established apple orchard. Any doubts they might have had over whether it was Yorkie's property vanished as they saw the oldster himself perched on a wicker ladder clipping away the uppermost branches from one of his trees.

"Ho!" Yorkie called, scrambling down the rungs with a smile. A worn basket filled to the brim with bright, yellow apples sat nearby. "I picked these for you. Some of them are going soft but yer horses won't mind, I guess."

Abner stared at the fruit and said, "I ain't never seen yeller ones before."

Yorkie picked an apple out of the basket and handed it to the young giant. "Try one, son, and you'll see why I have one of the best orchards around."

Abner took a bite and his eyes got big. Chewing, and wiping the fragrant juice off his chin he smiled and said, "Thank you, sir. That's the best apple I ever et!"

Matthew looked around, drinking in the scenery. It was a beautiful piece of land. To the north, he could see white, snow-capped mountains with skirts of red and gold...the dying, autumnal splendor of late season tamaracks, aspens and maple trees. He could also see a few farms here and there with livestock grazing on the lower slopes.

To the south, he saw the sapphire twinkle of rushing water. He realized it was the Wenatchee River which wound a sinuous path through the back edge of Yorkie Smith's orchard. Sending plumes of freshwater mist into the air, Matthew understood why the trees and meadows remained green and the trees still produced fruit despite the season.

Yorkie watched Matthew's face and beamed with

pride. "My pa settled here in 1832. I was ten years old at the time. I've worked this orchard my whole life."

"It's beautiful," Matthew murmured, then turned around when he heard Roy say, "Boss..."

Roy was pointing his finger to the east, further into the trees. Matthew looked and saw two women kneeling on the ground, talking to three small children. Skinny and ragged, they looked like urchins and he wondered where they came from.

Yorkie sighed, "Well, we're in luck, if you want to call it that," he said. Those two ladies live over there in an old farmhouse. Those young'uns belong to my neighbors to the west...the bastards I told you about."

Matthew was too far away to hear what they were saying but he saw one of the women hand a sack to the kids. With one feral glance over at the men who watched, the children took the sack and melted into the trees, disappearing from sight. The women looked as though they were going to run away as well, but Yorkie called out to them.

"Merrill, please come and talk to us before you go. These men...they're good men. You don't need to be afraid."

Matthew saw the two women whisper to each other, then one of them stepped away and faded into the tree line while the other walked slowly in their direction.

She was an older woman, wearing a blue chambray work shirt tucked into a pair of dungarees. Her long gray hair was loose down her back and she had a battered old kerchief around her neck. She was also attractive but for the tenseness in her face and the obvious fear in her eyes as she studied the men who surrounded Yorkie.

"Merrill, these are lawmen out of the Spokane area. They're here looking for some missing girls, including Sheriff Wilcox's niece."

Matthew stepped forward and extended his right hand, "Pleased to meet you, Ma'am."

Merrill stared at his hand as if it was a snake, then took a deep breath and clasped his hand in hers. "Merrill Sanders, Sheriff. Pleased to make your acquaintance."

"Is there anything you can tell us about the abductions in this area, Mrs...?" Matthew asked.

She interrupted him with flashing eyes. "Miss Sanders, if you please." He nodded and she turned to Yorkie. "Mr. Smith, would you be so kind as to donate a beef roast or the like if my girls and I match it with a cooked ham? You know those children have no way to cook the meat without being caught."

Yorkie said, "Sure, Meri. You know I will."

Turning back to Matthew, Merrill said, "Mr. Smith and I are trying to save the lives of a number of children who live across the way, Sheriff. I wish with all my heart that you and your men could put a stop to that devilry." She sighed. "As to your missing girls...yes, not only have my friends and I heard about it but we have lost some women as well."

Matthew's eyebrows rose as Merrill continued, "My property, about a half mile from here, is a haven for homeless women and girls. They don't always have it easy, you know. Sometimes they are left widowed and alone. Sometimes, though, they are abused by men who are no better than beasts. They are beaten, raped and left for dead by their husbands, or sold into slavery by a man's debtors."

She glared up at him and watched in satisfaction when his expression acknowledged the truth in her words.

Matthew wondered which category this handsome woman had once fit into. Despite her years, it was clear to the officers that she must have been a beauty in her youth. The only thing that marred her looks now was a long, jagged scar that ran from her left temple down to the corner of her mouth, like someone had taken a butcher knife to her pretty face.

"Anyway," she continued, "our guests come and go as they please. Some stay but others will run away again as soon as they heal up. Within the last four months, though, two women who went to town to fetch supplies never came back." Merrill turned away and studied the mist that rose from the river's passage at the back of Yorkie's property.

"Both of those women were here to stay, Sheriff. I would have bet my life on it!" She glared in frustration. "They were both deeply terrorized by their former existence and loved the peace and tranquility I was able to offer them here. That is why I believe they were kidnapped. They were both beautiful girls and, from what I hear, only the pretty ones are taken."

Shaking her head, Merrill added, "I have a personal stake in seeing those girls found. But before you go, please, please, do something to help those poor children next door."

11

THE SHE-DEVIL

MERRILL LEFT FOR HOME AFTER PROMISING TO DROP OFF a description and drawings of the girls gone missing before evening. After she had gone, Yorkie spoke to the lawmen about his suspicions.

"The Owens moved here about five years ago... spring of '87, I believe." Yorkie scratched his chin whiskers for a few seconds. "At first, I thought they was a fine addition to the neighborhood. He is some sort of pastor and he holds a revival meeting once a month in this big tent they brung up from California. Well, he did until a few months ago anyway.

"Like I said, they have a bunch of kids. Four or five of them, at least. I seen 'em myself when they first arrived. Lately, though, those children seem to have vanished." He squeezed his floppy felt hat in his hands. "Now, I know there are people who stick their big noses in each other's business when they ought not to but I swear, Sheriff, I think something terrible has happened.

"Where there used to be a passel of kids running around, climbing my trees and getting into mischief like healthy young'uns do, now there are only those two you saw earlier and they are nothing like what they used to be. They are the youngest, I believe...twin girls. I remember them being just as cute as buttons and now they are little better than feral animals."

Staring up at Matthew, the little old man whispered, "Could you just ride over there and ask after the children's health, maybe? See what happens, look into Frank and Mary's faces. You'll get my meaning, I know it!"

Matthew nodded and said, "We will, sir. Did you want to accompany us?"

Yorkie's eyes got big and he exclaimed, "No, siree. Those folks...well, I'm an old man and can't fight like I used to do. I'd just as soon stay back here at home."

"That's okay, Mr. Smith. My deputies and I will head over there now. Can we still expect the pleasure of you and your friends' company later on this evening?"

Yorkie brightened. "For sure. I told Pete, who told... well, like I said, you can count us in."

Mounting their horses, the lawmen traveled back out onto the road and turned right a mile and a half later onto an overgrown wagon trail. They passed under a stand of willow trees and entered a small meadow. A dilapidated farmhouse sat in the distance and a battered canvas tent took up space in the front yard.

It was close to eleven o'clock by now and the autumn sun had risen over the trees ringing the meadow with unusual intensity. Heat waves rose into the air and crickets sawed their legs together in a somnolent chorus.

"Matthew, look," Roy murmured.

Following his friend's gaze, the sheriff saw a teenaged girl hanging clothes on a line next to the dilapidated revival tent. He watched her start with surprise at their approach and run into the house.

"Watch out, boys, and hold up your stars so they can see them," Matthew said. Roy and Abner both unsnapped their holsters and laid ready hands on their pistols. All of them knew that surprising a criminal in his lair was a dangerous proposition. Even regular, law-abiding folk did not take kindly to trespassers and held the right to protect their holdings with whatever force they deemed necessary.

The men rode to the front of the house and sat their horses, well out of rifle range. All three of them held their badges up in the air and Matthew shouted, "Hello! I would like a word with Mr. Owens."

"What do you want?" a man's voice called out.

Thinking quickly, and remembering a story he once heard about a sheriff who played a trick in order to bag a train-robber, he answered, "Mr. Owens. My name is Matthew Wilcox - Sheriff Matthew Wilcox out of Spokane County. These are my deputies. We are here with a will that entitles you and your wife to over twenty thousand dollars. However, I need to serve these papers into your hands and you will need to sign them before the document is deemed legal."

There was a prolonged silence and then they heard Owens holler, "Who died?"

Matthew got down from his horse, rooted around in his saddlebags and found a sheath of arrest warrants. Holding the rolled bundle in the air and hoping Owens fell for the ruse, he thought, *This is tricky*. He had no idea where this so-called preacher came from and knew even less about the man's family. What he did know, though…

"Mr. Owens, the judge who gave me these papers told me that a wealthy parishioner from California left her fortune to you and your ministry."

Crossing mental fingers against the lie, Matthew waited. Ten seconds passed, then twenty seconds before the lawmen heard Owens shout, "Stay where you are. I'm comin' out there to look for myself."

Sighing with relief, he caught Roy's eye. The deputy suppressed a grin but winked once in acknowledgement of a gambit well played. "You want us up or down, boss?" he whispered.

Matthew watched the front door open and saw a gangly-looking man squeeze through the opening to stand on the porch. "You get down and stand by me, Roy. Abner, stay mounted, but back your horse up about twenty feet. Be ready for anything."

He heard the young deputy click his teeth and saw

the old draft horse move backwards. Staring at the dirty, middle-aged man who glared at him from the safety of the porch, he said, "I get the feeling these are bad people, Roy, and they aren't going to let us in. Agreed?"

Roy nodded. "Yep, I think you are right."

"We need to get Owens and his wife out here. Once they're close enough, I want them subdued. Let's try to do it without any gun play, but we can't let them get the drop on us either."

The pastor studied them and the papers Matthew held in his hand. He looked like a starved rat with long, yellow teeth and a sharp, pointy nose.

"Those papers in your hand," he growled. "Is that the will? I want to see it."

"Sure, Mr. Owens, you will." Matthew replied. "Both you and your wife need to sign, though, for the will to be bound by law."

Owens glared. "My wife don't write."

"That's alright, sir," the sheriff said. "I am here to witness her X."

Undecided, Owens wavered for a moment and then he hollered, "Mary, get out here! Now!"

"Here we go," Matthew said. "Get ready to move on my mark."

A well-fed, buxom woman exited the front door and went to stand by her husband's side. She wore a long, bloodstained apron and she scowled at the two lawmen with piggish, hostile eyes. After a brief conference, Frank and Mary Owens stepped off the porch and walked toward Matthew and Roy.

Matthew smiled at them. "Looks like this is your lucky day."

"Let me see them papers." Frank snarled as his wife studied them with a closed-lip frown.

Matthew adopted a wounded expression. "You seem a mite unfriendly for a man of the cloth, Mr. Owens."

The sheriff saw the couple hesitate and watched in fascination as they physically wrestled their faces into a parody of righteousness. Then Frank Owens smiled and said, "Our apologies, Sheriff. These are hard times and this country is a harsh place. Our flock has dispersed and we find ourselves ever on the lookout for fighting injuns."

Matthew bowed his head and held out the unfurled sheaf of papers, facedown, for them to see. He clasped a small bottle of ink and a pen in his other hand. "If you will, just come over here next to my horse. You can use the saddle as a desk to mark your names."

The man and woman approached, staring at the papers like thirsty pilgrims at a pool of cold water, and Matthew said, "Now!"

Immediately, Roy took two quick steps and placed his pistol up against Mary's dingy bonnet. The woman probably outweighed the deputy by fifty pounds but she was no fool. The Colt's cold kiss against her temple was equalizer enough, though, and she followed Roy's guiding hand down onto the ground.

The second Roy made his move, Matthew snapped his handcuffs around Frank Owens's wrist. The man lunged away but stopped when he felt Matthew's gun dig into his left kidney. Landing on the ground next to his wife, the pastor burst into tears.

"She made me do it! It was all her, the sick bitch!"

"Shut up, you bastard!" Mary Owens snarled. Then she wriggled close enough to sink her teeth into Frank's shoulder.

Growling, she worried at the man's body like a rabid hound while he screamed in terrified anguish. The two lawmen gaped in disbelief and then Roy cuffed the woman over the head with the butt of his pistol.

Mary fell into an unconscious heap next to her weeping spouse, her mouth wide open. Matthew and Roy bound the couple back-to-back hoping that, upon waking, the psychotic female would not try to eat her husband alive. Staring at her dirty, broken teeth, their hearts sank as they began to understand what might have happened to the children.

Looking up as Abner approached, Matthew said, "Abner, tie these horses onto that chew rail, please. Roy and I are going into the house to check on the kids." Studying the bloody bite on Frank Owens's shoulder, he shuddered. "If there are any kids left, that is."

Roy had the same sinking feeling and he glared down at the married couple in disgust. "You better hope and pray, Mr. Preacher Man, that we find all your kids present and accounted for." He spat on the ground and walked away up onto the front porch, Matthew following close behind.

"By any chance, did you see what happened to that girl?" Matthew hissed as they walked slowly into the house.

"Nah," Roy answered. "So we better look sharp."

The two men walked through the dark interior, their senses ringing with alarm. The place was filthy and they could smell the stench of death coming from the north end of the building. They ducked through an archway into a kitchen area and saw a door standing open at the back of the room.

The smell of decay rose from the open doorway like a steady stream of foul breath from the throat of hell. Exchanging a look of dismay, Matthew and Roy stepped through the doorway and descended a flight of rickety steps to the root cellar.

Both men already knew what they were going to find and their hearts were heavy with the savage knowledge of humanity's baser instincts.

FINALLY, A CLUE

Matthew and his deputies sat at a table in the back of Callie's Café, picking listlessly at the food on their plates. None of them had an appetite, although the beef pies sent up fragrant puffs of steam and their bellies cramped with hunger. Each of them struggled with what they had seen and experienced earlier that day.

Once Matthew and Roy found a lantern in the basement of Pastor Owens's house, they discovered wicker cages filled with pale fragile bones, scraps of leathery skin, and the remains of two small children. Their heads had been removed and sat on a high shelf, staring down at the lawmen in reproach.

Although Abner would never carry the weight of that spectacle, he was suffering as well. Mary Owens had awoken and lay trussed up against her husband, growling and hissing like a snake. Busy keeping one wary eye on her and the other on the darkened doorway through which his friends had disappeared,

Abner never saw the Owens's eldest daughter Prudence sneak around the back of the tent with a shotgun in her hands.

Following her father's instructions, she had grabbed the gun and snuck out the back door while her parents met the lawmen out front. She watched helplessly as the sheriff and his deputy seized Frank and Mary, but she didn't know what to do. The men moved so quickly there was no way she could debilitate them without doing the same to her folks. It wasn't until the tall sheriff and his deputy disappeared into the house that she seized her opportunity.

Abner was staring down at Mary Owens, trying to keep his skin from crawling away. She stared past his left shoulder and whispered an eerie language that made his heart stutter in fear; he'd heard his ma talk about holy men who sometimes "spoke in tongues" and wondered if that was what he was hearing now.

What he did not realize was that Prudence was creeping up on him with a shotgun aimed at his back. Her mother—who only tolerated the girl because she provided sexual relief for her father and Mary had no intention of allowing Frank access to her own private parts—was whispering encouragement to Prudence in a strange, sibilant language the Owens had perfected over their years of chicanery in the ministry circuit.

The only thing that saved Abner's life was, at the same moment she took aim and fired, Matthew and Roy stumbled out the front door onto the porch, saw the girl with her gun, and shouted for him to duck.

As it was, the shot grazed the young man's shoulder and the right side of his face. Roy and Matthew wrestled the girl to the ground before she had a chance to reload and heard her squeals of defiance and fury as she was tied up alongside her parents.

Matthew was able to pick most of the buckshot out of Abner's body but it wasn't until later—after Roy galloped into town, told young Dicky what had transpired and grabbed the sheriff's department paddy wagon for prisoner transport—that the town doc was able to dig some of the deeper pellets out of Abner's neck and jaw.

So now he sat, his shoulders slumped in misery and his spoon forgotten on his plate.

Yorkie and his friends had stopped by a little earlier. Most of them were agog at the news of the Owens's capture and the rumors of their foul deeds circling the small town like wildfire. Yorkie himself seemed both proud and saddened. He had known something was wrong and was glad that he had expressed his concerns to the first officers who acted as if they gave a good goddam. Still, if the stories were true, he kicked himself for the delay—maybe, if he had acted sooner, those two little boys might still be alive.

He told Sheriff Wilcox that the twin girls were safe with Merrill although there was no telling how long that might last. Yorkie recalled his own pa and how he used to beat both him and his ma senseless every other Sunday. *The Presbyterian Gospel,* Pa had called it with a smile. Yorkie remembered how he had wanted to run away; to just disappear from people like his father, who held him and his mother in helpless thrall.

"How long do you plan on staying, Sheriff?" Yorkie asked.

"We'll probably head out tomorrow, Mr. Smith," Matthew replied.

"Well, happy trails," Yorkie said. "I hope you find your niece."

Getting ready to leave, Matthew stared across the street at the silhouette of the telegraph officer who appeared to be closing up for the evening. Standing up suddenly, he said, "I have to go send my wife word about our whereabouts. You two have anything you want to add?"

Roy shook his head. "Nah, our families will know we're okay unless you say different."

Matthew nodded and clapped his hat on his head. Handing Roy a couple of silvers, he said, "Pay up for us, won't you? I'll be back in a few minutes." Then he headed out and crossed the dirt road to the telegraph office.

The door was opening just as Matthew jumped up on the boardwalk. Smiling, he said, "Sir, I know it's late in the day but I wondered if you could fire your machine up one last time?"

The portly man frowned. "Young man, I can see from your star that you are a lawman but I can't turn that machine back on. Not unless Sheriff Winslow says so, anyway. Sorry."

Matthew sighed with frustration. He had met

Winslow earlier and recalled withstanding the sharp edge of the man's reproach.

"How could you do such a thing in MY town, without MY permission? I have half a mind to let those two go free!" he had snarled while young Dicky—who had already experienced a similar tongue-lashing—wrung his hat in his hands with dismay.

Matthew had remained silent while Winslow ranted and raved but then something came over the Kittias County lawman's face and he stuttered to a stop, peering up at the young sheriff in sudden shock.

It was all Dicky could do to keep from laughing out loud. It was as if a tiny poodle had run up against a giant hound, barking and growling with territorial fear, only to realize his adversary was twice as big and a hundred times stronger than he was.

Taking a deep breath, Winslow backed away and muttered, "Well, of course, that ain't going to happen. The parents will hang. Don't know yet what will become of the girl."

Matthew stayed quiet while Winslow fiddled at his desk and then he said, "I believe that girl was as much a victim as her brothers and sisters were albeit in a different way, Sheriff. I hope you will give a true accounting when the circuit judge gets here?"

Winslow nodded. "Yes, yes, of course. When did you say you and your men are leaving town?"

"Tomorrow morning, we'll be on our way. One more time, *Sheriff...*" Dicky heard the insolence in Matthew's voice even if Winslow did not. "You and your men have heard *nothing* about any girls gone missing in the area?"

Winslow shook his head, jowls flapping. "No! I tell you, nothing like that is going on here." His face turned red, either in fear or outrage.

Now, standing on the boardwalk in front of the telegraph office, Matthew gritted his teeth in frustration. The agent's hands were apparently tied and there was no way he was going to test Winslow's will at this time of night. Sighing, Matthew said, "Well, I guess I'll have to come back in the morning then."

Bowing slightly, the man mumbled an apology and promised to open a little early; 6:30 rather than 7:00 am. Then, he took off down the street.

Matthew stared after him and shook his head. He had never felt so helpless in his adult life. This was the second full day of his search for Amelia Winters and he was no closer to finding her than he was two days ago. He knew that every day that passed lessened the chance of finding her at all but, time after time, he and his men seemed to be running up one blind alley into another.

Heading across the street, Matthew jumped a little when he saw Dicky's slight form materialize from thin air. Actually, Dicky had been hiding behind a tall sandwich board in front of the feed store trying to decide whether he wanted to tell Sheriff Wilcox what he had seen or not. He had just decided to plow ahead when the sheriff turned around, startling him.

"Oh, I'm ssssorry to snee..eak up on yyy…" his voice trailed off.

"Hello, Dicky. Did you want to speak with me?"

The young man nodded and Matthew said, "Well, let's head on inside the hotel, shall we? I think I can scrounge up some paper."

Dicky followed him and waited while the sheriff asked the clerk at the front desk for writing material. There was a small lobby with chairs, a couch and two round tables. He sat down at one of them, fidgeting nervously.

Matthew pulled up a chair, smiled and said, "Tell me what you know, Dicky."

For the first time since he had started working for Winslow, Dicky felt at ease and confident. There was something—a kindness maybe, or just a deeper under-standing in Matthew's eyes—that told the young man his word was valued…needed even. He grabbed the paper and pen and started scribbling.

He filled up three pieces of paper, read them and finally handed them back to the sheriff. Dicky watched Matthew and noticed when his eyes got big; he watched as the man bent over and started writing his own notes.

A few minutes passed in silence. Then, sitting back with a small smile on his face, Matthew asked, "Dicky, how would you like to work for me?

13

A KEEPSAKE

THE NEXT MORNING, DICKY STEPPED INSIDE CALLIE'S Café and saw Matthew and the deputies sitting at a table in the back. They smiled as he approached and Matthew said, "Pull up a stump, Dicky. Did you want to order something to eat?"

Dicky could not afford to eat out very often—not with what Winslow paid—and had packed a lunch. Having just ate half of it on his way to the restaurant, he grinned and shook his head.

Matthew said, "Welcome aboard, son. Since you are officially a part of my posse now, you will be eating and drinking compliments of the Spokane County sheriff's department. Okay?"

Dicky nodded, flushing with pleasure.

Matthew studied the young man's face and asked, "We may need to leave at the drop of a hat...are you fixed with your family and ready to go?"

Dicky pulled out a piece of scratch and wrote, "Yes sir!

My saddlebags are packed and my ma knows I took up a job with your outfit. Thanks again!"

"Good," Matthew said. "Here's our plan. First, I need to send a telegraph back home. We're waiting for the agent to show up, which he promised to do by 6:30. Then, once the Donnelly's come into town, we'll head out to their place and have a look around. Are you sure they don't have a lookout in place?"

Dicky shrugged and scribbled, "I don't think so. They have their two men, Dan O'Reilly and Fred Marston, but I am pretty sure they took off to the Donnelly's warehouse in Seattle. They usually head over there once a month or so to pick up handles and metal scrollwork for the caskets they make here in town."

Matthew nodded, remembering the conversation he'd overheard a couple of nights ago at the Shamrock Saloon; the bartender talking to Marston and his response about being gone for a week. Satisfied they wouldn't run into a shooting match on the Donnelly's property, he drank the last of his coffee and asked, "What time do the Donnellys usually show up for work?"

"Usually 8:00 or close to it," Dicky wrote.

Matthew sat up straight as he saw the telegraph agent scurrying toward his office. As promised, he was opening up early. Standing, he grabbed his hat and said, "You guys pay up and get the horses ready to head out. I'll meet you at the livery as soon as I'm done." He paused and added, "Pack your gear, too. No need to load your saddlebags quite yet, but have everything ready to grab."

The men stood to leave as Matthew went out and crossed the street. As soon as the telegraph machine warmed up, he sent his messages to the deputies in Granville and to Iris. Walking toward the town stable, he saw Dicky's little roan tied to the hitching rail out front and strained to see into the darkened interior. All three of the Spokane County sheriff department's horses were saddled. The mule nickered from his own stall.

"We're ready to go, Matthew," Roy called from inside the barn. "We were thinking this would be as good a place as any to wait. We can see out but the Donnelly's will have trouble seeing us here in the shade."

"Good idea. Dicky, please move your horse inside with the others."

Dicky quickly obeyed and the four men stood beside their mounts, waiting for the Donnelly's carriage to roll past.

"Watcher doin'?" The stable owner, a heavy-set man with a belly as big as a barrel, walked up from the back of the building with a bucket of oats in his hand.

Matthew turned around and smiled. "Nothing, really," he replied. "Just having a powwow before we hit the road."

"Well, okay...I guess. Just don't let these rigged up hoss's spook those left in their stalls. Once one goes, they all wanter take off in a bunch, you know."

Matthew *did* know that. Horses were such herders that they would all run straight over a cliff if the boss stallion told them to.

Pulling out his pocket watch, he peered at the time. 7:54...*Not too much longer*, he thought.

Ten minutes passed and Matthew started to wonder if the Donnelly's planned to stay home today. But then they heard the sound of hoof beats coming up the road. Standing back out of the light and staring through the big double doors of the barn, he saw a fancy black coach pass by. Looking down at Dicky, he saw the boy nod. "Wait here for a minute," he said, and went to the stable doors.

He watched the carriage pull to a stop in front of the flower shop. Margaret Donnelly stepped down and entered her business as the coach moved to the opposite side of the road and out of sight.

Earlier, Dicky had written that Patrick Donnelly always followed the same schedule. He would drop off his sister at her shop and then head across the street to mind the Shamrock and other business concerns from his office in the restaurant.

Hustling to where his men stood poised, Matthew said, "Let's go." All four lawmen mounted their horses, riding toward the cemetery and the Donnelly's home.

They rode about four miles, eventually coming up on a well-maintained piece of land. Most of the fencing was post and rail but soon turned to elaborate wrought iron with a beautiful, high archway surrounding the big white house. A discreet sign on top of the arch read, DONNELLY'S CEMETARY.

Staring past the fence, Matthew saw an elegant graveyard with a stone mausoleum, angelic statues and numerous marble headstones. Years ago, after Top Hat had decimated so much of his hometown and its population, the city of Spokane had donated wrought iron fencing for the local cemetery. Nicer than many towns boasted, there still wasn't enough money to maintain the grounds and there certainly wasn't enough cash left over for most folks in Granville to invest in statues or fancy tombstones.

He sighed and turned to Dicky. "Is there a groundskeeper?"

Dicky shook his head and stuttered, "Nnnno, sir. Just FFFred and Dan, I thth...ink."

"Okay, let's ride around the back of that barn," Matthew said. "We'll hide our horses there and if we hear anyone coming we can bail out down the road."

They rode slowly around the property, alert to anyone else's presence. Although there was a stand of tall, lilac bushes and a few fruit trees behind the house and barn, they could easily hit the road running if need be.

Matthew and his deputies got down from their mounts and tied them to whatever was handy on that side of the building. Then they peered around the corner, checking one last time for a guard or a lookout.

Finally satisfied they were alone, the men moved quickly to the big double doors in front of the barn, pushing one to the side. They slipped indoors and Matthew rolled the door closed again. Two horses whickered at them from their stalls and the lawmen let their eyes adjust to the dim. There was a large, well-maintained hayloft upstairs and the sun shone through the open slats, sending brilliant rays down through the shadowy interior.

There were six stalls on either side of the barn and the men searched them all. Matthew had hoped against hope that he would find Amelia stashed away somewhere inside but it didn't take long for them to see that wasn't the case. It was as clean as a whistle. So clean, in fact, that it seemed all wrong.

There was no dung anywhere and the hitching rails were spotless. Even the two windows set high up on either side of the sliding doors were shiny. It seemed like the entire place had been wiped down.

"What do you think, boss?" Roy looked as frustrated as Matthew felt. Although the barn's cleanliness was beyond reproach, it was a little too much so for Roy's taste.

"I think there was something here but the Donnelly's cleaned up the evidence."

Roy nodded. "Yup, I agree. Do you want to look inside the house?"

Matthew frowned. "I would like to but you know the law. The only thing we have is a gut feeling. I believe young Dicky but breaking and entering into the Donnelly's house without the sheriff's approval could get the bunch of us thrown in jail. And I don't think Winslow would grant us access."

Dicky glanced up at Matthew's words and his heart thumped with anxiety. He really had no proof of wrongdoing on the Donnelly's part and he would hate to get the Spokane County posse in trouble for a hunch.

"Boss, come and have a look!" Abner's normally placid face was alight with excitement.

Matthew, Roy and Dicky walked to where Abner stood by the last stall, staring down at the hay-covered floorboards. At first glance, the enclosure was immaculate…no dung, spilled oats, or trough water.

Yet Matthew followed Abner's gaze and spotted something strange. Moving closer, he knelt and peered at the place where a crossbeam held the wall upright. Crammed in between two pieces of lumber, there was a small piece of paper folded in two with only one corner showing.

He reached in and gently coaxed it out of its hidey-hole. Standing up, Matthew unfolded the square and beheld his own face along with that of his wife and infant son, Chance.

He remembered the day that photographer fellow had come out to the farm to take his family's pictures. To the amusement of Iris's other children, Chance had been in one of his rare rages. The little photographer was none too happy about the Wilcox family's nonchalant disrespect of his art: The more he squealed, "Please, no laughter, be more serious!" the more the family chuckled and smirked until, finally, he shot the image Matthew now held in his hand before he left in a huff.

The men crowded around him and Roy said, "Well, well. Looks like we finally found ourselves a trail to follow."

Matthew nodded silently and tucked the photograph in his vest pocket. Then he said, "Abner, great work...thank you."

The young man blushed with pride as Roy gave him a cuff on the arm. Dicky grinned up at the giant and said, "Gggg...ood eyes!"

Then Matthew said, "Let's go."

The lawmen walked to the barn doors and, after peering outside to check that they were still alone, pulled one panel sideways enough to squeeze through. Mounting their horses, the Spokane County sheriff and his deputies rode back through the yard and onto the road.

They kept their horses at a trot until they reached the town limits and then slowed to a walk. Once at the hotel, the officers moved swiftly upstairs, grabbed their kits, paid for their rooms, and were heading west toward Seattle before the sun hit high noon.

14

TROUBLE ON THE ROAD

DAN AND FRED STOPPED OUTSIDE OF A RAMSHACKLE cabin in the western foothills of the Cascade Mountains, about forty-five miles away from Seattle. It was still quite warm for September although the girls had shivered and quaked with the below freezing temperatures during the latter hours of the night's travels.

This was one of Donnelly's way stations. The men saw a paddock filled with horses, a milk cow and a flock of chickens in the side yard. As they inspected the property, an old man stepped out on the porch.

"Hello! I was beginning to think you weren't comin'!" he hollered.

"Smitty, you old dog!" Dan responded. Then he and his partner climbed down off the wagon, stretching their legs. Fred heard the captive girls in back of the wagon, whispering amongst themselves and complaining of their need to pee.

He rapped sharply on the back entrance port and hissed, "Shut up! We'll let you out in a minute."

Dan walked up to Smitty Threwgard and said, "You got some coffee made, by any chance?"

Smitty nodded. "Yup, sure do, although it's a mite strong by now. What kept you men? I expected you last night."

Dan rubbed the whiskers on his face. "We had to stop every other minute for these bitches to pee, or take care of their bleedin' or what have you," he swore. "We always used to dope 'em up for the trip but, this time, Mr. Donnelly said there wasn't any dope to spare. Probably Margaret got ahold of what there was. She never could keep her fingers out of the cookie jar, you know."

Smitty gestured and Dan followed him inside the cabin, accepting a cup of stout black coffee. Taking a noisy slurp, he continued. "Anyway, maybe it was a good thing we stopped. About thirty miles back, Fred glassed our back trail and saw four riders coming up fast behind us." Smitty raised an eyebrow.

"Reason I mention it is," Dan continued, "Fred thought he saw a man he recognized. They was a good ways back, about twenty miles, but he thought he saw a rider that's as big as a house and rides a draft horse. If that's him, it means there is a band of lawmen—probably those deputies out of Spokane—hot on our trail."

"You think they're after you?" Smitty wanted to know.

Dan shook his head. "Fred thinks so but you know

he's always worried about this thing and that. Anyway, there's no way to tell, really. But it don't help that this is such a lively bunch. Last thing we need is an inquisitive bunch of lawmen sniffin' around this wagon."

Moving to the open door, he peered outside and saw that Fred was herding the girls down a plank to the grass. He watched as a number of the females squatted in place to relieve their bladders.

Smitty whistled. "Lookit that penny-headed girl there…she's a beaut!"

Dan nodded. "Yep, that's the newest acquisition. Her name is…" He stopped talking as both men heard Fred start to yell. The tall, skinny man ran back down the plank from inside the wagon and accosted the redhead just as she started standing up from her squat.

"What do you mean, you don't know?" they heard Fred's voice bellowing through the still, morning air.

"Ooops, looks like we might have us a problem," Dan muttered and strode off the porch to where Fred stood screaming into the frightened girl's face.

"What's going on here?" he asked his friend and partner.

Fred turned around. "One of the girls is missing!" he hissed. "The little squaw…"

Dan's heart skipped a beat. "What? How can that be?" Now he was getting mad and wanted to shake some information loose from the mute, terror-stricken girls. Donnelly did not suffer losses well and would not hesitate to take his anger out on their hides.

Staring at Amelia, he asked, "When was the last time you saw the squaw?"

The disheveled young beauty looked down at the ground and replied, "I really don't remember since it was dark when we last stopped. I thought she was asleep under her blanket but maybe she left while we were busy."

Dan frowned. "And you didn't think to alert us when you saw she was no longer in our company?"

Amelia's cheeks turned red. "No! Like I said, it was dark. For all I knew, she had changed positions while I was outside. I didn't even know she wasn't there anymore!"

The girl made a reasonable argument, but she was too young and inexperienced to dissemble well. Although her eyes were wide with innocence, she kept glancing down and sideways...a sure "tell" if Dan ever saw one.

Stepping forward, he raised his right hand and slapped the furtive look right off her face. She fell down with a cry and the other girls gasped with dismay. Amelia stared at the bright red blood that spotted her hand from the split on her lower lip and then glared up at her tormenter. "Okay," she spat. "She escaped a long time ago, maybe thirty miles back. And I hope she gets away for good!"

Dan stood over her, fighting his desire to kick her in the ribs. He and Fred were under strict orders to take as good a care as possible with this latest bunch since the Sultan's auction was coming up quick so a bunch of broken bones would be frowned upon for sure. Taking a deep breath, he turned to Smitty and said, "Let's change this horseflesh out. We got to get a move on."

The old man tossed his coffee cup dregs on the ground and walked as swiftly as he could into the paddock. Fred moved to the traces and started to unhitch their tired stock from the wagon.

Dan growled, "You bitches get up in that wagon. There will be no more kindnesses for you from now on as I see you can't be trusted. Now git!"

The young women fled as quickly as possible up the plank. One girl yelled, "You ain't even going to give us any water?"

"No! Now, shut yer mouths!" Dan snarled. He had to feed and water them and he knew it. Still, he thought the fear of going without food and drink might deter the prisoners from doing anything stupid, at least until they made it to the warehouse.

He and Fred got their new team harnessed and took a quick lunch. Then, after throwing two full canteens of water and a loaf of bread into the back of the wagon, they took off on the final leg of their journey into Seattle.

Approximately twenty-five miles away, Matthew

held up one hand and whispered, "Whoa, boys. There's something over there in the trees."

The men pulled up their horses and stared into the woods to their right. Shadows intersected with shafts of sunlight that shot down out of the sky like golden arrows. It was pretty but hard to distinguish what was what. They strained their eyes and all of them drew their pistols in readiness. Then a branch cracked, sending chipmunks to chattering overhead.

"There!" Matthew pointed and slid down off his saddle. The lawmen crept into the brush, keeping their eyes on a few low bushes that quaked with constant, unnatural movement. Matthew signaled for the men to stop and moved forward on his own. Peering over a fallen log, he saw an Indian woman curled up on the forest floor. She was so thin he could see her bones pushing against her flesh. Her eyes were huge and stared up at him as if her last hope had just died.

He held out a hand and said, "Hold on there. We aren't going to hurt you." He squatted down, staying on the opposite side of the large, fallen tree and called, "One of you, give me some water."

Someone thrust a canteen over his shoulder and he uncapped it, watching as the girl's eyes tracked his every move and licked her lips in thirst. He handed the water over the log for her to grab. Wary as a hungry hawk, she reached up and took the canteen out of his hands. Tipping it to her mouth, she took a number of short sips and Matthew nodded in approval.

"Good. She knows not to drink so fast that she founders," he murmured.

"What ya got there, boss?" Roy asked softly.

"An Indian girl. Looks like she has been used rough, too." He glanced over his shoulder at the deputies. "Listen, why don't we stop here for a few hours? The horses need a rest, and we could use the time to try and figure out how to help this little squaw."

"Okay," Roy agreed.

Matthew heard the three men walk away to set up a temporary camp. He gazed down at the girl who had finished drinking and was trying to get comfortable on the ground. Her eyes were heavy and it looked like she was about to fall right over in exhaustion.

Clearing his throat, he asked, "Can you understand me?"

The young woman stared up at him and then, to his shock, she smiled. "Yes, I think you are Uncle Matthew."

15

CHASING WEST

Matthew felt a sense of relief that he had chosen correctly. Sometimes a posse had no more to go on than a sixth sense when it came time to cut sign. Animals left a trail to follow: broken twigs; hoof or paw prints; drops of blood. However, when it came to humans—especially those that did not want to be found—the trail could sometimes become impossible to find, much less follow.

Although he was shocked when the Indian girl spoke his name, he also realized that this girl must have seen the picture tucked in his vest pocket. Pulling it out, Matthew unfolded the photograph and showed it to her.

"Do you know the girl who left this?"

Pushing her long, black hair away from her face with shaking fingers, she nodded and answered. "Yes, it was Amelia."

Ashamed, Matthew swore under his breath and

apologized. "I'm sorry. You're hurt and tired. Let's go over here and get you something to eat."

Abner and Dicky had just gotten a small fire lit in a clearing about thirty feet away and Matthew could see Roy fixing a fresh pot of coffee. The girl looked famished but she eyed the other members of his party with distrust. "It's okay, Miss. Those are Spokane County deputies...my friends. They would never hurt you."

She stared up into his eyes and then took a step toward the fire. Letting out a cry, she stumbled, wobbling in pain.

Looking down, Matthew frowned. Despite her long dress, he could see her right ankle was at least twice as big as the left.

"Whoa! Let me help you," he said as she grimaced in pain. Not knowing what else to do until they were able to dress and wrap her injury, he scooped her into his arms. She struggled briefly, then went limp as he strode toward the fire.

As the deputies watched them approach, Dicky appeared worried but Roy, as usual, was all business. He took one look at her ankle and walked over to the mule to get his medical kit.

"Knock it off!" he snapped when the animal laid its ears back and bared its teeth. Quieting, it allowed the deputy to rummage around in the bags. A moment later, Roy knelt by the girl with long strips of wrapping material. Gazing down, he said, "This is either a break or a really bad sprain. Look at that swelling!"

The girl's ankle was as big around as a cantaloupe, and blue and purple with bruises. Her toes were turning white which Matthew knew was a bad sign. He had the feeling this young woman had walked for many miles when she should have been resting and letting her injury recover.

"Lie down for a minute and let us wrap this ankle," he murmured.

She gazed at the four men and sighed, knowing she required assistance in order to make it back home to her people. "Thank you" she whispered and laid down, allowing one of the men to place her foot in his lap.

Matthew held her hand as Abner and Dicky chopped stout branches into splints and Roy wrapped soft cloth rags all around those branches for support.

"What's your name?" he asked.

Biting her lip to keep from crying aloud in pain, she looked up and smiled. "My people call me Little Deer, but the teacher at my school says my name is now Sarah."

"Well…," Matthew paused, "you are very brave, Little Deer. Can you tell us what happened to you and Amelia?"

At that moment, Abner walked up with a steaming cup of fresh coffee and handed it to Sarah. She took a drink, grimacing at the bitterness, but Matthew could see the ashy color leave her complexion almost immediately.

Roy finished wrapping her ankle and stood up. "I think this is a bad sprain. Maybe, if she lets it rest for a while and keeps the splint on, the swelling will go down. She's not walking anywhere though...not for a while anyway." He glared down at the young woman with his stern words, making sure she got his message.

Sarah struggled to sit up and Abner put one of their saddlebags behind her back for support. Looking over at the sheriff, she said, "I was walking to school. I'm not a student anymore, but I help the white-lady teacher with some of the Indian children who need to learn English so they can succeed in their studies." She took another sip of her coffee and continued.

"The school is just outside of Walla Walla. It is about three miles away from my family home, on the outskirts of my people's reservation. It takes me about an hour and a half to walk there so it was just breaking dawn when a carriage came up the road behind me. Normally, that would not be a problem for me. I will walk off the road and let wagons or buggies pass but..." A tear trickled from her eye and she whisked it away with an angry swipe of her arm.

Sarah stopped talking and lifted her nose like an inquisitive hound as Abner had just put some bacon in a fry pan, the smell wafting through the air. She looked so starved, Matthew wondered how long it had been since she filled her belly.

Turning to Dicky, he said, "Would you bring Miss Little Deer a piece of bread soaked in that bacon fat?"

Nodding, the young deputy hustled off and Sarah looked up at the sheriff. Smiling, she said, "Sir, I appreciate your efforts to honor me and my people by using my Indian name but it's really not necessary. Mine was one of the first tribes to go willingly to the reservation. We were dying, you see, and most of our men were killed either on Bear Paw Mountain or fighting against Custer and his troops."

Dicky brought a piece of hard bread liberally soaked with bacon fat and the young woman tore into it like a hungry wolf. While she ate, Matthew walked over to the coffeepot and poured himself a cup.

Turning to Roy, he said, "We'll stay for a while longer, then we need to move out." Glancing at the two younger men, he added, "Get some shut-eye if you can. Once we get going, I don't plan on stopping until we reach Seattle."

Roy handed him a small cup of water and winked. Knowing what it contained, Matthew nodded his thanks and walked back to where Sarah sat on the ground. Handing her the laudanum-laced drink, he said, "Do you remember who took you?"

She drank the liquid, and sat back against the saddlebag with a sigh. Nodding, she said, "Yes. It was a man named Fred, and another named Dan. They put something over my mouth and then I slept. When I woke up later, I was in a big barn with some other girls."

Sarah's eyelids started to droop. "I was there for many days and nights, and I am sure that the woman drugged us to keep us quiet. Finally, though, Amelia came. That was..." It was all she could do now to keep her eyes open. "… three days ago, I think." She laid her head back and started to nod off.

Matthew leaned forward and said, "Sarah. Do you know where those men were taking you girls?"

Startled awake, she answered, "Yes…I think so." She struggled to sit upright. "Most of the time when I was held captive in the barn, I slept and slept. Last week, though, I started to wake up. I think the woman who watched us was using the drugs meant for us."

Sarah gazed off into the distance for a moment, then said, "I heard the big boss—the woman's brother, Mr. Donnelly—say that a cheek was holding an auction where girls would be bartered off to the highest bidder."

Matthew grinned. *Proof!* he thought. *If worse came to worst, he could call Miss Little Deer to court as a witness.* Then he frowned and asked, "A cheek? You mean a sheik or a sultan?"

She nodded. "Yes. I don't know what kind of man that is exactly but I heard our captives talking about it a lot." This time, when Sarah laid her head back on the saddlebag, she fell into a deep slumber.

Matthew knew perfectly well what a sultan was. He also knew that if he and his men did not move quickly, they would lose Amelia forever to the Far Eastern sands of time.

"What do you mean he left?" Winslow snarled.

The deputy shuffled his feet and mumbled, "Sir, what I meant to say is I saw the little bastard riding off down the road with that Spokane sheriff's posse about noon. I thought you knew!"

Winslow glared at the man and then said, "I gotta go. You sit here while I'm gone and mind the office. I'll be back in a little while."

The portly sheriff stood up and plucked a handkerchief out of his coat pocket. It was, of a sudden, unbearably hot and he knew that his sweat had more to do with facing Donnelly than the warm weather conditions. Still, he was dripping like a pig.

He mopped his brow and the back of his neck as he walked down the boardwalk to the Shamrock Saloon. Winslow had known for a long time that Donnelly was a crook. Although he didn't quite know what the man did, he was not blind as he had often seen the Donnelly's black coaches coming and going in the dark of night. He had also seen the furtive glances and witnessed too many episodes of clandestine, criminal behavior to be innocent of the man's activities.

Still, the minute the sheriff had let his own greed and ambition get in the way of his duties, Donnelly had owned him lock, stock and barrel. Two years earlier, when the Irish siblings first came to town, Patrick had offered Winslow a hundred dollars a month to oversee some of his enterprises. In other words, look the other way.

At first, Winslow thought the man was running guns. And maybe he was. But the sheriff also "looked away" when a wagonload of painted ladies showed up just after the Shamrock's doors opened. Prostitution was against town policy—it was 1889 in the town of Wenatchee, after all, not some backwater burg in the 1860s.

But a hundred bucks was a hundred bucks. So, despite a number of town hall meetings and a rowdy protest by the Ladies Auxiliary Club, Winslow pocketed the cash and allowed a brothel into the city limits only two blocks away from both the Lutheran and Presbyterian churches.

Over the last few months, word had reached his ears about a series of kidnappings taking place in eastern Washington. His first thought was that Donnelly was behind it and Winslow decided, if he knew what was good for him and his family, he would keep his suspicions to himself.

Now, though, the pigeons had come home to roost in the form of Matthew Wilcox and his Spokane County deputies. *Damn their do-good hides!* he thought as he kicked at a small clod of mud so hard, he almost fell over backward.

Hiring young Dicky had been a bad mistake, as well, Winslow acknowledged with a sigh of self-disgust. The kid was too smart by half and had noticed almost immediately that something was off about the town's newest benefactors. Every time the boy came a runnin' to tell him what he already knew, though, Winslow would put the fear of God into him, warning Dicky that he didn't know nothing and to keep his big yap shut.

Still, he acknowledged that he might have been a little too rough with the kid this last time. Especially since that damn nosy sheriff, Matthew Wilcox, was standing right there with his cold emerald eyes drilling holes into Winslow's soul. He had come off sounding like a liar, even to his own jaded ears.

He strode up to the Shamrock Saloon and was about to step inside when one of the doors swung outward. Patrick Donnelly was standing there, glaring at where Winslow stood wiping the sweat from his face.

"About time you showed up, Sheriff. I was just coming to fetch you." Patrick's large face was red with fury and his hazel eyes bored into Winslow's like two bullets.

Although Winslow felt like running and screaming away from the gangster, he followed Donnelly into his office and gulped when the huge man locked the door.

Patrick turned to him and said, "You need to gather up some evidence against those Spokane County lawmen. Rape, murder, I don't care what you come up with." He grinned and added, "Then send a telegraph to the King County sheriff's department demanding an arrest."

16

AN IMPORTANT MESSAGE

SEVEN HOURS AFTER SARAH FELL INTO AN EXHAUSTED slumber, she woke up in the arms of a young giant. She remembered his name was Abner and he smiled bashfully as she squirmed around in his arms.

"It's all right, Ma'am. We're just coming into a town now," he murmured.

Facing forward, and painfully aware of her throbbing ankle, Sarah saw a little town not too far off. It was a ramshackle place, surrounded by tall fir and cedar trees with a tumbling waterfall in the distance. The streets were muddy and there seemed to be more saloons than houses.

Matthew recalled there was some trouble here a couple of years back involving itinerate Chinese railroad workers but things seemed to have settled down now. At least, he hoped so.

He stopped his horse and, reining the animal around, asked Sarah, "How are you feeling?"

"I'm better, thanks." Amelia was right...her uncle Matthew was a very handsome man even if he was white. Gazing past him, she frowned. "Where are we? I was hoping to go home to my people in Walla Walla but this is different country. Very, um, green."

Matthew nodded. "Yes. If time wasn't of the essence, my men and I would have taken you home but we don't have that luxury. I have decided to install you in the closest hotel and find you some medical attention. Then I'm sending for my wife, who will come and take you back to your family. Is that okay with you?"

Sarah had never—not even once—been asked if she approved of a man's plans or not. Startled and pleased, she nodded her agreement. The sheriff winked and trotted back to the front of their party. Walking slowly, they entered the town known as Gold Bar.

Originally a gold miner's camp, it probably would have dried up and blown away if not for the railroad depot and a few new buildings designed to accommodate travelers. Matthew saw a decent hotel, a restaurant and a large church. Sighing with relief, he felt sure he could find accommodations for Sarah until Iris arrived by train to accompany her back home.

Gasping, Dicky pointed and stuttered, "Loo-oo-ok!"

They had come down from a tangle of trees and high bluffs but now they could see a gigantic mountain come into view. It was ungodly huge and rose like a frosty iceberg over the hills and treetops.

Turning to Dicky, Matthew said, "I believe that is Mount Rainier. It's a volcano."

Dicky looked half-ill with awe. For that matter, so did Roy who asked, "It ain't going to explode on us, I suppose?" He eyed the looming mountain with distrust.

"No. It's dormant, from what I've read," Matthew supplied with a grin.

"Well, it better just stay that way," Roy responded.

They pulled up in front of the only hotel in the rough little town. The proprietor sat on the front porch, eyeing them in an unfriendly manner. "How do you do?" Matthew called out. "My name is Matthew Wilcox. I am a Spokane County sheriff and these are my deputies. Do you have a room available?"

The middle-aged man spat chew on the boardwalk by his chair and said, "I got rooms, but we don't let Injuns in."

Matthew's pleasant expression darkened. "Is that right? How much money would it take for you to have a change of heart on that score?"

The proprietor scowled. "There's not enough money in the world to make me change my mind. Now git!"

Matthew sat rigid in his saddle. He understood that, for some, bad blood between white settlers and the natives would never wipe clean. Still, he hated rude behavior in a man. Glancing over at Sarah, he saw that her cheeks were flushed with fear and shame.

"You run an unfriendly establishment, sir," he snarled.

The man just shrugged and spat upon his own porch again with contempt.

"Sheriff, I got a room you can use." A woman's voice came from across the street. Matthew turned in his saddle and saw an older woman with a broom in her hands standing in front of a large gray house. She waved, gesturing him closer.

Giving the hotel owner one last glare, Matthew reined his horse around and trotted about fifty feet down the muddy road. His deputies followed and they pulled up in front of the house. "Hello!" Matthew smiled. "Did I hear you say that you have a room available?"

The woman grinned. She was missing many teeth and her face was as wrinkled as an old pear but her eyes were merry. "Yes, I do…four rooms to be exact."

"That's wonderful, Ma'am. We'll only be needing two, though. One for little Sarah and one for Abner who will be staying on to watch over her until my wife arrives."

"Name's Gertie Mumford. This is my home. Used to be just me and my family but, once the mister passed on and the young'uns married, I've been letting rooms out." She gazed down the road at the hotel and frowned. "Gotta say, I've been making a pretty good living at it, too. Don't know why that rascal George Libby keeps turning away paying customers the way he does but I'm not complaining neither."

She stepped off her porch and walked over to peer up at Sarah. "Oh, my. Looks like you have a hurt hoof, dear. Son, hand that girl down to me so I can get her into bed."

Abner glanced at his boss who nodded in agreement. Sliding down off the huge draft horse with Sarah in his arms, he allowed her feet to drop and held her upright as she tried to put weight on it. Gasping in pain, Sarah clutched Abner's arm.

"Well, this girl needs the doc," Gertie exclaimed. Turning to Matthew, she said, "His office is down the road, there on the corner. Why don't …?" She gazed at the four men and her eyes landed on the smallest of them. "You," she said to Dicky, "run down and fetch him here."

Dicky grinned. "Y-y-yes, Ma'am!" he said and took off down the street.

Abner picked up Sarah again and they trooped into Gertie's house. It was a homely place but very clean with sparse furniture and a warm fire flickering in the woodstove. Although Indian summer had kept the temperatures moderate, Matthew had felt autumn's inevitable approach in the early-morning frosts and red leaves falling from the deciduous trees.

They helped Sarah into a small bedroom and then Matthew went back out the door just as Dicky and the town's doctor stepped up on the front porch. Matthew stuck out his hand to shake and introduced himself. Then he said, "I was hoping you could check Sarah's ankle. I suspect it's broken, which is why there's so much swelling. How much do I owe you for your services?"

The doctor, a young man with ginger hair and a harried expression, replied, "Well, two dollars is my standard fee. But if I need to do a procedure, it'll be more."

Matthew said, "Do what you need to do, Doc. Say, can you tell me where the telegraph office is?"

The doctor frowned. "It's in the hotel lobby, Sheriff, sorry to say. George is not a friendly fellow and neither is the company he keeps."

"Lucky for me, I don't need a new friend right now." Turning to Dicky, he said, "You and Abner stay here with Sarah. Roy and I are going to send a telegraph. We'll be right back."

Roy, who had been standing behind Matthew, slapped his hat on his head and stepped off the porch. Matthew followed and the two men walked across the street trying in vain to avoid the numerous mud-filled puddles and potholes.

Three men darkened the hotel's front porch as the lawmen approached. They were a rough lot with dark, mud-splattered clothing and cold expressions on their faces. They stared at Matthew and Roy a little too closely for comfort and the sheriff felt a chill warning.

Stepping inside the hotel, Matthew saw a caged-off area with a telegraph machine and a portly woman inside. He walked up and cleared his throat. She looked at him and he saw that her large, watery blue eyes were wide with fear.

"I would like to send a telegraph, please," he said.

She pulled a piece of paper toward herself and held her quill in readiness. Her fat cheeks quivered with anxiety and Matthew knew that something was *very* wrong. Standing up straight, he turned around just as Roy murmured, "Boss..."

Two men were walking up behind them. They both wore stars on their coats and one of them held a cocked and loaded pistol in his right hand. "Put your hands in the air!" one of them barked. "You are under arrest for the rape and murder of one Prudence Owens!"

Matthew and Roy glanced at one another in shock, knowing that things had just become much more complicated.

Later that afternoon, as Matthew and Roy sat together in one cell, Gertie Mumford entered the jailhouse with a large shallow bowl of food in her arms.

"I brung the sheriff and his deputy some supper," she announced.

The Gold Bar deputy, a handsome kid who seemed confused by the whole affair, said, "Mrs. Mumford. You know that food ain't allowed in here or regular civilians neither on account of the bad sorts we get."

Gertie rolled her eyes and said, "These two men aren't bad sorts, Davey. This whole arrest has been a mistake, you'll see. Meanwhile, they need to eat something. So let me pass!"

She marched past the deputy and approached their

cell. Shoving a bowl filled with stew and bread under the metal bars, she asked, "Boys, I'm operating under the assumption that these allegations against you are a bunch of bull?"

Matthew felt the heat of false accusation warm his face. He nodded and said, "Yes, Ma'am. We arrested her parents for malicious mischief and murder in Wenatchee but, when we left, the girl was safe and awaiting the circuit judge's arrival. If that girl *was* raped and murdered, I aim to find out who actually did the deed, if it's the last thing I ever do."

Gertie stood in front of them and her shoulders sagged in frustration. "I thought so, Sheriff. No man takes such good care of a stray Indian girl only to rape and murder another." Glancing over her shoulder at the deputy who stood by the front door looking like he didn't know which way to turn, Gertie stepped up close to the bars and whispered, "What can I do to help?"

Matthew smiled. "Here's money," he said, reaching into his money-belt and withdrawing some bills. "Please send a telegraph to Spokane informing my wife and my deputies what has happened. Tell my wife, Iris, that I need her to board a train to come and fetch Sarah back home to her tribe." He glanced up at the deputy who was walking toward them with alarm in his eyes.

"Hey, Mrs. Mumford," the young man cautioned. "Don't get too close to those prisoners. They're dangerous men!"

Gertie turned around and said, "Foo!"

Turning back, she added, "Davey-boy is getting a mite nervous, Sheriff, so I really *should* be on my way. Anything else I can do?"

Matthew eyed Davey and said, "Just tell Iris to contact the Washington State Governor, Elisha Ferry, about what has happened, okay?"

Gertie's eyes got big and so did the deputy's. Then, the old woman grinned and said, "I sure will, Sheriff. Now eat up that dinner. I'll be back in the morning to fetch the bowl.

17

IT'S A TRICK!

MATTHEW AND ROY HAD STAYED UP LATE TALKING AND making plans but now they lay quietly, trying to get a little shut-eye before morning. Matthew, however, was too keyed up to rest. He was worried that he would never be able to find Iris's niece. They'd had a good start but there were too many obstacles—being six hours or so behind the wagon didn't help, and neither did finding and taking care of Sarah.

This latest development was the real deal-breaker though. Matthew knew that Donnelly had set this game in play. The man was covering his ass, plain and simple, and would stop at nothing—even the rape and murder of a defenseless girl—to sell his kidnapped victims to the highest bidder for a profit.

Matthew also realized that Winslow must be on the take and he swore vengeance against the man's crooked hide. Only a lawman could swear a warrant out on another officer and most sworn sheriffs hesitated to do so, at least not without solid proof. This was the work of a desperate man.

He almost grinned. *Well,* he thought with a certain amount of pleasure, *it was a bad move.* Especially since the Washington State governor had once been a close, personal friend of his deceased uncle, Jonathon Wilcox.

Matthew held no doubt that, as soon as Governor Ferry heard about what had happened, he and Roy would be free to pursue their objectives. But he worried that, by then, it would be too little, too late as he had heard about the flesh-market auctions that took place all over the country.

It had started early in the century when pioneers first stared heading west. White girls were beautifully exotic and, to many Indians and Mexicans, as easy to pick as apples off the tree. The girls were often swept away forever, either to serve as slaves or sexual bond-servants to whoever was able to pay the highest price.

Then, many a Middle Eastern sheik and even some Far Eastern princes started sending agents to the new world to procure the finest female flesh for their assorted temples and harems. Countless thousands of young women had met their fate at the hands of unscrupulous dealers over the last six or seven decades. It wasn't until the Pinkerton agency grew in strength and stamina, and telegraph machines opened commu-nication from coast to coast, that open abductions finally tapered off.

Which wasn't to say that flesh trading was over...far from it. Matthew grimaced in the darkness, trying not to let his imagination get the better of him. Amelia was only seventeen years old. She might be smart and, according to Iris, full of beans. But she was ill-equipped to deal with the men who sought to buy her services.

He sat up on his cot and stared over at the young deputy, Davey Humphries. The boy was asleep with his head down on the desk. He was green, Matthew acknowledged with a sigh, but nobody's fool. Although he was drooling like a baby on the sheriff's desk blotter, the keys to the jail cells were clutched tightly in his hand.

Damnit! he swore. Both he and Roy knew they would eventually get out of this mess, but it would probably take days...days they did not have to spare.

Suddenly he heard a light clatter by the cell's window. Looking up at the ceiling where the barred window let in air and some meager sunlight during the daytime hours, Matthew watched as a small rock sailed through the enclosure. Standing, he walked to the opening and whispered, "Who's there?"

"It's Abner, boss. I need to tell you something."

Looking over his shoulder at the still-sleeping Davey, Matthew stepped up on Roy's cot.

"Hold on a minute, Abner," he said and bent down to shake Roy awake. The deputy's eyes opened in alarm and then focused on Matthew's face.

"Shhh!" he whispered with his index finger on his lips for emphasis.

Roy nodded and scooted over to the foot of the cot

so Matthew could get as close to the window opening as possible.

"What is it, Abner?"

"Sir, because of his speech problems, Dicky wanted me to tell you what he found out a little while ago." There was a slight pause as Abner tried to get the message right. "Sir, according to Dicky, this arrest...this whole thing is a trick."

Matthew felt a thrill of alarm. Being arrested was one thing, especially since he knew the warrants would soon be rendered useless. Being set up for assassination was another thing entirely. "How is this a trick, Abner? Did Dicky say?"

"Yes. He said the three men who reported your so-called crimes to the sheriff here in town are Donnelly's men and they're not lawmen at all. Sir, you and Roy need to get out of there right now! Dicky and I fear an ambush!"

Matthew bit his lip in frustration. They had no guns, no knives, no way to get out of the spot they were in. Then he heard something outside the window that made his lips turn up in a smile. A soft nicker and Abner's voice crooning, "Come on, Baby. That's a good girl!"

Matthew couldn't see out the window but he could hear as the 6'8" Abner walked his giant Percheron to the outside wall and slowly climbed onto the mare's back. "Stand still...that's my good girl!"

Suddenly, two pistols appeared on the other side of the bars. They were clutched in Abner's big none-too-steady hand and Matthew quickly seized the weapons and handed them to Roy.

"Abner, you're a genius," Matthew whispered.

"What do you want us to do now, boss?" the young man asked.

"Head back to the house and be ready to leave at a moment's notice. Make sure you're both armed, Abner. It might get a little exciting around here."

"What about Sarah, sir?"

"Leave her where she is. I'm sure Gertie will take good care of her until Iris gets here."

"Okay. Good luck!"

Matthew heard the clop of the draft horse's hooves moving away. Then he looked Roy in the eye and said, "You ready to break out of here?"

"Yup," Roy responded, staring out at the snoozing deputy. "How should we do this?"

He thought for a moment. "I really don't think that kid is in on this. Maybe his sheriff is innocent, too. I can't know for sure but I don't want Davey to get hurt, so follow my lead."

Matthew sat down on his bunk, hiding his pistol behind his back, and Roy followed suit. Then, affecting a terrified and pain-filled voice he called out, "Deputy! Wake up, please! I'm sick!"

Matthew huddled on the side of the cot with his thin blanket pulled up over his shoulders like a shawl. He shivered dramatically and pulled a long, sick face.

Davey startled awake, stood up, and moved in their direction. "What's the matter with you?"

Matthew groaned in reply and Roy said, "Maybe it was something he ate."

Davey frowned down at the prisoner and wondered what to do. Clearing his throat, he said, "You want me to fetch the doc?"

Matthew shook his head. "Nah, just bring me a bucket. Think I'm going to throw up."

Davey nodded and walked a few feet away to fetch a slop pail. When he turned back around, he saw Matthew and Roy standing upright, pointing pistols at his belly. Realizing he'd been duped, he dropped the bucket and held his hands in the air.

"Don't shoot!" he pleaded. "I got a wife and two little'uns!"

"Son, we don't want to hurt you," Matthew said, softly. "We just need you to let us out of here. There's been a terrible mistake and I think that men are coming—soon—to kill us. I don't doubt for a minute they will kill you, too, if you get in their way."

Davey looked undecided for a moment until the two lawmen cocked their pistols. The sound echoed in the hallway and the young man blanched. Then he stepped up to the lock and inserted the key.

When the door swung open, Matthew said, "Head on over to that chair, Davey. I'm going to tie you in."

Fear made him chatty. "Do you have to, Sheriff? What if I need to piss? Hey, how did you get those pistols? I know for a fact that I took your firearms myself. It was that giant that rides with you, wasn't it?"

Matthew nodded his head at Roy who immediately

walked over to the desk and opened the bottom drawer. Pulling out their own gun belts and pistols, he slung them over his shoulder. Then he turned the lantern low and twitched the front window curtains closed.

As Matthew tied Davey's wrists together, he said, "Listen up, Deputy. My men and I were falsely accused. We are searching for a bunch of missing girls and need to hurry out of here. But you need to tell your boss that the men who leveled charges at us are NOT lawmen at all. Sheriff Winslow of Wenatchee is in cahoots with their boss, though, so you need to be careful!"

"But..." Davey stopped talking and his eyes got big when a volley of gunfire erupted in the street. They heard a wretched screech and angry shouting. Matthew and Roy ducked and moved swiftly to the window. Peering outside, they saw three shadowy figures walking up the boardwalk on the opposite side of the road.

They also saw Baby, Abner's draft horse, on the ground thrashing her legs and squealing in agony. It was hard to see through the darkness with only a few storefront lanterns lighting the hour but Roy hissed in anger, "Goddammit, Matthew! That's Abner underneath his horse. He's stuck and he looks injured!"

Turning around, Matthew ran to where Davey sat agog and dragged the man, chair and all, to the back. Taking a deep breath, he tried the door and it opened into an alley.

"Come on!" he cried and the two men took the

deputy out and sat him on the stoop. Then Matthew threw a blanket over the kid so he blended into the night.

He whispered, "Davey, this is a showdown. It has nothing to do with you but, if you shout out, I think they will shut you up forever. Got me?"

Matthew saw the boy's head bob up and down in agreement. "Good, you stay as quiet as a mouse and, when this is all over, you tell your boss what I said. Okay?" Another nod and the two lawmen ran away into the night.

Donnelly's crew stepped up on the boardwalk in front of the jailhouse. They opened the door with their pistols cocked and ready to fire but stopped in confusion when they saw the empty cells plus the local deputy was nowhere to be seen.

Frustrated, they glared at one another with displeasure. Their orders were clear: Find and do away with the Spokane County sheriff's posse. The Gold Bar sheriff, Troy Duncan, was now dead and so was his wife. Deputy Davey Humphries should have been easy pickings, too, but he was gone as were the men they were ordered to kill.

Swearing, the outlaws stepped back outside. It was too late and too dark to find the missing prisoners but they could kill the giant man pinned underneath his horse and move on to kill the Wenatchee deputy-turned-traitor, Dicky McNulty.

Stepping down onto the muddy street, they froze

when they heard the words, "Don't move or I'll shoot you where you stand!"

Frozen in place, Donnelly's henchmen understood that the Spokane County sheriff had somehow gotten the drop on them.

18

A BLOODY MESS

DONNELLY'S MEN WERE AT A DISTINCT DISADVANTAGE. Roy stood behind them in the dark and Matthew faced them with both pistols clutched in his hands. And unbeknownst to the outlaws, Dicky had run out of Gertie's house and hidden behind Abner's horse. Baby had trembled and moaned, jerking as her blood spilled into the dirt. She had been shot several times but now, mercifully, the big mare lay dead on top of her owner.

Feeling remorseful about using Abner's horse as a hide, Dicky inched his rifle up and over the animal's belly until the barrel site was set dead center on one of Donnelly's crew...a particularly cruel specimen who had often ridiculed Dicky's stutter. He closed one eye and hoped he wouldn't need to shoot. Although he had often imagined getting even with his tormentors, Dicky had never shot a man before.

Meanwhile, Abner lay stock-still. His left leg was numb now but he had no doubt that it had been broken in the fall. He'd heard two distinct cracks as Baby keeled over, pinning him on the road under her weight. Unwanted tears filled his eyes, both from the agony of his injury and the loss of his loyal mare. He didn't have time to waste on emotions, though, as his boss held the three bogus officers in his sights. Unfortunately, one of those men already had his gun out and was aiming it at Abner's head.

"I'm gonna plug that boy of yours, less you drop your guns!" he shouted.

"Don't think so." Matthew pulled the trigger and watched as the man's pistol flew out of his hand onto the road.

The man screeched and jumped up and down, shouting, "Aw, shitfire! My hand! He shot my hand!"

His companions opened fire. But it was too dark for them to take good aim, a fact for which Matthew was profoundly grateful. Fortunately, the lantern light on the front of the hotel illuminated his attackers enough to give him a clear line of sight. He lifted his pistol, aimed and fired. One of the taller men, the one who seemed to be the boss of this outfit, clutched at his left shoulder with a cry of pain.

Matthew felt a line of fire scorch across his left thigh. *Goddammit!* he cursed and stumbled, ducking behind a water trough. He wasn't sure who had shot him but it didn't matter at this point.

He heard the staccato percussion of pistol shots and then an enormous bellow of rifle fire that seemed to serve as an exclamation point to the night's proceedings. Except for a shuffle of feet and assorted gasps of shock from the townsfolk who had awoken to the ruckus and come outside to investigate, silence reigned.

Struggling to his feet, Matthew peered over the trough and saw Roy and Dicky standing over Donnelly's men. Two of them looked to be dead and the other one was huddled in the mud rocking back and forth and cradling the shattered mess that used to be his gun hand. He groaned with shock and pain, muttering, "Look at my hand...my poor hand is shot to shit!"

Roy walked up to Matthew. His grim look of resolve was replaced with alarm when he saw the dark, bloody stain on Matthew's leg. "You're hit. Why didn't you say something?"

"It's nothing, Roy. Just a graze." Looking around at the prone bodies, he said, "Well, this is a bloody mess."

Roy nodded in agreement, then added, "Better thank Dicky when you get the chance, Matthew. I got off a good shot and killed one man but the skunk you wounded had you in his sights. I think he woulda got you in the back but Dicky laid him low with the rifle."

Matthew stared across the street at the young deputy. He was kneeling over Abner now and something he said made the bigger man grin with delight despite his injury and the dead horse pinning him to the ground.

He was about to call out to Dicky when a man came running up the street, shouting, "The sheriff! The sheriff and his wife are both dead!"

Shouts of astonishment and outrage filled the air as the people in town took in what had just happened. More than one angry set of eyes landed on Matthew and his deputies in accusation.

Holding his hands in the air, Matthew yelled, "In case some of you don't know, I am a Spokane County sheriff and these are my deputies! The men you see here in the street set an ambush for us and we dealt with them accordingly!"

About thirty men and women dressed in assorted nightwear stared back and forth at the dead and wounded to the tin stars Matthew, Roy and Dicky held in the air. Abner tried to lift his star as well but kept falling into a woozy doze.

Matthew spoke once more. "If you're thinking that me and my men had anything to do with your sheriff's death, you should know that Roy and I have been locked up in jail most of yesterday and last night. Go around back and you'll find Davey Humphries tied up on a chair, covered with a blanket for his own safety. Ask him if what I say isn't true."

Two men ran around to the back of the jailhouse while the other citizens stared at Matthew in consternation. Then Gertie's voice rang out. "He's right! These are good men in pursuit of the law. I, myself, sent a telegraph to the sheriff's office in Spokane just a few hours ago, not to mention the Washington State governor!" She drew herself up to her full height and added, "They put a stop to these villains and God bless 'em!"

Matthew saw Davey Humphries and his two escorts

walk around the side of the jailhouse. The deputy walked up to him a few seconds later. shaking his head in shock. "I can't believe that the sheriff is dead," he whispered. "Him and his wife both. And looks like you've been shot, too. Let's get you fixed up."

Glancing at Roy, Matthew said, "We have to help Abner. I think his leg is busted."

"Don't worry about it. We'll get him out from under that horse and install him next to Sarah," Roy said. "Don't think he will mind *that* development."

Matthew wondered for a moment what Roy was talking about but then he grinned. Abner *had* been acting half-moonstruck the last couple of days. Maybe he was sweet on the little Indian gal.

Now that it was determined the Spokane sheriff and his posse were not a threat, the townsfolk sprang into action. The men managed to pull Abner's horse off his leg and carry him into a bedroom in Gertie's house. Sure enough, according to the doc, Abner's tibia was broken in two places and he would need a couple of weeks rest before he was able to walk.

At the same time, the doctor's wife took a critical look at the long, bloody welt on Matthew's thigh. Having decided the wound was not serious, she poured straight alcohol on the graze and wrapped it up in clean bandages. Matthew sucked air and sweated, then took a long slug of whiskey. *It might not be a serious wound,* he thought with a grimace, *but it still stings like blazes!*

Davey, Roy and Dicky dragged Donnelly's men out

of the muddy street and ensconced the wounded man in one of the vacant jail cells. Telegraphs went flying, and food was prepared and served up to the survivors. Matthew limped outside and marveled at the carnival atmosphere.

Roy walked up to where Matthew stood and said, "What now, boss?"

"Let's go have a chat with the man I shot." Matthew glared.

"Okay," Roy replied and the two men walked up the road and into the jailhouse.

Davey and the doctor stood by the desk talking but, when the officers stepped in the door, they turned their way.

The doctor said, "The man's name is Bill Arlington. I got the bleeding to stop but that wrist is so shot up I'm going to have to amputate and, possibly, brand the wound closed. The blacksmith is building up his fire now."

Matthew didn't give a hoot about the man's hand. The way he figured it, if you ran with criminals, you'd best be prepared for the consequences. Still, he needed that man's intelligence right now—at least for a few minutes. "Do you mind if I have a word with him? He might be able to help us with our investigation."

The doctor nodded. "He's pretty doped up but do what you need to do."

The prisoner was lying on the cot, still as death. Matthew wondered if he had died but, when he walked up to the bars, the man turned his head and stared.

"You shot my hand, you piece of shit!" he mumbled.

"That's right, Bill," Matthew said. "My aim was off. I meant to shoot you in the heart."

The prisoner scowled and turned his face away but did a double take when the sheriff entered the cell. Matthew stood over him and said, "I want to know where the girls are."

"Screw you! I ain't saying nuthin'!" Bill snarled.

Matthew bent over a little and gave the man's bloody wrist a light tap. Stepping back, he watched and listened as Arlington screamed in agony. "You *are* going to tell me what I want to know or you'll be losing more than one puny hand."

The man shivered and tried staring in defiance. But Matthew bent over again, his index finger extended and aiming for the bloody wound.

"Alright! Alright, sweet Jesus, don't touch me again!" he whimpered.

Matthew stood straight and said, "Well? Where are the girls?"

Bill Arlington knew what would happen if he squealed...Donnelly would have his hide. Not knowing who was worse—Donnelly or this hard-faced sheriff— he said, "Fred and Dan are taking them down to the docks in Seattle. There's a place there, a warehouse, where they fix the girls up pretty for auction."

"Where is it? I need an address," Matthew snarled.

"I don't know...I DON'T!" Bill squealed as the sheriff made to touch his wound again. "It's by the ferry, though…the big ferry that heads west over the sound."

The pain of his injury was leaching all the color out of the man's face. Matthew heard the doctor say, "Sheriff, this is my patient and I want you to leave him alone now. He's not out of the woods yet."

Matthew glared and then his shoulders slumped. *What am I doing?* he thought. *This is not like me, at all.* Still, there came a time in every man's life—especially one like him—who waded through criminal bullshit for a living; where you just had to shake some of the stuff off your boots or you would be sucked into the muck.

"Just one more question, Doc, and we'll be on our way," Matthew said. Turning to Bill, he asked, "I've been to the docks so I know it's a big area. How will I recognize the place?"

Bill's eyes were drifting shut; whatever the doctor had administered for the pain was taking effect. Opening his lids at Matthew's words, he thought about it for a moment and then said, "There is another building, right down the road from the warehouse. It's a small place where they hold the auctions."

His eyes drifted shut again but popped open when Matthew hollered, "And?"

"There's a dragon. A pretty blue and green dragon painted on a sign outside the door. That's where you'll find the girls."

19

THE PLOT THICKENS

MATTHEW AND DICKY RODE THEIR HORSES AS HARD AND fast as they dared toward the shoreline of Lake Washington and the ferry steamer that would take them into the city of Seattle. The sheriff felt the clock ticking in his heart as well as the hot pulsing pain that throbbed along the top of his thigh. If his team had been able to ride unhindered after the wagonload of girls, they might have stood a chance. But one delay after another made Matthew feel they might be too late.

After the furor had died down the night before, Matthew ordered his men to catch some sleep. Then, at 5:30 that morning, he told Roy to stand guard over Abner and Sarah while he and Dicky made their way to the auction house. Matthew would have preferred Roy's company—he was as quick and tough as it came in a pinch. He needed that toughness, though, to handle the law enforcement officers and the political dignitaries that were sure to show up today in Gold

Bar. Someone with solid experience to sort out the mess Donnelly's men had created.

He also trusted Roy to watch over Iris when she arrived later by train and also to see that both Abner and Sarah arrived home safely. Thinking of Iris made Matthew's gut feel tight with longing and the need for council. One thing he had learned after marrying the widow Imes was that, although she had come from a long line of vaudeville actors and "showmen", she had a level, no-nonsense approach to life and its foibles.

Often, while dealing with some of the shadier characters in his hometown and surrounding area, Matthew had sought his wife's advice. It was one thing to hear a woman's complaints about her lousy, no-good, son-of-a-bitch husband but quite another to learn from Iris that the woman in question was known in ladies' circles as a bully and an abuser.

Sometimes, she also seemed to understand men better than Matthew did. He had been taught how to act and behave by his grandfather and his uncle Jonathon—both southern-born with a rigid set of "old-world" rules. Matthew was often blinded by his own expectations; Iris, on the other hand, was able to point out when a man's surly attitude masked a timid and fearful heart.

Many, many people had fled west after the Civil War and still lived in fear of aggression. It didn't really matter by now which "side" had won that conflict as emotions ran deep and memories were long. And some newcomers to Granville were refugees of that war, viewing lawmen as no more than a different kind of soldier...hard and cruel men who were to be avoided at all cost.

Iris had taught Matthew that many men were not as lucky as he had been and reminded him to look to his heart, rather than his moral upbringing, while dealing with the citizens of his town. How he missed her!

Shifting uncomfortably in his saddle, Matthew glanced at his companion. He couldn't help but shake his head in wonder. *If nothing else,* he mused, *my instincts were right about this kid.*

Dicky was as fresh as a new blade of grass but he was proving his mettle. Interestingly enough, he also seemed to be losing his stutter although Matthew was loath to point it out lest the boy's unruly tongue remember its old tricks. Just last night, after Dicky and a number of other men had hauled Abner to a bed in Gertie's house, he had reportedly said, "Sorry those men killed your horse, Abner" without stuttering at all.

Abner had stared him and said, "That's okay, Dicky, I'm better now. Hey, what happened to your stutter?"

Roy told Matthew that the boy blushed as red as a beet and slapped his hand over his mouth in shock. He had made no reply, but his face was wreathed in smiles this morning and he sat tall in his saddle even though the day was getting long. It seemed to Matthew that being needed and respected was all it took to loosen the knot in the boy's throat, and he was happy for Dicky that it had finally happened.

They had another ten miles or so to go before they

hit the dock. According to the locals, depending on the weather, the steamboat made three trips back and forth across Lake Washington per day and the last trip was just before sunset. Pulling his watch out of his pocket, Matthew saw that it was almost 3:15. Touching his rowels to his horse, he said, "We're running out of time, Dicky. We have to make that boat."

Glancing down at the bulge of bandages on Matthew's thigh, Dicky asked, "How you holding up, sir?"

Matthew said, "I'm fine, Dicky. Let's keep going."

The young deputy clicked his tongue and their tired animals put on one last burst of speed. Cantering steadily through the drizzling rain, they gained a low hill and Matthew saw a vast body of water in the distance. He also saw a rickety paddleboat coming towards them about three hundred yards out from the shore. Black smoke belched from two tall stacks and a horse on deck reared and whinnied at the noise. *We're going to make it!* Matthew thought.

They crested the hill and trotted down to where the old boat was just docking at a pier. Two farm wagons, a couple of pedestrians, and an elegant buggy waited to embark. A Negro man shuffled off the vessel and went from one customer to the next collecting fares while a number of small, dark children scrambled here and there, grabbing the bridles of reluctant mounts, tossing wood into the boiler and squirting grease on the paddle assembly.

Matthew heard the old man tell one of the walking

customers, "Storm's a blowin' in. Y'all need to hold on tight to the rails."

Matthew studied the water and saw that, indeed, whitecaps were frosting the swells and wavelets were starting to reach high enough to drench the ferryboat's wooden deck. He was used to water but Dicky was looking green around the gills. "No problem, kid. We'll be across in no time."

Dicky glanced sideways at his boss and said, "If you say so, sir."

Grinning, Matthew said, "I do. Let's go!"

Handing some money to the old ferry captain, they led their mounts onto the boat. "You need 'em stalled, Mister?" one little girl asked.

Matthew responded, "That's alright...these horses can cope, I think."

The child grinned. Her black hair was twisted into tiny spikes and her gap-toothed grin made Matthew miss his son, Chance, who had the same twinkle in his eye when he smiled. She gestured to her left and said, "You tie 'em up on the portside rail, okay? Tie 'em tight!"

"Will do," he replied and led his horse to the left.

Dicky followed and soon they had both horses secured and hooded. A few more fares squeezed onto the boat before the paddles started spinning. Four young boys balanced precariously on the rails and stuck long wooden poles into the water. There was a slight resistance and then the boat floated free, moving into the currents.

Matthew stood close to his horse's head and crooned meaningless words into its ear. If he wasn't so worried, he would have felt a certain amount of excitement. He had been to the big city of Seattle once but that was years ago. He vowed now that he would bring Iris and the kids back for a visit someday. There were fine shops, shows, plays...even an opera house.

As the old boat did a steady clip despite the heavy current, the distance to the far shore diminished rapidly. He saw that the city was shrouded in fog, the gusty winds apparently isolated on the water.

He decided he needed a map. Or maybe they should ditch the horses and ride a trolley to the wharf area. *I could use some time off this horse's back,* he thought as an off-tune horn bleated from the prow of the ferry. Matthew stared at the fast approaching shoreline and gritted his teeth in a grim smile. *If Dicky and I made it in time, the chase is on now.*

Approximately a half hour after Matthew and Dicky left the town of Gold Bar behind, George Libby's wife Naomi scurried out of the large downstairs room where they made their home and into the telegraph booth. Her right cheek still stung from where George had struck her after she complained about his extracurricular criminal activities.

She couldn't understand why he felt the need to line his pockets with Donnelly's money, especially since their hotel was making a profit now that the railroad tracks were down and the train station was just up the road. She suspected that George had borrowed more than he could repay and was forever in the man's debt.

Shaking her head in disgust, Naomi let the machine warm up and doodled a few lines while she waited. MEN DOWN>STOP>> SHERIFF LEFT FOR SEAT-TLE>STOP>>HAVE A ROTTEN DAY> STOP>> Grinning, she crossed the last few words off her message. Deciding that "Men Down" was too provocative, she wrote, LAWMEN SHOT> STOP>>

"You sent it yet?" George was standing just outside the wire cage, glaring in at her. She jumped and said, "I'm sending it now. The machine had to warm up first."

"Well, hurry!" her husband snarled. "We got customers stirring and you haven't even got the coffee started yet." Grumbling, he stalked off as Naomi stared after him with resentment.

Don't suppose you could do it, she thought, and then bent to her task. It didn't take too long to send her message but even as she tapped out the letters, her heart filled with fury at being made an accomplice to her husband's nefarious schemes.

George was too dumb and far too lazy to learn how to run the telegraph machine so she was the one who had sent Gertie's messages far afield of Spokane. She had also made sure that the telegraph to the governor's office flew to an unknown party in Portland, Oregon rather than to Elisha Ferry.

There would be no investigation into what happened here last night; no King County sheriff nosing about and no help from the Spokane County sheriff's wife, Iris Wilcox. Naomi had made certain of that and her heart broke. She had always been a good girl—a church-going girl—but George was turning her into a crook.

She finished sending her messages to Sheriff Winslow and Patrick Donnelly, then took her scratch paper and set it alight. Letting the ashes fall into a metal tray, Naomi heard one of their patrons clattering down the stairs.

"Oh, Mr. Partridge! I am so sorry the coffee is not on yet," she called out. Standing up, she squeezed out of booth, locked the cage door and swept ahead of the middle-aged man into the dining area. "Please, sit down. I'll bring you a cold glass of milk and some bread and jam. The coffee will be ready in a few minutes."

"Can hardly function of a morning without coffee," she heard the bewhiskered gentleman complain. But he shut up soon enough when she brought in the promised treats.

Heading back into the kitchen, Naomi measured coffee into the pot and set it on the stove to boil. Stepping up to the window, she peered out the right edge of the pane and saw the tips of her husband's boots as he sat rocking on the porch.

She took another step sideways into the pantry and pulled out one of the messages she had re-routed yesterday, the one Sheriff Wilcox had sent to his wife Iris. Looking down at the man's hasty scrawl, she bit her lip in envy. What a handsome man he was and the way he had written, *I love you and miss you more than I can convey, remember our secret vow,* set her heart aflutter.

Knowing that she was risking her husband's wrath and possible reprisal from Donnelly, Naomi decided to re-send the telegraph to Iris Wilcox in Spokane. What could it hurt? It was just a love letter, after all, and instructions to come and fetch the little squaw. Those things surely had nothing to do with Donnelly and his ruffians.

Glancing outside again, she walked through the swinging door to the hotel's main lobby and into the telegraph booth. The machine was ready so it took no time at all to send the message. Then she hurried back into the kitchen, threw the scratch paper into the woodstove and removed the coffee pot just as it began to boil.

20

A SECRET VOW

IRIS WAS HELPING ABBY PUT AWAY BOOKS AND PAPERS from the day's classroom activities when Samuel ran in the back door of the schoolhouse. He clutched a brownish-yellow envelope in his right fist and blurted, "Ma! Pa sent a telegraph!"

Her heart skipped a beat and she knew her cheeks flushed red. *Lord,* she thought, *when is my passion for that man going to fade?* Taking three long steps towards her eldest son, Iris snatched the paper out of his hand and ripped it open. She read Matthew's words while her children watched her face anxiously.

Most of the message was straightforward: Mattie needed her to board a train and come west to the town of Gold Bar. Once there, she was supposed to escort a young Indian woman back home to Walla Walla. That was simple enough, Iris knew, but the last line in the message made her heart pound with dread.

Years ago, when she and Matthew first married,

they were both still reeling from the attack on their hometown by the outlaw known as Top Hat. Many of their friends and family members had perished as the gang took over their town in retaliation against the young sheriff. Matthew and the town's citizens were ultimately triumphant but at great personal cost.

A week before Matthew and Iris tied the knot, he came out to her farm and asked to speak with her alone. Shooing the children away, Iris stared at her groom-to-be as he gazed up at the setting sun. There was such sorrow in his green eyes, she wondered if Matthew was about to call off the wedding entirely. Heart aching in her chest, Iris had clasped her hands together in her lap and waited.

Matthew turned to her and said, "You know I'm not cut out to be a farmer, right?"

Iris couldn't help but smirk. Matthew was certainly capable of farming…she had never met a more intelligent or canny man. He just didn't want to do it and that was fine with her. She had two good, steady farmhands already and enough money to sell—even at a loss—if that's what Matthew wanted to do.

Still, realizing the seriousness of his question, she nodded and said, "I know that, Mattie, and I've never asked you to farm this land. Why is that fact bothering you now?"

His eyes locked on hers and he said, "The town fathers have asked me to stay on as sheriff here in Granville and, eventually, they want to put my name up as a Washington State Marshal. I guess old Steve

McChord is fixing to retire in the next few years and they want me to replace him when he goes."

Iris frowned. "Are you telling me something new, Mattie? I knew going in you were going to be a lawman for as long as you're able."

Matthew leaned over and kissed her. Then he sat back and said, "We're entering into a new, modern age, Iris. It's an exciting time to be alive but also a perilous time—especially for lawmen. Used to be a sheriff could chase a bunch of outlaws down with a decent posse and a good team of horses." He sighed. "Some outlaws were worse than others though...and you know about that."

Iris nodded in agreement.

"But, for the most part, the outlaws operated under the same principles as those who chased them —a good horse, a hidey-hole, and a fast gun. Things are different now." Matthew sat up straight. "Trains are here and telegraph machines...things move quicker than they used to for both the good guys and the bad.

"If you still want to marry me, knowing what my chosen profession is, then you and I need to have a code. Some sort of secret warning system in place so you and the kids and everyone else in this town will never be taken by surprise again." Matthew's eyes looked deeply into hers and he clasped both of her hands tightly in his own.

Iris had thought her young husband was erring toward the side of caution. After all, she mused silently, what are the

odds of another outside attack? Especially since Top Hat is
dead and gone, along with the rest of his gang?

She watched as Matthew pulled a piece of paper out
of his pants pocket and listened as he started reciting
some phrases he thought suitable. There were quite a
number of key words on his list but she liked the one
that said, "Remember our secret vow."

Reading those words now, Iris realized the only
reason she had chosen that phrase over the others was
because she had thought of nothing else for weeks but
her marriage vows to Matthew. Just that morning,
before Matthew showed up at the farm, she had
scratched out one line and added another to the little
poem she would read to him during their wedding the
following week.

Five years later, she studied the telegraph again. Dear
Iris>Stop. Please board the train to Gold Bar>Stop. Roy will
meet you>Stop. Escort the young woman, Sarah, back home
to Walla Walla>Stop. Dicky and I will follow Amelia's trail
into Seattle>Stop. I love you and miss you more than I can
convey. Remember our secret vow> Stop.

"What is it, Ma?" Abigail's frightened voice pene-
trated her concentration and Iris stared at her children's faces.

"Your father is okay but I have to leave town." Iris's
mind was awhirl with everything she needed to do
before the train arrived at 7:00 tomorrow morning.
First and foremost, though, was keeping her family
safe.

It hardly mattered why she had originally agreed to

the wording of Matthew's secret code, the message now was loud and clear: They were in danger. The outlaws Matthew chased were cunning and ruthless, and Iris needed to inform the authorities about the situation as this meant the posse was compromised.

Iris's brown eyes flashed and she said, "Sammy, you and Abby need to pack up a few things and get some clothes and toys gathered up for Chance, too. You're going to stay with Auntie Louise for a few days. Won't that be nice?"

"But Ma!" all three kids cried in near perfect unison.

"No buts!" Iris knew that if her children had their way, they too would ride along to try and help but there was no way she would let that happen. "I want to see your bags packed and loaded in the wagon within the hour. I also want to see all three of you in the back of that wagon when I show up or I'll have your pa give you a whippin' when he gets back home!"

The children managed to keep their eyes from rolling. Matthew's whippings were notoriously easy, usually resulting in a piece of hard rock candy and a long talk rather than a hot bottom. Iris, on the other hand, was a force to be reckoned with when angered.

So, within minutes of receiving Matthew's telegraph, his family was on the move.

ROY STEPPED out on the front porch of Gertie's house and lit a stogie, something he only did when he was out of Louise's line of sight. It had been a long morning since Matthew and Dicky left. Abner's leg was giving him fits although he tried to deny it, and Sarah was not helping herself either, hobbling back and forth from her own room to help Gertie care for the stricken young man.

Roy gazed up and down the street, momentarily catching the eye of the hotel proprietor, George Libby. The middle-aged man glared back at him and leaned forward, allowing a long string of spit to drizzle through his two front teeth and land on the boardwalk in front of his chair.

Rolling his eyes in disgust, Roy acknowledged the insult with a raised middle finger and stepped back inside Gertie's house. Seeing the old woman bustling around the long plank table with a large pot of oatmeal, he called out, "Gertie, when did you say the westbound train should arrive?"

She set the pot down on the table and frowned in concentration. "Well, seems to me the westbound arrives about 3:30 or 4:00 every afternoon. That's if there's no breakdowns and the weather's fair."

Checking the small clock on the mantelpiece, Roy saw that it was almost 3:00. Chances were the train would not roll in precisely on time but he figured he would get a head start. That way he'd be the first to see Iris when she stepped onto the platform.

"I'll be back shortly, Gertie. Hopefully, with Sheriff Wilcox's wife," he said.

Roy sauntered down the boardwalk, keeping an eye on Libby as he walked past. The man stared at him with dead, cold eyes and he wondered again if the hotel owner was somehow involved with Donnelly's crew.

Just as he arrived at the train station, he heard a distant whistle coming from the east. He could hardly believe it but the train was actually running ahead of schedule. Stepping up onto the wooden deck next to the rails, Roy stood behind a pallet stacked high with barrels. From the smell of them and the white crust rimming the tops of each, he figured that the containers held salted fish.

If asked, Roy could not have told you why he hid instead of mingling with the small crowd that was starting to show up in readiness of the train's arrival. It was a habit with him, one that had first started when he took up his deputy's star for Spokane County. Over the years, he had found that standing back and getting the "lay of the land" before any confrontation served him well in staying alive.

This cautious "look first" tendency was a defense mechanism that had become second nature by now. He was not a big man nor was he quick with a gun. But he had managed to keep himself and his best friend Matthew out of a few jams by approaching every situation with careful consideration. He watched as the black and gray train approached from around a tall bluff. It's "cow-catcher" was rusty with dried blood and the smoke belching out of the stack was smelly with the acidic odor of coal.

The train squealed against the rails and sighed to a stop in front of the station. Standing up straight and peering between the barrels, Roy watched as a number of people climbed off; men, women, children, and one old granny carrying a caged chicken in each hand. He tried looking for Iris through the windows but smoke and steam obscured his sight. Then his eyes got big and he knelt in the shadows.

A number of men, two of whom he recognized from Wenatchee, disembarked and stood by the steps as Patrick and Margaret Donnelly made an appearance. Roy watched Donnelly look around and then focus his attention on George Libby as the man scurried up with his hat in his hands.

Well, I was right! he thought. *That son of a bitch is in on things with Donnelly. And to think Iris is on that train with the man who stole her niece. Or is she?*

Roy squinted and saw the conductor get off. Usually the last person to leave, he shook his head in dismay. *What in the hell is going on here?* he wondered. *Where is Iris?*

The passengers were making their way slowly down the street toward the town's hotel and restaurant. Donnelly and his sister, along with their henchmen, strolled toward the hotel as well while Libby talked a mile a minute about what had happened in town the night before. Roy could hear every word the man said and listened to him jabber until he heard the conductor shout, "Train leaves in one half an hour folks! Better be back here on time or you'll have to catch the next westbound tomorrow!"

After the small rush of people disappeared, Roy sat in the shadows, gritting his teeth in rage. Suddenly he understood that the telegraphs Matthew had written had never been sent and he would bet his bottom dollar that Libby's wife was responsible.

This meant that Matthew and Dicky were out on their own with no back-up. And he was stuck here with two injured people to care for and Iris had no clue she was needed. So, essentially, there would be no help from the governor, King County, Iris...or anyone.

21

A SERIOUS COMPLICATION

ROY HAD A DECISION TO MAKE, BUT EVERYTHING HINGED on what that skunk Libby had to say to Donnelly about Roy's presence here in town. Fearing that Donnelly might seize the opportunity to get rid of at least Abner, he scurried across the street and headed toward the sheriff's office where he had earlier seen Davey sitting at his former boss's desk.

Stepping inside, Davey smiled and said, "Good morning, Roy. What can I do for you?"

"You can go over to Gertie's house and watch over Abner and Sarah for a bit while I rent a coach. And while you're there, would you please ask Gertie to make sure those kids are ready to leave at a moment's notice?"

Davey looked alarmed. "Why? What's going on now?"

Roy shook his head. "The boss of the men who killed your sheriff and his wife just got off the train. I guess he'll be heading on in to Seattle but I wouldn't put it past him to eliminate anyone he feels is a threat to his plans. He brought four men with him and I want to make sure they can't get to Abner or Sarah...or me, for that matter."

Davey stood up and Roy saw a remarkable transformation come over the young man's face. He suddenly looked much older than his years and pissed as hell.

"Damn them! I've had enough. This isn't some back alley juke-house...this is my hometown! I think I'll serve an arrest warrant while I'm there." He reached over, grabbed his hat, a rifle, and was about to leave when Roy stopped him.

"Deputy, please don't do that. At least not now as Matthew and I don't have enough solid proof yet. I fear you'll just set yourself and your family up as targets and I don't want to see any of you get hurt. Just stand outside on Gertie's porch with your star showing, okay? I have a feeling that Donnelly's boys won't want to tangle with the law during the light of day. If they do, though, I'll be right behind you."

He nodded and Roy watched as Davey walked down the street and stepped up on Gertie's front porch. Then he turned and ran to the livery where a man and two boys were shoeing a big gelding by the side of a large barn. As he walked up, Roy saw the horse pin its ears back and nip at the boy who held its halter.

"Gawd-dangit, Clarence, hold that hoss still!" the man barked.

"Excuse me but do you have a buggy or a wagon to rent?" Roy called out.

Wiping sweat from his brow, the man peered at Roy and asked, "Where you fixin' to go?"

"I need to get to Spokane as fast as possible. I would wait on tomorrow's train but my fellow deputy and I are needed back home." Roy knew he wasn't making any sense as even the fastest carriage would travel slower than a train. Still, he didn't want to advertise that he and his company were on the run. The livery owner was no fool though and he scratched his ear thoughtfully.

"Listen. I got a couple of wagons I would be willing to rent but you would do better, I think, to wait for the eastbound stagecoaches. They're part of a new outfit out of Seattle. They travel in tandem with six horses each...fastest rigs I've ever seen and can almost beat a train when they're running strong. They should be rolling in about 5:00 and usually travel another fifty miles into the town of Index where there's a pretty decent hotel."

Roy nodded and smiled. "Thank you kindly. I'll do that."

Turning around, he frowned. Sure enough, two of the men he'd seen accompanying the Donnellys stood on the boardwalk in front of the hotel, staring across the street at Davey who glared right back with a belligerent expression on his face.

Deciding from the stance of both parties that he'd better go give the deputy a hand, Roy walked swiftly up the street. One of Donnelly's thugs, an older man with silver hair and fancy clothes, was fingering the pistol on his gun belt. Pulling his own revolver, he hollered, "Davey, get inside, if you please!"

Roy came to a halt, lifted his gun and pointed it in the general direction of Donnelly's two henchmen. Studying Roy's face and the easy way he held his firearm, the older man held his hands out from his body. Then Donnelly came out the front door and grinned.

"Where's your sheriff this fine afternoon?" he asked.

Roy glared. "That ain't none of your damn business!"

Donnelly shrugged, still grinning. "Well," he drawled. "I'm sure me and my boys will meet up with him soon."

Davey had ignored Roy's request and stepped up next to him. "I'd like for you and your party to leave my town right now," he snarled.

From the expression on Donnelly's face, Roy figured that a gun battle was a forgone conclusion. But then the train's whistle blew and a couple of passengers hurried out of the restaurant, followed closely by three more.

"Train leaves in five minutes, folks!" the conductor bellowed. "All aboard!"

Roy glanced toward the locomotive and saw a plume of black smoke rise from the stack as the engineer stoked the boiler for the last pull into Seattle. More customers began filing toward the depot and he saw Donnelly speak to his men, who started walking toward the train. A couple of minutes later—as he and Donnelly stared each other down—Margaret joined her brother.

Tipping his hat, Patrick Donnelly winked and followed his sister down the road toward the train.

"...and don't come back!" Davey yelled at Donnelly's back.

Watching as they boarded the train, he asked, "Will you and Matthew stand witness if I call on the King County sheriff to investigate the deaths of my boss and his wife?"

Although Roy was pissed at the kid for almost getting them into a fight they couldn't hope to win, he replied, "Yes. Just give us a few days to get things sorted out, okay?"

"Okay. It'll be a couple weeks before they make it out here anyway. There's such a population boom going on in Seattle right now, us smalltime folks are pretty much on our own but once a month when the police commissioner and a few of his deputies show up."

All of a sudden they heard a racket at the far end of town just as the train started chugging away from the depot. Staring, Roy saw that two coaches were approaching fast. Piled high with trunks and luggage, he could see faces peering out the window openings.

Turning to Davey, he said, "I have to get Abner and Sarah on one of those." Reaching into his pocket, he pulled out some coin and asked, "Could I trouble you to purchase fare for three passengers?"

"Sure," Davey said and strode to where the conveyances were skidding to a stop in front of the livery.

Roy walked back to Gertie's home, told her what he was doing and enlisted her assistance in gathering up his two charges. He thanked the woman for all her help and scratched a hasty letter just in case Iris did show up after all. Handing the note and some extra cash to Gertie, he shook her hand and took his leave.

It took some doing and a lot of extra coin but two passengers in one coach squeezed in with the people on the other, leaving one empty. Abner sat on the back-bench with his broken leg stretched across it while Roy and Sarah shared the seat facing him.

Although beads of clammy sweat dotted Abner's forehead, he insisted on holding a shotgun in case Donnelly's men tried pulling a fast one and returned to finish what they'd tried to start.

Roy watched closely as the train pulled out and saw no sign of such subterfuge but he let Abner act as he saw fit—some sort of affirmative action seemed prefer-able to the young man than just lying around waiting for the other shoe to drop. Roy planned on riding with them as far as Ellensburg, where they would transfer to a train heading into Spokane; he felt they would be safe enough by then to go ahead alone while he doubled back and went after Matthew and Dicky.

As they took off with a lurch, Roy closed his eyes

and tried not to worry about the seemingly impossible task of finding Matthew before Donnelly got to him.

———

The next day, Iris stepped off the train in Gold Bar along with a number of other weary travelers. Hearing the conductor yell that the passengers had a half an hour to eat and relax before they departed for Seattle, she searched the small crowd looking for Roy.

She knew Mattie and a young fellow by the name of Dicky had gone ahead to the city but, as the departing passengers dispersed, she could not understand where Roy had got off to. She stood still, wondering what to do, when she saw an old lady scurrying in her direction.

The skinny little woman came to a stop in front of Iris and grinned up at her with a toothless mouth. "Well, I guess the sheriff wasn't exaggerating when he said you was real purty with copper-colored hair!" she said.

Self-consciously, Iris fingered her messy hair. Train travel was never the cleanest affair as there were usually too many passengers—and sometimes animals —stuffed into the cars; it was also always too hot and the open windows—the only feasible way to get a breath of fresh air—let in smoke and ash from the stack.

Iris felt certain that the back of her dress was splattered with baby urp and she suspected her bonnet was sprinkled with tobacco chaff from the kind but incessant pipe smoker who had shared the bench with her. Still, the old lady was nice to compliment her and Iris held out her hand in introduction.

"If you are referring to Matthew Wilcox, then yes. I'm his wife, Iris, come to take young Abner home, and a girl named Sarah to Walla Walla.

"My name is Gertie, honey. Here," she said, fumbling in her apron pocket and pulling out a scrap of paper. "The last thing Roy did before he left with Abner and Sarah yesterday was write you this letter."

Iris started to open it but Gertie put a hand out and touched her arm. "Before you read it, let me fill you in on what I know. I think things have changed for your husband and his posse, and NOT for the better. Let's sit right here. That way, if you decide to head on in to Seattle tonight, you won't miss the train when it leaves. If'n you decide to go home, you can come and stay with me—I own that boarding house just down the street—and then take the next train back east."

The woman guided Iris toward a long bench and she sat down with a plop. Although she knew something was wrong, it wasn't until Gertie articulated the words that her heart accepted the truth of the matter.

Early that morning before she boarded the train, Iris had informed Bean Tolson and two Spokane deputies that she wasn't familiar with that their boss might be in some trouble. Not sure of the circumstances, she had asked them to please get a hold of the county marshal so that he could inform the authorities in King County to keep an eye on Matthew's whereabouts and spring into action if necessary.

The two fill-ins seemed skeptical but Bean, having known Matthew most of his life, looked alarmed and knew Iris would never raise a red flag unless it was absolutely called for. So she hoped he'd somehow gotten word to the marshal and that the King County lawmen were aware one of their sworn officers might be in need of assistance.

Gertie filled Iris in on what had transpired the last couple of days. She assured the younger woman that Abner and Sarah were safe and, although Matthew had been wounded in the shoot-out, he was in good health; she talked about Matthew's suspicions and shared what she knew about the Donnellys; and she again offered Iris a place to stay, stating that she might do better going home and taking care of her family while her husband got rid of the crooks.

Iris shook her head. "I will go on into Seattle, Gertie. It sounds like Roy has things handled with Abner and Sarah, and my place is by my husband's side. I know the Washington state governor and many state representatives as well."

The train whistle blew and, with it, a plume of smoke rose up into the evening sky. The conductor started ringing a bell by the passenger door and Iris bent close to the older woman so Gertie could hear over the sudden racket.

"The girl Matthew is looking for is my niece," Iris said. "She was apparently abducted by this Donnelly fellow and his henchmen. Now I hear that she is only one girl out of many and I know that Matthew will not rest until he gets them all back home where they belong." Iris saw the ongoing travelers approaching the train station and stood up.

She gave the little old lady a hug and whispered in her ear, "Thank you so much for helping my husband and me, Gertie. If you see Roy, please tell him I've gone on. And also tell him..." She paused a moment. "Tell him to go to the opera house in the downtown area. He can't miss it. Tell him to go around back to the stage entrance. He will either find me there, or people who know me and are willing to help."

Then Iris gave Gertie another hug and boarded the westbound train.

22

MARGARET...IF ONLY

TWENTY-NINE HOURS EARLIER, MARGARET DONNELLY disembarked the same train in Seattle. It was 7:48 pm according to Da's old watch and rain fell from the murky sky in sheets, making two of the tall lampposts on the edge of the platform sputter and hiss. Everything sparkled.

She acknowledged that the tarry ball of opium she had bought from an old Chinese man in Gold Bar might be adding to the carnival gleam. Yet she still enjoyed the vivid colors, allowing herself to revel in the rushing feeling of goodwill that suffused her entire being.

Margaret peered through the gloom as Patrick barked orders to the men and boys who had come to the station to take them to their warehouse. Grinning in relief, she saw Earl Dickson standing close to one of their black carriages, smoking a cheroot; she had no doubt her brother would shoot the man dead if he knew that Dickson was her main narcotic supplier.

She felt confident, however, that Patrick didn't know. As far as he was concerned, Dickson was his sister's main squeeze and as long as their relationship did not get in the way of business, he didn't care. Making a mental note to hide her poppy intoxication from the ever-vigilant eyes of her brother, she walked up to Earl with a smile.

He did not return her grin but stared meaningfully up and down her body. She squirmed under his inspection, knowing that hours on the train had done nothing to improve her appearance. Angry and on the verge of tears, she returned his scornful assessment.

Dickson might have been handsome once, but years of living dangerously had taken their toll. He was as skinny as a stick, with long ape-like arms and hunched shoulders. His eyes were his best feature—as blue and luminous as a summer sky—but they nestled blearily in darkened wrinkled pouches. He had also lost another tooth since their last encounter.

Her good mood dissipated. Just a few minutes ago, she had been more than willing to trade sexual favors in lieu of cash for the fine quality opium he supplied. But now the very thought of those dirty hands on her once-beautiful body made her skin crawl with disgust...both for him and herself. Ignoring him, she got into the closed carriage and watched as Patrick gave final orders to his assorted lackeys and then walked up to where she sat.

He glanced at Earl who had climbed up onto the driver's bench and said, "Take her to the warehouse and make sure she doesn't leave." Earl nodded.

Turning to Margaret, Patrick said, "You have the rest of the night off. Do what you want...?" He wiggled his eyebrows lasciviously, cutting his eyes toward Dickson. "But if I hear that you stepped out to...you know...I'll give you a whipping you'll never forget. Got it?"

Margaret nodded and thought, *how I used to love this boyo with his bright green eyes and jet-black hair, his skinny arms wrapped around me in fierce but futile protection.* But now, whatever good was ever in Patrick was gone, leaving an empty husk of a man whose only care was the acquisition of money no matter the cost to those who once loved him above all others.

"I have business to take care of tonight, but I'll be at the warehouse by noon tomorrow. I expect the girls to be dressed and ready for inspection by then," he said and stepped away.

Margaret saw his face and felt a chill. Lantern light from above etched his bloated cheeks, leaving his eyes and mouth in shadow; it gave her the vision of a skull floating in the dark. Then he grinned, dispelling the image with his once irresistible charm before the carriage jerked forward.

She sat back on the plush leather seat and prayed for the time to move forward swiftly. It was about eight miles from the train station to the warehouse. Sometimes the journey could take two or three hours, especially if the market was busy or if there was too much traffic for the narrow, congested streets.

Hopefully, because it was evening, the trip would only take a little while. Then she would immerse herself in the warm, soft cocoon of opium's embrace...even as she endured the more carnal embrace of the man who kept her habit alive and well.

The next morning, Margaret awoke and sat up in bed with a groan. She felt both light-headed and heavy, her mouth tasted like ashes, and every square inch of her flesh prickled painfully. She had chewed the last of her poppy ball on the way to the warehouse, depending on Dickson to supply her with more once she availed him of her charms. But the cad had tricked her instead.

He followed her into the Donnelly's living chambers; a three-room suite in back of the warehouse consisting of a parlor/office and two small bedrooms. Usually they partook of a little brandy and opium before doing the deed but, this time, he had grabbed her shoulder from behind, wrenched her around and took her on the floor.

Even as he grunted and wheezed in her ear, she told herself it would be over soon and then she could commence to feeling good but it didn't go the way she had planned. Once Earl finished, he got to his feet, buttoned up his fly and said, "I got word from that dick Freddy Marston that giving you any kind of drug would get me shot so you can forget about getting high."

Margaret glared up at him from where she lay in a sweaty, rumpled mess on the floor. "You might have mentioned this before you raped me!"

Dickson shrugged. "Figured there ain't no love lost between you and me. Also, I know you can't do nuthin' about it since you'd only implicate yerself in the process. So tough titties, Mags." Then he stepped over her and walked out the door.

She managed to hit him in the back with a porcelain figurine as he left her bedroom but he didn't even flinch. Margaret, however, sobbed and sobbed— more from fear of being deprived of her precious medicine than her erstwhile lover's rejection. In addition, the little keepsake she had thrown was one of the few prized possessions she owned, an item more valued for its sentimental history than its monetary worth.

Staring down at the powdery shards still left on the floor, she closed her eyes and mourned the wreck her life had become. She remembered the day Patrick had given her the porcelain ballerina.

She was only a couple of years into her life as a whore and still in good spirits, as fresh and vibrant as a spring daisy. And healthy, despite the odds. In addition, opium had yet to enter her life. Spoiled and decadent, she was lounging in bed when there was a knock on her door.

"Come," she called and, to her surprise, Patrick entered her room. She had hardly seen hide nor hair of her brother since she was first sold to the highest bidder downstairs in the auction room, but she had heard that he was doing well and rising rapidly in the ranks of Banyan's Irish mob.

She had often wondered if Patrick was disgusted by her now—or angry—but it wasn't as if she'd had any choice in the matter. Those thoughts filled her mind as Patrick came to stand by the side of her bed. He looked down at the rumpled sheets and she thought she saw him sniff inquisitively. Stung, she said, "For pity's sake, Patrick! This is my private chamber, not where I work. As you would know if you ever came for a proper visit!"

He had blushed and mumbled, "Sorry, sis...here." He pulled a small package from his pocket and thrust it in her face.

She studied the grimy paper and the limp bow for a moment, then took it from his hand and opened it. The involuntary gasp that escaped her lips made him grin with pride. "Patrick! How did you get this?"

"Nicked it, o'course. But when I saw it, I thought you should have it."

Margaret turned the exquisite piece over and over. The words *Havilland and Co. Limoges* were etched into the bottom of the china figurine of a ballerina with swirling skirts, creamy white skin, emerald chips for eyes, and long black hair; her skirts were many shades of purple and her tiny toe-shoes were a satiny pink. There was such beauty and grace in her attitude, it looked to Margaret as if she was ready to pirouette right off the palm of her hand and dance through the air.

Gazing up at her brother with tears of gratitude in her eyes, Margaret whispered, "Thank you so much, Patrick. She's beautiful!" Placing the tiny ballerina carefully on her nightstand, she put her left hand on his arm, adding, "But, please, don't take such a chance again." She had no idea how much something like this cost but guessed it was enough to feed them both for a year, if not more.

Patrick shook his head. "Nay, I won't. Sister, I..." He stared down at her for a second with wide, frightened eyes. "I'm sorry about what happened to you, okay? I really am and I'm gonna get us out of here as soon as I can."

Touched, Margaret nodded and said, "That's good, Patty. But we're doing all right, aren't we? You're getting ahead and I'm well." She blushed as her brother's eyes narrowed. "I'm only saying things could be worse."

"Aye, that's true. But I want you to be ready to go when I say go, you hear me?"

She had nodded then, thinking why rock the boat now? But that was before she had her first of many rough customers and got hooked on opium.

Two long years passed before Patrick flew into her

room without knocking and said, "Pack your things! We're leaving now!"

They got away safely but lived on the run for the next twenty years. Margaret never knew if old man Banyan had died or been killed yet, finally, his henchmen seemed to give up the chase. That was when they settled in Washington state and started living in relative peace. Margaret had a reliable source for dope and, for the most part, she enjoyed working in the flower end of the funeral business. She even appreciated the hunt when Patrick decided it was time to supplement their income by nabbing unsuspecting girls.

Now, shaking and sweating on her rumpled sheets, she understood her motivations were fueled by her addiction to opium. Although occasionally Patrick sold a girl at an unbelievably high price, they never really made that much money in the kidnapping business...not enough to justify the risks. She suspected that, for Patrick, the thrill of the hunt and his desire to feel all-powerful—along with his subjugation of the weaker sex—prompted his latest career choice.

If only we had not been born in famine-stricken Ireland, Margaret mourned. If only Da hadn't died leaving Patrick and me alone in this God-forsaken country. If only we hadn't fallen into Banyan's hands. If only...if only I'd never been born at all!

She wept for a few minutes, hugging her arms to her chest in grief, and then she sighed. The little clock on the highboy dresser in the corner read 8:30 am and she was supposed to have the girls ready for inspection by noon.

She needed to stop feeling sorry for herself and find new sources for her dope or things were going to get rough.

Amelia heard the bitch enter the warehouse and wished she wasn't feeling so helpless; she grimaced, wishing she could wrap her fingers around Margaret Donnelly's throat and squeeze until the woman was dead.

Instead, she sagged against the back of her chair and tried to keep from vomiting. The girls' keeper, a dried up old prune who called herself Holms, kept forcing them to drink a foul-tasting green concoction that made them sleepy and too weak to fight back.

Amelia had tried to refuse a couple of times but whenever she pressed her lips together to keep the potion from going down her throat, one of the two men who watched their every move would simply step in and poke his fingers hard into her cheeks, forcing her teeth apart. By now, Amelia's face was black and blue with finger-shaped bruises.

That didn't stop Holms from painting her cheeks bright red though, or putting some sort of lurid purple paint around her eyes. She was also adorned in a peacock blue dress with a neckline that fell almost to her waist, showing her ample freckled breasts through black lace. Amelia felt like dying from the shame of it.

She knew by now that she was about to be sold to serve as a prostitute and her dreams of becoming a doctor were fading by the day. She had been so sure that her uncle Matthew would come to save her but she'd lost track of how many days had passed since she was kidnapped and her hopes were fading, too.

Allowing a tear to escape, she looked around at the girls imprisoned with her and gave herself a mental slap. She, at least, was still fairly healthy but many of the others were obviously quite ill. Some were so doped up they could hardly keep their eyes open or their heads upright; the rest were either stricken with some sort of disease or they had been injured before their arrival here.

Amelia wondered how Sarah was doing or if she had survived at all. She remembered how brave and strong the girl was and briefly entertained the thought of a whole tribe of fierce Indian braves coming to Seattle to rescue her and her fellow captives. Realizing her ruminations were ridiculously fanciful, she closed her eyes against the reality.

She heard footsteps approaching and opened her eyes to see Margaret standing in the doorway of the small room. The woman was nicely dressed in a gown of gray wool and a plumed hat. Her cheeks were very pale, though, and Amelia could see the woman's hands trembling from where she sat. Strangely, Amelia saw something approaching concern—even pity—in Margaret's eyes as she stared at one girl after another.

Holms rushed up and cried, "Miss Donnelly, I don't know how these girls got to be in such rough shape! The doc has been in and says there's no disease as far as he can tell. But there's certainly something wrong with this lot." Wringing her bony hands together, she added, "And it ain't my fault!"

Ignoring the woman's denial of guilt, Margaret stepped past her and approached Amelia. Standing before her, Margaret lifted the girl's chin.

"What happened to her face?" she asked.

"Ack! That one's a fighter! Every time, she rejects the fairy juice…she keeps her lips sealed or tries to spit it out! We can't have that, of course, so Harry pries her mouth open. That's all."

Margaret could think of nothing but her own girl-hood…the terror, the cruelty and the hopelessness of her situation after she started her first menstrual period. She remembered her own auction, and how it had made her feel. She recalled the pity and revulsion shining from her brother's eyes, a look that had never quite gone away.

Her heart thumped loudly in her ears and, for a second, Margaret couldn't breathe. She stared at the sick, grief-stricken girls and understood she was visiting her own demons upon these innocents; she wanted to run screaming from the room in horror and shame.

She snapped back into the present and, rounding

on Holms, she snarled, "Never put your hands on this girl again! Do you hear me? The auction is in two days. If this one is passed over by the sheik, I will hold you personally to blame."

Margaret looked at the owlish, lavender circles ringing Amelia's eyes. "And for heaven's sake, remove this horrible paint. You've made her look like a circus clown!"

She glared at Holms' ugly, pinched face. "Take these three girls up front," she said as she pointed to Amelia, a Chinese girl by the name of Han Lin, and a beautiful Latin girl with glossy, black hair. "Put some proper clothing on them and stop giving them the Green Fairy juice. It's obviously making them ill. Feed them well and let them rest."

Starting to leave, Margaret stopped and turned around. "Remember this, Holms. These girls are not your playthings to ruin as you see fit. If anyone around here is a sad, silly clown, it is you, not them."

Holms, the men who assisted her in her duties, and the prisoners watched as Margaret Donnelly swept from the room. Holms' cheeks were flushed bright red with embarrassment and she snapped, "Alright, then. Help me get these three into the front of the warehouse while I find some different clothes for them to wear."

Swaying, Amelia stood up from her chair and thought about the look on Margaret's face and the words she had said. Warning herself, she nevertheless felt there might be some hope after all.

23

A FAMILY GATHERING

IRIS STEPPED OFF THE TRAIN INTO THE WAITING ARMS OF her sister-in-law, Muriel Winters. The plump, matronly woman was trembling with fear and sorrow, but her embrace was warm. Giving her another hug, Muriel stepped back and searched Iris's face.

"Have you heard anything yet?" she asked.

Iris shook her head. "Matthew is still looking for her and he is close, dear. But, no, I have no good news yet."

Right after she had boarded the westbound train in Gold Bar, Gertie had rushed to the hotel and sent a telegram to Iris's brother, Lewis, in Marysville.

But Iris felt terrible about the delay. The first couple of days after Amelia's abduction, she had stalled, thinking that Matthew would catch up to the girl sooner rather than later and there was no need to worry her parents. Then, after she received her husband's telegram, she had simply forgotten in the mad dash to help Matthew in his search. Now though —with her sister-in-law's wide brown eyes staring into her own—Iris knew her hesitation to contact them was unforgivable. Lewis and Muriel were angry and hurt at Iris's seemingly callous behavior.

Clearing her throat, she decided to take the bull by the horns. "I am SO sorry that I didn't let you know about what happened sooner. Please know, though, that Matthew and his deputies are hot on Amelia's trail. We will get her back, I promise!"

Her brother stood behind his wife, hat in hand, looking as lost and forlorn as a man could be. He blamed himself for his daughter's disappearance and Iris was determined not to let him wallow in self-recrimination. Stepping forward, she took his hand and said, "Lewis, this is NOT your fault! Matthew believes these thugs have been doing this for quite some time and to many young girls."

Lewis's eyes grew damp. "I was the one who said she could go alone to Spokane. Muriel told me Amelia was…is too young." A tear trickled down his whiskered cheek and Muriel stepped to his side.

"Doctor, what your sister says is true. This is not our fault!"

Muriel had met Lewis Winters when she was twenty-six years old, an overweight and lonesome woman without prospects or fortune. From the Ozark Mountains and poor as dirt, she had left home at eigh-teen and, through sheer guts and determination, trained to be a nurse. Little did she know that she would meet the man of her dreams during one of the ugliest battles of the Civil War...the battle of Antietam in Sharpsburg, near Maryland.

She was assigned to the medical tent of a new doctor named Lewis Winters. Although tall and hand-some, the poor man was afflicted with a nervous dispo-sition and a lisp from the slight cleft in his upper lip. Knowing she stood no chance with this aristocratic northern gentleman, Muriel had nevertheless stepped forward with brisk efficiency, taking the place of younger and prettier nurses assigned to the tent.

After a while, he requested Muriel's presence as head nurse and they worked side by side for the dura-tion of the war. After hostilities ended, Lewis asked her to be his bride and she accepted his proposal with barely masked disbelief. Muriel never stopped calling her husband Doctor, even after following him and his father to California, then to the Pacific Northwest, and giving him two children.

Lewis drew himself up to his full height and declared, "Iris, I know you asked me not to call on the authorities but I did anyway. Matthew is a capable man but this is my daughter we're talking about."

Iris sighed. She didn't blame her brother; if it was one of her children, she would have done the same thing. Still, she understood that her husband some-times operated on the far edges of the law. He did things in a roundabout manner that cut straight through legal machinations and by-passed dictated rules and regulations to gain maximum results.

Although Matthew had received many accolades during his career as sheriff, he had received almost as many citations for his unorthodox methods.

She smiled. "That's fine, Lewis. Believe me, I understand."

He gave her a nod and muttered, "We're ready to go. I know you must be tired after your journey but I'm scheduled to meet with the King County Sheriff's Department tomorrow at 9:00 am." Lewis gestured toward a carriage and four horses standing in wait about twenty feet away. Iris returned his nod and started walking toward it as her brother picked up her valise.

"When was the last time you saw your father, dear?" Muriel asked.

"He came to call after Chance was born but that was about four years ago. How is he these days?" Iris asked.

Muriel grinned. "Oh, as flamboyant as ever, I'm afraid. The Doctor keeps telling him to cut back on the brandy but..."

"Yes...but!" Iris finished her sister-in-law's sentence with a sigh of disgust.

"Oh well, you'll see for yourself soon enough." Muriel gave Iris's arm a squeeze and stepped up into the carriage.

Iris and Lewis followed and the driver gave the horses' rumps a light slap.

Awhile later, the carriage pulled up in front of the opera house in downtown Seattle. Iris watched as Lewis paid the driver his fee, plus a handsome tip.

Her nostrils were instantly assaulted by the smell of a show night and, for a moment, her heart yearned to be back in the business. Shaking her head ruefully, she allowed the fragrance of caramel apples, kerosene, and the sharp, yeasty aroma of ale, perfume and popcorn to fill her up. As her nose identified each specific odor, Iris's mind traveled back in time to when she was a young girl in her teens.

When Iris was eleven years old, her beautiful mother died. Martha Winters had always been frail but scarlet fever left her already thin body emaciated and her nerves in a constant state of high anxiety. Trembling with fear and pain, she wasted away in front of Lewis and Iris. To make matters even worse, Martha seemed to blame her husband Gerald for her ill health. When the end finally came after a bout with pneumonia, it was a blessing for her and her small family.

Guilt-stricken and remorseful, Gerald couldn't help but sigh with relief when his lovely bride finally succumbed to death's early embrace. Martha was one of the most gorgeous women he had ever clapped eyes on. With her long red hair, green eyes and rosebud mouth, her fair, flawless skin gleamed with a light of its own. She seemed infused with a steady, solemn wisdom that appealed to his own reckless nature like a ballast on the high seas.

Gerald—better known then as Gerry—had arrived from London with his father, a stern and formidable professor of English literature. They were moving to Boston where Edward Winters would teach English at Harvard University. Much to his father's dismay, Gerry yawned at the study of that subject and shuddered at the thought of entering law school. What he did enjoy, however, was drama. He read every play he could get his hands on and never missed the chance to see Shakespeare performed. Still, being his father's son, Gerry was expected to finish and graduate from college, and he did so with honors.

Then, one rainy afternoon, Edward was run over by a half-broken gelding while shopping for new clothes for the upcoming school year. Although teaching English literature was the last thing Gerry wanted to do with his life, he stepped into his father's shoes after Edward's untimely demise.

Three years after he started teaching for a living, he met Martha—the daughter of one of his father's colleagues—at a school function. Although she seemed a rather solemn sort, he was overwhelmed by her physical beauty and, after only five or six chaperoned meetings, he proposed marriage. At first, he was delirious with joy. Martha was the epitome of charm and she came from a well-to-do Boston family. It didn't take long, though, for Gerry to understand that Martha was one of the grimmest and unhappiest people he had ever met.

She seemed to think his fascination with the arts—and brandy—would fade with time and that his unseemly fondness of the theater could at some point be drummed out of his head. He, in turn, tried everything he could think of to interest her in the finer arts but she remained unimpressed. Finally, he stopped talking to her about the theater and eventually stopped talking to her about anything at all.

Understanding that she was driving her husband away, Martha tried to interest Gerald in "society" but he just laughed at her, stating she was free to pursue her own interests but not to expect him to fit into her schemes. They were at an impasse by then and the only thing that bound them together was their children. Try as they might, the husband and wife were polar opposites and would probably have ended up hating each other had the fates not intervened.

Although Gerald missed Martha's soft voice and beautiful visage, he finally decided to follow his dreams after her death. He quit his job, emptied his bank account and started up his own group of players. Luckily, he had enough money to buy entrance into society's best theaters. Although he and his troupe endured hard times and "the assorted slings and arrows of outrageous fortune", he and Iris traveled about the country in peace and happiness. Lewis, much more staid in his approach to life, elected to stay behind in Boston and study for his medical license.

Gerald followed his dreams all the way to California and opened a small theater. He did not strike it rich but genuinely felt that he was a wealthy man, surrounded as he was with good friends, culture and the love of his beautiful daughter. And it was there that Iris met her future husband, Kevin Imes, a gold miner who had indeed struck it rich just outside of the San Francisco Bay area.

When Lewis and his new family moved from Boston to the Seattle area, Iris and Kevin followed them to Washington. Not long after, so did Gerald and his players. Gerald bought the little theater next to the opera house and had been in business ever since, catering to the cultural needs of the masses rather than the high-brow needs of the city's elite.

Glancing up at the billboard, Iris saw that "A Midsummer Night's Dream" was in its second week of production and she grinned. Of all of Shakespeare's plays, "Dream" was the most popular but it was also the most controversial. The goat-headed Pan and the blatant sexual overtones in the bard's play often drove the more conservative citizens in town mad with fear and self-righteous indignation.

It was October though, which meant that the more free-spirited people in town were allowed their excesses while God-fearing citizens stayed home safe and sound behind locked doors.

There was a flutter of activity as their bags were handed down from the top of the carriage and then Iris and her family walked toward the Globe Theater. Weaving their way through the vendors, the barkers, the finely dressed and the not-so-fine citizens that milled about in front, Iris saw her father come around from the stage entrance in the alley.

His cheeks were bright red from too much brandy and hypertension, and his tall body seemed more stooped than ever. But he was smiling and his hazel eyes were alight with love. His long-time companion Trudy Showls, a gray-haired woman with heavy make-up and deep cleavage, stood by his side and they welcomed everyone with open arms.

Iris felt equal parts exasperation and a deep upwelling of love for her brilliant but wayward Papa. She stepped into his hug with tears in her eyes and he held her tight, even as he stared at his son's stricken face.

"There, there now, it's going to be alright. We'll get Amelia back and soon, too. Look who's here to see justice done!"

Iris had to peer past her father's jacket and squint into the shadows, but then she gasped with joy. "Mattie!"

Matthew was walking slowly toward them. He had

a cane in one hand and seemed to be moving gingerly. Yet his eyes were as hot as coals and the way he gazed at her turned her guts to jelly with longing.

Breaking away from her Papa's embrace, Iris dropped her valise and ran to her husband with a cry of delight. They kissed, deeply and passionately, as a few theater-goers clapped and hooted. A tiny, red-haired man standing behind Matthew stared at his new boss and his lovely wife, his mouth open in shock and awe.

24

A NEW PLAN

MATTHEW AND IRIS SNUGGLED TOGETHER ON THE HOTEL bed, breathing hard and smiling in the afterglow of their frenzied lovemaking.

When Matthew had first dropped his britches, Iris gasped out loud in shock, "Oh my God, Mattie!"

He shrugged. "It's only a flesh wound, wife. Nothing to be concerned over. Now come here!"

Iris pushed his hands away, staring at the seven-inch long, bright red gash on her husband's inner thigh. The still-seeping scar contrasted sickeningly with the lurid blue, purple and green bruises surrounding it, and Iris winced in sympathy.

"Mattie," she said, "lie down on the bed. We'll do this, of course, but we'll do it my way. Okay?"

And so Iris brought her husband to a shuddering climax with the deft use of her sure hands, soft lips and oh, so clever tongue. However, Matthew did not stay idle. Taking one then another nipple into his mouth, he licked her breasts until she gasped and squirmed, crying out as he worked sensuous magic with two of his fingers in a different place on her body.

The young couple had rocked together in ecstasy, pouring every ounce of their love into each other until they finally fell back in exhausted laughter.

"I needed that," Matthew groaned happily.

Iris smiled. "Me, too, my love." Turning on her side, she faced him and propped her head on one hand. "Not to change the subject but are you angry that Lewis called in the King County sheriff?"

Matthew winced a little as a trickle of sweat stung the raw scrape on his thigh. Standing up, he walked over to the basin and wetted a washcloth. Wiping the sweat away, he answered, "I don't blame him, Iris. It's just that I don't think we're dealing with your average criminal here. If the sheriffs start snooping around, I'm afraid that the quarry will go to ground. It's a lot harder to find someone who is running than someone who is hunkered down and hidden." He soaked the washcloth again and added some soap, running it over his chest and shoulders. "A lot more expensive, too," he added.

"I'm sorry." Iris flopped back on her pillow in frustration. "I swear, I told him to keep quiet for the time being but he's never listened to me!"

Matthew grinned. "A full-grown man taking orders from his little sister? Surely you jest!" He walked back over to the bed and stared down at her face. "Seriously, maybe this is for the best. One way or the other, this gang has to be stopped. You know, don't you, that prostitution is not considered a crime in this state...at least, not yet. Kidnapping is, though, and so is human trafficking." Running his thumb up and down his wife's cheek, he sighed.

"Maybe this way the sheriffs can find some of the girls and return them to their homes and families. And that will give credence to the story I have to tell because, surely, they will have some questions for me to answer." He shrugged. "And who knows? Maybe we'll catch them with their guard down. Pray to God I'm wrong and we find Amelia in the morning."

He looked very tired and Iris patted the mattress. "Come to bed and sleep. It's late and we're both weary. Hopefully by tomorrow afternoon, Roy will be back and then we can all sit down together and make some plans. You did say that the auction is taking place two days from now?"

"Last I heard, yes. That's only if they don't get scared off, though," he said as he climbed into bed next to her.

They kissed and, within seconds, Matthew was snoring while Iris stared up at the ceiling and wondered if her meddling hadn't just cost her and her family Amelia's life.

Early the next afternoon, two young street urchins darted down an alleyway in Chinatown. They both wore rags and watch caps, although one set of clothes was cleaner than the other. Dicky, who had always tried to dress well, felt daring and liberated...something needed for his diminutive size rather than being overlooked and smirked at.

He was on a mission assigned to him by his boss, Matthew Wilcox: Hang around by the purported auction house and gather as much intelligence as possible; hover close to the door with the dragon insignia and see if the Donnelly's or their henchmen showed up; watch and see if the King County lawmen raided the place; and report back immediately with any new information.

Although it wasn't stated, Dicky knew the wound on Matthew's thigh was paining him something awful. This was simply a way to keep an eye on the crooks and their nefarious endeavors while the sheriff recovered from being shot. The auction wasn't supposed to take place until tomorrow night, after all, and this bought a little recovery time.

The boy Dicky ran with really was a street urchin, although young Peter Elliot was a canny customer who preferred honest employment to a life of crime and had managed to find work with Mr. Winters' theater performers. He did many things, like handing out flyers, running sundry errands, fetching fresh fruit and fish from the market, and taking the actors' costumes back and forth to the Chinese laundry twice a week.

He had also worked out a lucrative deal with the flower-seller down the street. Sometimes, especially during a grand opening, Mr. Winters ordered dozens of roses delivered to the actors. Everyone in the troupe knew it was only a ruse but the patrons would watch the expensive bouquets being delivered back-stage and become convinced that the play was being well-received and the players were earning high acco-lades. Peter earned a two-bit tip every time he deliv-ered the roses—both from the florist and Mr. Winters.

Dicky had to give the teenager credit. Peter was smart as a whip, fleet as a deer and possessed of a sunny, affable nature despite being alone in the world and as poor as a church mouse. Although he had been born in less than fortunate circumstances, the thirteen-year-old boy did not seem inclined to let his station in life dictate what he might become.

The two young men darted here and there like wraiths, avoiding the crowds of people who sold their wares or those shopping. They dodged the farms carts and fancy broughams that filled the narrow lanes and finally emerged close to the door with the dragon emblem painted on its surface.

"Hold up here," Peter hissed and ducked down behind a pile of rubbish that nearly filled the mouth of the alleyway. Dicky ducked in next to the youngster and followed Peter's pointing finger with his eyes. They were about three blocks away from Chinatown and closer to the briny inland waters of Puget Sound where businesses were giving way to large warehouses and distributing outfits.

The air was thick with the odors of fish, hops, tar, horse and cattle manure, flowers, and rubbish. A thin, sweet fragrance wafted through it all—one Dicky's nose couldn't identify.

Leaning close to Peter, he whispered, "What's that smell?"

The teen grinned. "Incense. A couple of old Chinese men run a shop here. They sell all sorts of herbs and medicines and they make the joss sticks the Chinks like so much."

Dicky stared through the fog and saw a bright red lacquered door incongruously nestled in the front façade of a weathered building that looked as if the slightest wind might blow it down. Even as he watched, an elderly Oriental man with a long, white pigtail stepped out the door with a broom in his hand and started sweeping the front stoop.

Then Dicky saw something out of the corner of his eye. Three men were loitering outside of a saloon across the street about a hundred feet away from where he and Peter crouched. Two of the men were unfamiliar but the third man was none other than Fred Marston, one of Donnelly's henchmen.

All three were watching the surrounding area closely and Dicky was glad Matthew's wife had suggested dressing in disguise. With his penny-red hair and short stature, Dicky stood out like a sore thumb and he knew if he had strolled down the street in his usual garb, Fred would have recognized him immediately. He shuddered, knowing that he would probably be gasping his last breath while his bullet-riddled body bled out on these muddy city streets if not for Iris's timely advice.

Squatting even lower on his heels, Dicky moved forward a little and searched the area again. Sure enough, he spied two more "lookouts", one perched on the roof of a warehouse about fifty feet away and another standing behind an ivy-covered lattice screen very close to where he and Peter hid.

Settling down on his heels to wait and watch, Dicky hoped he would be able to bring good news to his boss and an expedient end to this whole sorry affair.

Dan O'Reilly grinned. He had been patrolling the perimeter as ordered and look what he found. It was that little bastard Dicky McNulty in the flesh. He might not have noticed at all, if it were not for the fact the deputy doffed his watch cap and swiped one spindly arm over his forehead, exposing that carrot-top for all the world to see.

Dan ducked out of sight around the edge of the alley and removed his boots. After checking to see if either of the men were glancing over their shoulders, he ran swiftly and silently down the cobblestones and gravel. He had a six-inch-long Bowie knife in one hand and a sap in the other.

Dicky had moved ahead a couple of feet, leaving the other man alone and in line for attack. Hoping it was Matthew Wilcox, Dan stepped up close, put one hand over the man's mouth and pulled his head back, exposing his throat. Then he drew his blade across the soft, white skin and moved away as a spray of dark blood flew into the air.

Staring at his victim's face, O'Reilly's victory turned sour as he saw that he had not just killed a sworn enemy but a young teen-ager. He heard a voice say, "You bastard! Why did you have to kill that kid?"

Although the deed had been done in almost perfect silence, Dicky had heard something—a scuffle perhaps or a sigh—and he now stood with a gun that was almost bigger than the hand that held it, pointing at Dan's face.

Dicky was filled with anger and remorse but his aim was steady, his brown eyes cold. But Dan had been in tighter places than this; he feinted to the right with his knife hand and, at the same time, chopped down with the cudgel hitting Dicky a glancing blow across the right temple.

O'Reilly grinned as he saw Dicky's eyes grow unfocused and seized the opportunity to end things once and for all time. Lunging forward, he sunk the blade into the little man's left shoulder. The blade was so slick, though, the point of it sunk into the tough muscles of Dicky's upper back rather than the tender arteries of his neck or the nerves in his spine.

Still, Dicky's face turned white and he started swaying on his feet. He could hear some sort of strange music in the distance and wondered if he was hearing an angelic choir. He hoped not, for this music was beyond his reckoning—eerie with wild piping and short staccato drumbeats. He grimaced, thinking he didn't much like the sounds these particular angels made. Besides, he wasn't ready to listen to their songs quite yet...he had work to do.

Clapping his left hand over the blade sticking out of his shoulder, Dicky lifted his pistol and again pointed it at O'Reilly who was watching him with a smile on his smug face, a smile that began to fade as the diminutive deputy cocked the hammer.

Before Dan could turn and run away, Dicky stuttered, "You are a bbbad, bbbad man." A roar filled the alley as he shot O'Reilly right between the eyes.

Dicky then glanced at the bright, beautiful boy who had tried so hard to succeed in life but now lay still and wide-eyed in death. Wincing in pain, he closed Peter's eyes and whispered, "I'm sorry, kid...so very sorry."

Then he ran for his life as he heard bullets fired behind him.

"Hey! Is that you, McNulty? Come back here, you little prick!"

Dicky recognized Fred's voice...a deep, raspy rumble filled with rage and surprise. There was more gunfire and he felt a tug at his shirtsleeve. Knowing he'd almost been hit, he ran even faster and gasped as a large crowd turned a corner.

They all wore bright, exotic costumes and a huge, multi-colored paper dragon danced in their midst. Many of the people played flutes, beat on drums, then screamed as Dicky staggered into their midst.

The sounds rang in his ears and buffeted his soul as tiny pinpricks of light floated around the corners of his eyes. He saw the Oriental people's heavily made-up faces and watched as their eyes stared, their fingers pointing at the long blade that stuck out from his left shoulder. Then the parade was behind him and he stumbled up the street toward the little playhouse.

His legs growing weaker, Dicky could only hope and pray that he would find Matthew—and sanctuary —before it was too late.

25

THE GAUNTLET IS DOWN

MATTHEW PACED THE FLOOR IN FRUSTRATION. HE HAD awoken earlier feeling rested for the first time in days. His leg felt better as well. Iris's brother had used some sort of soothing unguent on the torn skin and wrapped his upper thigh in soft bandages. While Lewis administered his services, one of the troupe's tailors let out the seams on Matthew's jeans so, for the first time since sustaining the bullet wound, the stiff material didn't chafe.

The King County sheriff and his men had just left. Matthew grimaced with disgust, and a vague sense of rage. It seemed that these officers were picking the battles they thought they could win rather than doing the right thing. Although Matthew had known that selling their case might be a tough proposition, he still gritted his teeth in anger at how dismissive the local constabulary had been.

The only girl they took the slightest interest in was

Amelia. But that was because Dr. Winters had some influence in the community and, better yet, money to put up for a reward. The rest of the girls would be shrugged off as a loss. Although Sheriff Adams had seemed interested, his desire for warrant money was not enough to convince him to send his men to investigate.

Matthew had not wanted to call the authorities in at all but, when confronted with their willful ignorance and greed, he lost his temper.

"I know prostitution isn't illegal, you imbecile!" he raged. "But Amelia is only a young woman who was going to train to be a doctor's assistant. She is NOT a whore!"

This invective was directed at one of the police commissioners, a sour-faced little man with a too-large hat by the name of Marty LeVesque. He had strutted about the parlor as if Matthew was a criminal somehow responsible for the death of the Gold Bar sheriff. It seemed to Matthew that the King County sheriff and his deputies were not overly fond of the commissioner either but when Matthew called the weasel an imbecile, Sheriff Adams had called a halt to the meeting.

"I am sorry, Sheriff Wilcox," he grumbled. "However, we have enough work on our hands right now, what with the striking union workers trying to shut down streetcar service and the heavy drug trafficking going on in this town." He clapped his derby hat on his head. "We simply don't have the manpower to chase down a bunch of missing girls...especially without any proof."

He went on to add, "Again, I am sorry for your loss. So go ahead and see what you can find. If you come up with something valid, send word and maybe I can muster a man or two to help out. Until then though, don't do anything illegal in your search or I'll be forced to apprehend you and your deputies."

Adams and his cohorts made ready to leave even as the commissioner sneered. "I will be keeping an eye on you and your activities while you are in my town, Sheriff Wilcox," he snapped. "Furthermore, you can expect a full inquiry into the death of Sheriff Duncan."

Matthew watched the men file out of the room and sighed. Dammit, I could have probably used their help but my big mouth just put an end to that notion, he silently swore.

Iris's father and brother had been present during the interview; Lewis had turned to Matthew after the lawmen left with wide, angry eyes but his father-in-law smiled. "Well, we didn't really want their help anyway. Did we, son?"

"I don't care what he wants, Father! This is my daughter we're talking about and Matthew just chased off what little help we had!" The normally placid man was quivering with wrath and Matthew bowed his head in acknowledgment.

"I apologize for losing my temper, Lewis," he said. "But they weren't really interested in this case. Please, though, don't think we are giving up!"

In answer, Lewis stormed out of the room, slamming the oak door as he left.

Matthew felt a wave of weariness rise up in his chest and then he threw his shoulders back, turned to his father-in-law and said, "Sir, we *will* do better on our own. I have always felt that if the people who run these kinds of auctions sense the law on their tails, they will rabbit. Now we have a chance to catch them in the act and maybe save all the girls in the process."

Pulling his pocket watch out of his vest, he looked at the time and frowned. "Sir, when did my deputy leave?"

The old man replied, "We dressed up Dicky as a ragamuffin so he would blend in better with Peter and that took a little time. But I think it was about three hours ago. Why? Did you expect him back by now?"

Matthew had set no time limit on Dicky's reconnaissance mission but something was bothering him… some sixth sense that had always alerted him in the past when things were going wrong. He shook his head. "No, but I think something has happened. When you see Iris, please tell her I walked down to the wharves to check up on things. Okay?"

Because Peter was going to be otherwise occupied, Iris had left earlier with Muriel to fetch some of the actors' costumes and to pick up some fresh fish for today's supper. Matthew was sure his wife would be unhappy with him for leaving after he had promised to stay in and rest but that "feeling"—that awful crawling sensation of alarm—was growing stronger by the minute.

He knew that Roy would be arriving around 8:00 that evening. The deputy's telegraph had expressed frustration at the delay but comforting words as well: Abner was safe and sound by all accounts and Sarah was well, too, although she had chosen to accompany Abner back home to Granville rather than proceed to Walla Walla.

Still, Matthew realized he wasn't at his finest right now and wished for Roy's steady hand. Sometimes he acted quickly when his boss had one of his feelings; other times, he would just shrug and tell him to calm down. Either way, the sheriff wanted his best deputy and closest friend by his side.

Iris's father frowned and asked, "Didn't you tell her you'd wait for Roy to arrive?"

Matthew sighed. "Yes, I did. And I won't go far or get into any trouble, I promise. Really, I just need some air," he lied.

Moving swiftly down the stairs, he peered through the door window and saw that the heavy morning fog was starting to dissipate, long lines of golden sunlight gleaming through the low clouds. He grabbed his jacket and stepped outside just in time to hear the low-pitched rumble of a large crowd coming his way. Walking toward the street, Matthew stared to his left at a strange and ominous parade; they were obviously Orientals and most seemed to be dressed in their finest, most colorful clothes.

The group was very quiet except for a steady stream of gasps and whispers. They were also moving quite slowly and Matthew strained to see what was going on at the front of the solemn procession. *Is it a funeral rite?* he wondered and then noticed a small but tough-looking Chinese man carrying something in his arms.

It looked like a bundle of rags until Matthew saw a shock of bright, red hair and he took off running despite the pain it caused him. The approaching crowd slowed and stopped as he reached them.

The Chinese man paused and looked down at his burden. "Is this him?" he asked in heavily-accented English.

Dicky opened his eyes and smiled. "Yes, this is my boss. Th,th,thank y-y-you!"

Bowing, he promptly deposited the deputy's body into Matthew's arms and said, "He stabbed, better help. Quick, quick!"

Matthew barely had a chance to express his gratitude before the man turned around, growled something unintelligible in his own tongue, and led his people back down the street from whence they came. Glancing at Dicky, his heart sank.

The young man's face was so white that his freckles stood out like splatters of orange paint and both of his eyes were ringed with purple bruises. A grimy, leather knife grip stuck out from his shoulder and seemed to be wedged into the flesh so tightly that it served as a cork against the blood of the injury.

Dicky didn't weigh much more than a hundred and twenty-five pounds but Matthew's arms trembled.

"I thought I told you to stay out of trouble!" was the only thing Matthew could think of to say and the deputy grinned.

"I tried to, boss, but they got me anyway. Sir...the boy. Little Peter, he's dead!" Tears welled in Dicky's eyes and Matthew gave him a gentle squeeze.

"Don't worry about that right now. Let's get you inside first, okay? My wife's brother is a helluva doc!"

Dicky's eyes closed as Matthew spun on his heels and walked quickly down the road. The sheriff started calling for help as soon as he got to within twenty feet of the show house and, within minutes, Dicky was passed out on the kitchen table while the people by his side studied O'Reilly's knife, pondering the best way to remove it from the young man's neck.

Patrick Donnelly swept everything off his desk in rage and shouted, "Goddammit to hell, Freddie! How could you let this happen?"

Fred Marston bowed his head, silently. He knew his boss was just letting off steam but he couldn't help but resent the histrionics. After all, Dan had been Fred's best friend for almost as long as he could remember; he could hardly believe that old Danny Boy was actually gone and knew he would see that third eye drilled into the center of his good friend's forehead all his living days.

But Patrick was like a sick bull, rampaging around his small office, tearing pictures off the walls, and kicking out at anything his feet could reach. He had always let anger take the place of fear, sorrow and uncertainty and—for the most part—that anger had kept them in good stead through hard times. Now, though, Fred just wanted to cry for his loss.

He clenched his fists as an ink blotter flew through the air, almost hitting him on the ear. Taking a deep breath, he said, "Honestly, Patrick, I didn't think you would want us shooting into a whole herd of Chinks and that's what woulda happened if we hadn't stood down!" He paused for a moment, then asked, "What are we gonna do, boss?"

Fred's question seemed to briefly quell Patrick's fury and he sat down at his desk with a huff. Reaching inside one of the drawers, he pulled out a bottle of good scotch and two glasses. Pouring a drink for both of them, he gave one to Fred and lifted his own in a toast.

"To Danny Boy!" he said and drained the scotch in one gulp, immediately pouring another.

Fred followed suit and the two men sat in silence for a moment. Then Patrick said, "We get even, that's what we're gonna do."

Fred smiled and nodded his head in agreement. "I

know where the kid's at. And that prick, Matthew Wilcox, too!"

Patrick stared at the flames that licked the front of the woodstove and murmured, "We have to do this right, though, and not let our emotions get in the way of good business."

Fred narrowed his eyes. Business...it's always business with Patrick and the devil take the hindmost, he thought.

As if he had heard the words, Patrick glanced his way. "Freddie, you know I loved Dan, too. But we have to attend the auction first. Surely you can see that. From the sound of things, that kid is probably already dead and will never utter a word against you or me. We'll sell off those little twats, make a load of cash, and then we'll hunt down that sheriff and shut his mouth permanently, too."

Donnelly swallowed the rest of his drink and stood up. "And while we're at it, we'll rob him of someone dear, just like he done to us. We'll make sure that person suffers, just like Danny did and make certain, before we kill him, that Wilcox feels the loss just as keenly as we do now."

Fred Marston smiled.

26

MAGIC POTIONS

MATTHEW KNELT AT THE HEAD OF THE TABLE BY DICKY'S head and Iris sat on the young man's chest; the doctor took a deep breath, grabbing the knife by the hilt.

"Now remember," he murmured, "blood is going to gush when I pull this blade out...lots of blood. In a way, that's for the best since we need to drain this wound of infection. Too much, though, and Dicky will bleed to death. So, when I say bear down, do it quickly. This boy's life depends on what we do in the next few minutes."

Dicky had woken up long enough to take a stiff shot of whiskey and a few drops of laudanum. He gazed up at Matthew's beautiful wife and wondered if he had already died and gone to heaven, such was the angelic vision perched over him. He heard someone say, "Ready?" and saw the angel nod, then his eyes flew open in agony.

Dr. Winters pulled the knife straight up and out.

Both Matthew and Iris pounced, pushing the flesh forward and pressing down against the blood that welled up out of the two-inch gash. Lewis threw the offending weapon into the corner and Muriel rushed forward with a washbasin filled with soapy water and another bowl filled with herb-soaked compresses.

Matthew and Iris winced at the foul-smelling concoction but knew that Lewis was quite adept at using herbs to cure his patients. Iris asked Muriel what was in this particular batch and she replied, "Many of these things are new to me but I do know there's vinegar, charcoal, honey, Cat's Claw, dandelion and chamomile in this batch. One of the newer things Lewis is trying is moldy bread which sounds terrible, I know, but seems to work wonders."

The doctor pressed the wet cloths to the injury and opened the lips of the gash, letting blood ooze out and pushing more of his medicine into the deep cut with a long, bulb-ended tube. Then he smeared a brownish paste, which brought tears to the eye with its astringent fumes, around the wound. Glancing up at his sister, Lewis said, "You can get down now, Iris. You're squashing the kid."

Iris blushed and scrambled down off the table into her husband's arms. They watched as Dr. Winters continued to clean the area and finally, after applying more paste, bandaged it and gave the patient a shot of morphine.

Dicky gazed up at the doctor and tried to speak but

Lewis said, "Don't try to speak right now, son. Listen, can you move your fingers for me?"

Dicky frowned and concentrated. After a moment, they saw him move his thumb and fingers. The doctor smiled and said, "Very good. Now how about your toes?"

There was the slightest motion in his right foot and then the young man closed his eyes in exhaustion. Dr. Winters took Dicky's hand and whispered, "Just close your eyes now and let the medicine do its work."

Dicky was already asleep, though, and Lewis stepped toward the kitchen sink with a sigh. "That could have gone worse, you know," he said. "There are so many arteries and nerves in the neck area, just pulling out the knife could have killed him. Also, I could have severed the nerves in his spine which he needs in order to walk." He shook his head. "Luckily, I think the blade came out without doing permanent damage."

He scrubbed his hands briskly and dried them on a stack of clean, cotton bandages. Then he turned and stared at his brother-in-law. Lewis was still angry over Matthew's high-handedness but grateful nonetheless at how hard the young sheriff was working to find Amelia.

Putting his resentment aside, he continued, "The real risk now, of course, is infection. That blade was filthy and it went deep. I tried to wash out the area as much as possible but puncture wounds are the most difficult to treat."

Looking at his patient, Lewis added, "Dicky is a healthy young man though. With proper care—and luck—he will pull out of this."

Matthew smiled. "Thank you very much. I am so glad you were here to help. This kid has had it rough and I want him to have a place by my side...if he recovers."

Lewis nodded. "Well, time will tell. In the meanwhile, why don't you help me get him into a nice soft, bed? He needs rest more than anything."

Matthew picked up the deputy and walked down the hallway toward the small room that had been set aside for him and Roy. Placing Dicky on the bed and noting the pallor in the young man's cheeks, he sent up a silent prayer. Remembering the boy who had died during the altercation, Matthew fervently hoped that Dicky would not follow that path.

Iris's father had wept when he heard the news and swore that Peter would have a proper burial rather than be planted in "Potter's Field". Wondering if the two men Gerald Winters had sent to find the body were successful, Matthew again hoped those men would not be found out by Donnelly's ruffians and suffer the same terrible fate.

Leaving the doctor and his wife behind with their ointments and salves, he went back to the kitchen area and heard a violin squawk downstairs as the actors warmed up for tonight's performance. Glancing at his pocket watch, Matthew saw the hour was growing late and what little daylight remained was succumbing to winter's early dusk.

Stepping into the kitchen, he saw Iris at the woodstove putting clams, potatoes and onions into a large pot. Turning around, she smiled. "I pray Dicky pulls through, Mattie."

Sitting down at the table, he said, "Me, too. He is a good kid."

Iris wiped her hands clean with a towel and asked, "And how is *your* wound?"

He had almost forgotten about it over the last few hours. "It's good, really! Your brother is a fine doctor."

She nodded and then a frown marred her expression. "Mattie, are you serious about going to that auction tomorrow...alone?"

"Well, Roy will be with me. But, yes, I am."

Iris bowed her head. She did not want to quarrel with her husband but her heart was filling with ice and a premonition of doom. "Mattie, I don't want you to go!" she blurted.

Matthew frowned in consternation. It was not like Iris to question his decisions or to act squeamish when it came time to get things done. It was especially disconcerting now as the prize in this endeavor was her own niece. He took her hand in his.

"Iris, from what I've been able to gather, these sorts of auctions are pretty high-class. There's a lot of money at stake and, often, the men who gather to do the bidding are considered "the elite". He shrugged at her exclamation of disgust.

"I know," he agreed. "There is nothing classy about what they are doing but, in this case, money speaks volumes and your brother has given me a lot of money. If it's not enough, you and I can add to the pot. So I truly believe Roy and I can waltz in there and buy Amelia's freedom without firing a shot."

Iris sat up straight. "But what about the other girls, Matthew? Will you just leave them behind?"

Matthew flushed. "I don't plan on leaving anyone behind!" he snapped. "But, first things first, don't you agree? We get Amelia out of there and away from harm. Then, she can stand as proof—and a witness—against the Donnelly's!" He glared at his wife for a moment as he struggled with his own frustrations.

"I am sorry I wasn't able to remedy this situation sooner," he added. "But the Donnelly's have proven to be tough customers. I simply need more help to bring their enterprise down."

Iris stared at her husband, then stood up and rushed to his side. Falling on her knees, she grasped his hand in hers and said, "Mattie, I am so sorry! Honestly, I didn't mean my words to come out the way they did!" She kissed his knuckles. "It's just that I have such a bad feeling...a feeling that something horrible is going to happen, even if you DO manage to buy Amelia back!" Tears filled her large brown eyes from both the fear she felt and the hurt she saw on her husband's face.

Matthew's expression softened and he pulled his wife into his arms. "I understand, Iris," he murmured. "Patrick Donnelly seems willing to do just about anything to get what he wants. Fortunately, I think what he wants right now is a good payoff for those girls, plain and simple."

Iris shook her head. "But Dicky told us he killed one of Donnelly's closest friends! Maybe I'm wrong, Mattie, but he seems like the sort of man who would seek revenge."

Matthew drew back and looked his wife in the eyes. "That's why Roy and I are going in disguise, dear. The make-up artists here will color my hair, shave off my mustache and put me in fancy clothes so I look like landed gentry. They are planning to alter Roy's appearance as well." He gave her arms a little squeeze. "We'll be fine. Just a couple of rich strangers who trade in the flesh market."

Iris hugged her husband once more as she wiped away her tears. Walking to the stove, she stirred the clam chowder that was starting to fill the room with fragrant steam.

Matthew watched her for a few moments and said, "It's a little early yet, but I'm heading down to the livery to pick up our horses for transport back home to Granville. I also need to telegraph the sheriff in Gold Bar and have him send the mule back home by train." He added, "That dang old beast is as ornery as they come but he belongs to our department and my bosses won't take kindly to the loss of him."

"Is there someone around here who can go with you?" Iris asked.

Matthew nodded. "Yes. Your father is sending one

of his drivers with me, along with one of his best stage-hands. I hear that both men are handy with a gun although I sincerely doubt that Donnelly will do anything tonight about what happened." He put on his hat and walked over to the stove where Iris stood.

Giving her a hug, he murmured, "I could be wrong, Iris. And because of that, I will use extreme caution. Still, I believe that most of Donnelly's energy will be spent on getting the girls he kidnapped ready to sell tomorrow."

Matthew kissed her cheek and stepped away. Winking, he grinned. "I'll be back soon with Roy. And, like I said, I am feeling so much better."

Iris returned his grin and said, "I plan to test that assertion, husband, just as soon as you return."

Two men stood in the shadows across the street from the opera house and the little theater next to it. They were well hidden from prying eyes and lost in the masses as carriage after carriage pulled up in front of the playhouse, disgorging gaily-clad patrons.

The vendors were hard at work, selling popped corn, hard candies, ale and oranges from their stalls. Earl Dickson's practiced eye also saw busy pickpockets lifting watches, coin purses and wallets away from the crowd of rubes milling around in front of the theater.

Ignoring the familiar sight, he kept focused on the alleyway to the side of the building. He had been to a couple of shows in the past and knew it was also the stage entrance as well as the actors' way in and out of their quarters located upstairs.

Dickson gritted his teeth. Donnelly had somehow found out that he was Margaret's opium supplier. He had experienced a few sweaty moments when he was first confronted and honestly thought Patrick was going to make good on his threats and have him shot.

Only genuine contrition on his part and the promise to work for no wages for the next year stilled Donnelly's hand. That and the fact Earl had the presence of mind to follow the Chink parade—and the wounded deputy—back to this very same spot. Seattle was a big place, big enough for that Dicky kid to have gotten lost for good and his boss was grateful for Earl's quick thinking.

Now he was back in good standing with Donnelly and—along with Fred Marston—he watched as a carriage emerged from the alleyway. Two men sat on the front bench and Marston grunted with malicious delight.

"There he is...that dirty, low-down bastard Matthew Wilcox," he hissed. "That lawman has been a thorn in our side since we left Wenatchee and, by God, I would like to put an end to his miserable existence right now!"

Fred actually had his pistol out and was aiming at the carriage when Earl put a restraining hand on his arm. "Not here and not now!" he snarled. "There are too many witnesses, Freddie."

Marston lowered the gun. "Gawd-dammit, you're right. Better wait for orders, I guess."

The carriage moved slowly into the street, weaving through the crowds. Then it picked up speed and was lost to the darkness. Earl sighed with relief. That was too close for comfort and he wished again that Dan O'Reilly was the one standing by his side rather than the hothead Marston.

"Come on. Let's go tell the boss we found what he's looking for." He stepped away and Freddie soon followed.

BIZARRE BAZAAR

LATE IN THE AFTERNOON THE NEXT DAY, THE RENTED carriage moved slowly down the road toward China-town. Fog swirled and danced ahead of them, pooling under the gaslights. Vague shapes darted here and there in the mist, causing the matched pair of roans to shudder and snort with tension. The driver soothed them with a whisper, his soft Irish lilt submerged under a harsher accent, one melodious and foreign.

The resplendent coach pulled to a stop in front of a weathered door with a green dragon painted on its peeling surface. The men who stood in the shadows chatting, smoking, and placing side bets on tonight's auction stopped what they were doing and watched as three passengers disembarked from the fancy conveyance.

They studied one man in particular who was quite tall with bronze-colored skin, long black hair and mustaches. He wore a dark gray derby, an eye-patch and a wool suit; his embroidered vest made many who watched fairly drool with envy as did his knee-length kid boots. With leather buttons from toe to mid-calf, his shoes spoke of wealth as most of the men in attendance knew it required at least two servants to secure the wearer into such elaborate footwear.

The aristocrat was accompanied by two Mideastern men wearing desert caftans and colorful head scarves; one of them carried a valise no doubt filled with cash, and the other appeared to be the bookkeeper clutching a sheaf of papers in his arms.

The bystanders grinned in anticipation. *This ought to be good,* they thought as the sheik's men had arrived a little while ago, a scruffy lot that didn't look even half as rich as these newcomers.

The lesser players in this passion play had seen it all before. Princes from the far eastern deserts would compete against one another, betting fortunes beyond imagining in order to best one royal house over the other. Sometimes—depending upon the merchandise— the bids for new female slaves came in hot and heavy, far outpacing the value of the goods on display. The side bets grew exponentially and many of the spectators who stood about in the fog rushed to the door in order to watch the action up close.

Matthew, Roy and Gerald stepped inside the painted door and found themselves in a tiny shop. Floor-to-ceiling shelves filled with jars and pots took up the back wall. A waist-high counter separated the customers from the stock and a small Chinese man hurried out from behind it, bowing profusely.

"Ah so, you men come for auction, yes?" he squeaked.

Matthew kept his face schooled into a haughty frown. "Yes, and we do not like to be kept waiting!" he snapped.

The man almost touched his nose to the floor in humility, then sprang upright and said, "Prease, come with me."

He moved swiftly through a doorway and down a dim, cluttered hall to a set of stairs. As soon as Matthew entered the hallway, he heard a tide of voices ebb and flow like the briny seas only a few blocks away. There were other, stranger sounds as well; high-pitched warbling flutes, explosive laughter and the percussive rhythm of exotic drumbeats.

They followed the Chinese man downstairs and waited while he opened a set of double doors into a vast chamber. As soon as the doors opened, Matthew tried to hide his shock at the bizarre spectacle that met his eyes. Gerald gripped his son-in-law's arm and murmured, "Well, well. It seems that Muhammad has moved his mountain…here."

Indeed, Matthew silently agreed. He had no way of knowing whether the Chinese who sponsored this affair were catering to the sheik's desires or if the sheik himself had brought the Mideastern bazaar to Seattle's wharf for the occasion. But he felt as though he and his friends had just been transported to the Arabian sands.

Staring through the haze of smoke from coppery braziers, large hookahs, smoldering cheroots, and tobacco pipes, Matthew saw that at least a hundred men and women had come for the auction. There were dusky-skinned Asians in attendance as well as Americans, Englishmen, haughty Spaniards and foppish Frenchmen. A group of Native Americans stood apart from the others—buckskins, elaborate chest-plates and feathered braids announced their intention to either buy or sell.

A group of fur-clad mountain men clustered around a small, fenced enclosure, shouting encouragement to those betting on the fighting dogs locked in mortal battle within. Even as he watched, Matthew heard a high-pitched, agonized howl when one of the dogs locked its jaws on the other's throat. Human cries of delight and growls of dismay rose into the air as the vanquished animal bled to death on the floor at their feet. Matthew saw men dismantling the makeshift cage and noticed a teenaged boy lifting the dead dog—a thin but lovely German shepherd—into his arms as tears streamed down his cheeks.

The sheriff turned away in disgust. He knew that if he were so inclined, he could arrest at least twenty people on the spot but, for now, he must play his part in this sham. Although many of the people in attendance today were obviously rich, they were spoiled and rotten from self-indulgence and a clear disregard for the law or societal morality.

Most of them were already drunk on whiskey or

sucking on little green-tinged sugar cubes. Dancers wove their way through the crowds, jerking their lithe bellies in parodies of passion and ringing tiny finger chimes in paying customers' ears. One of those dancers saw Matthew and sidled up to him. Smoldering, kohl-ringed eyes gazed into his and her sinuous form almost, but not quite, touched his in eager invitation.

He gulped and waved his hand dismissively. The dancer paused and melted away into the seething crowd. Their Chinese escort raised his voice slightly in order to be heard over the noise. "Come this way, prease. The auction starts soon."

Matthew and his companions followed to a section of high-backed, padded chairs and small, round tables —a concession to the wealthier patrons—and many more people were finding seats, benches and stools to sit on.

He gazed to his left and saw another grouping of chairs and tables. Many foreigners were gathered together along with another whose face looked quite familiar and he growled under his breath. *It was that weasel of a police commissioner, LeVesque!* No wonder the pseudo-lawman had objected so fervently against any action regarding this farce; he not only didn't care about the fate of the girls who were about to be auctioned off like prize cattle but chances were he was lining his pockets with every sale made.

Matthew looked away quickly when LeVesque and two others glanced his way, then remembered he and his men were in disguise; maybe their showy entrance had caught the attention of the sheik and his minions. *Probably worried we have more money than they do*, he thought and prayed that was the case.

He continued to search for the Donnellys but there were so many people in attendance he couldn't tell if they were there or not. Roy was searching the crowd as well and he leaned in and whispered, "I saw the Donnelly woman, boss...she's behind us. But I haven't seen Patrick."

Spotlights suddenly illuminated the area and the gaslights around the room sputtered and dimmed. There was a lull in the action, then a middle-aged Chinese man led a teenaged girl through a back door and onto the stage.

The young woman was wearing a knee-length silk robe and her long black hair gleamed with blue points of light, her small face sweet with dark eyes and a rosebud mouth; Matthew judged her to be an Indian of no more than thirteen or fourteen years. Her expression was both terror-stricken and dazed, and he realized that she was doped up on something as the poor little thing stared out at the excited audience as if she were lost in some outlandish and hideous nightmare.

The lights on stage were strategically placed and although the robe covered most of her body, it was so sheer that nothing was left to the imagination as she stood trembling under the spotlight. The Chinese man smiled out at the crowd, winked, and stepped up behind her. Then he grasped the robe with a flourish and yanked it away from the girl's grasping fingers.

Although she tried to hide her nakedness behind her hands, two more men stepped up and pulled her hands behind her back so her nudity was displayed to the lascivious eyes of the bidding crowd. Matthew heard gasps and excited titters ripple around him as the young girl's breasts were revealed as well as the soft, black patch of hair between her thighs.

Matthew saw the group of Indians gesture in angry excitement and one of them—an older fellow with an elaborate chest-plate—waved his money in the air. In stilted English, he yelled, "We buy! We got cash! We buy that one!"

Matthew couldn't help but wonder if the natives were doing the same thing he was...attempting to buy back what had been stolen; a daughter, perhaps, or a wife. However, the sheaf of dollars clutched in the man's hand was pitifully thin and, after one of the auctioneers inspected the cash offering, the real bidding began.

The Indian slumped in misery and his companions led him away as the bids grew higher and higher. Finally, cheers and jeers rolled across the room as the sheik raised one finger, buying the girl for one thousand dollars cash.

Another young woman was led to the stage; this one as fair as the other was dark. Long blonde hair fell in ripples down her back and, although her breasts were small, her hips were shapely and her long legs made every man in the room squirm with desire. Another flurry of activity ensued and, again, the sheik prevailed. One thousand dollars changed hands and the blonde was led off stage, her head held high and her eyes as clear and cold as an artic wind. Three more girls were offered but the sheik took a rest, allowing others in the room to barter and buy.

Drinks circulated and food was brought to the more elite patrons. When a tray of seafood landed on their table, Matthew turned away in disgust but Gerald picked up a shrimp and bit into it with gusto.

"Cheer up, son. The high mark on these bids seems to be one thousand dollars and we can match that handily."

Matthew thought the show was just warming up but he was loath to scare his father-in-law. Nodding, he replied, "I'm just not hungry, sir."

"Suit yourself then," Gerald said and bit into another shrimp.

A few minutes later, the Chinese man walked back onto the stage. The lights dimmed again and he said, "Now, for our better stock. Bidding starts at one thousand dorrars!"

A thrill of excitement and anxiety rippled through the crowd as another girl stumbled onto the stage. This one was obviously Chinese with black hair rippling to the floor and tiny bound feet. Her face was doll-like with white pancake make-up and she had huge, black eyes. Standing as still as a statue, her silk kimono fluttered to the ground.

There was a collective sigh as her body was revealed. She was so slender she looked almost boyish but her skin was as pale and luminescent as the finest pearl and her nether region had been plucked of all hair. Matthew felt his cheeks heat up and heard Roy mutter, "Holy Moses…"

Then the bidding started in earnest. One thousand dollars quickly turned into two, three and four until she was sold to the sheik for four thousand, six hundred and fifty dollars.

Five more young women came and went; they were different colors, shapes and sizes but they were all beautiful. Thousands of dollars changed hands as the girls were auctioned off to the highest bidder. Any sensual desire Matthew might have felt at their erotic beauty faded to pity as he saw the looks of fear, shame and loss in the girls' faces. Each and every one of them knew that their lives had just been reduced to nothing more than sexual bondage.

Finally, an hour or so later, Amelia Winters was brought on stage. Matthew couldn't help but grin as he saw her jerk away from the much smaller Chinese man who held her arm; for a moment, she looked just like Iris. Then her long robe was stripped from her body and what bravado she possessed fled. Standing naked in front of the audience, her cheeks blazed in shame.

Amelia was tall with large round breasts, a waspishly thin waist and wide, flaring hips. Her red hair fell in abundant curls to the small of her back and her many freckles gleamed under the spotlights. Her brown eyes stared over the top of the crowd and

Matthew's heart clenched as he realized she was reciting the "Lord's Prayer" under her breath.

The crowd reacted with feverish intensity. Men, as well as women, were standing up and waving cash in the air. Matthew saw one of the fur-traders reach under his bearskin and fondle himself for all the world to see. Glancing to his left, he noticed the sheik sitting straight up in his chair and whispering into his agent's ear. Knowing that the bidding would quickly get out of hand, he said, "Now, Gerald!"

Amelia's grandfather rose to his feet and shouted, "Ten thousand dollars!"

Gerald was—first and foremost—a consummate actor and his guttural, Mideastern accent fell over the crowd like a dash of cold water. A groan rose up from the spectators and the sheik stared over at them with malicious eyes. Amelia was staring as well and, for a moment, Matthew thought she might have recognized her grand-papa but her expression was bleak.

The sheik whispered into his agent's ear again and, looking as though he might have an apoplectic fit, LeVesque cried out, "Eleven thousand!"

Back and forth the bidding went until beads of nervous sweat dotted Matthew's forehead. Iris was a fairly, rich woman but how much was too much? Yet he had not come this far to quibble over the outrageous price. Nudging his father-in-law's elbow again, the old man shouted, "Eighteen thousand dollars!"

A stunned silence fell over the crowd and Amelia turned to face their table. In his nervous anxiety,

Gerald had almost forgotten to use his Arabian accent and Matthew could see the sudden hope blooming in the girl's eyes. She was smart enough, though, to keep her suspicions to herself and she let her gaze drop to the floor.

The auctioneer said, "The bid is eighteen thousand dollars! Do I have a counter?"

The crowd held its collective breath and stared as the sheik consulted with his agent.

Once again, the auctioneer cried, "The bid is eighteen thousand dollars for this red-haired beauty...do I have a counter?"

The sheik shook his head and the auctioneer shouted, "Sold to the gentleman for eighteen thousand dollars!"

28

CHECK

WHEN DICKY WAS A SMALL BOY, HE USED TO GO FISHING with his pa on Icicle Creek. They'd board a tiny rowboat and float close to shore, keeping far away from the rapid currents and eddies that muscled their way through the high gorge on either side of the water. They caught trout, sturgeon and even the occasional red-fleshed silver salmon that had traveled far inland from the Pacific Ocean to spawn.

In Dicky's mind, those occasional days of recreation with his pa counted as some of the best times of his life. Whenever he felt low—or frightened or confused—he would close his eyes and remember those days of instruction, laughter and love and knew he'd been blessed.

Those recollections filled the young man's mind now, but they were warped and horrifying. He found himself in that tiny skiff again, facing the seething rapids in the middle of blood-red rushing waters. Heat beat down from the searing sun overhead and he saw that the boat had drifted far from shore and was quickly being sucked into the raging currents.

His pa sat behind him in the boat, shouting frantic orders but his words were garbled, lost in the echoing roar of the water's swift passage. Trying to turn around, Dicky found himself strangely rooted into place. Forced to stare straight ahead at the jagged, toothy rocks jutting up from the water, he yelled, "Pa! What should I do?"

Dicky heard his father's panicked screams but he was stuck like glue, unable to turn around or pick up an oar or do anything at all. Then he saw a sight that turned his heart to ice. A huge tree was toppling over the river—a fork-shaped jack pine with blackened, gnarled branches... the same tree that had killed his father so many years before.

"No!" he groaned, shaking his head back and forth in an attempt to stave off the nightmare. His eyelids fluttered and he sucked in a great breath of air as consciousness returned to his mind. The back of his neck and the top of his left shoulder throbbed in agony. He knew something terrible had happened, then remembered he had been stabbed.

Gagging at the pain that pulsed through his system, Dicky knew he was quite ill. The frightful dream must have been brought on by the fever that raged through his blood. Vaguely surprised he was even alive, the young man swallowed painfully. His throat was parched and his right hand fumbled at the bedside table for a glass of water. Then he heard another scream.

Thinking for a moment that he was re-entering that awful dream, he opened his eyes wide as he realized the screams were actually happening. Dicky heard the sound of an orchestra coming from downstairs; fiddles sawed, French horns bleated, and muffled laughter greeted the actors in Gerald's troupe. One of their shows was in full swing.

Although his eyes felt as if someone had put glue in them, Dicky gazed about the darkened bedroom, trying to see what had awoken him. The door was ajar, casting a wedge of light across the floor, and he saw somebody there—a tall, lean figure of a man with a grizzled beard and a white coat...Dr. Winters!

Then he glanced to his left, where he could hear the grunts of a struggle. Dicky peered into the shadows and saw Iris heaving against the arms of Freddie Marston who held one hand over her mouth, a blade against her throat. He had already drawn blood despite the fact Iris was kicking like an angry mule, making her captor wince with pain as her heels connected with his shins.

"Let her g-g-go!" Dicky cried and struggled to sit up, but he fell back in a woozy daze. The room swam about his head, much like the one time his pa had let him drink a few shots of good whiskey, and his stomach lurched as his eyes spotted another form on the floor by his bed. The light from the hallway illuminated her face and Dicky saw that the doctor's wife

Muriel lay in a pool of her own blood, leaking from the ear-to-ear slash in her throat.

Dicky had thought the woman a sweet saint a couple of times over the last few hours. Whenever he opened his eyes she was there, whispering words of encouragement in her soft, Southern drawl. Now she was gone and Dicky knew Marston had done the horrible deed.

A dark form materialized in the doorway and he heard an unfamiliar voice say, "Hurry up! The show's almost over!"

Dicky closed his eyes, hoping the intruders would think he was dead or at least too far gone to hinder their plans. His heart ached as there was no way he could help Matthew's wife; he couldn't even sit up without the whole world turning upside down. Still, he hoped against hope that he would survive long enough to tell Mr. Wilcox what had happened and who had taken his dear Iris.

Sensing a presence by the side of the bed, he held his breath. Now was the moment, he knew, that his life truly hung in the balance and Dicky waited for his fate to be sealed. He heard the man step away and say, "I think the show's over, Freddie. Get a hold of that bitch now and we'll take her to Potter's Field like we promised."

Dicky heard more struggling and then the harsh sound of flesh hitting flesh. "There!" the man hissed. "That's how you take care of women who fight back!"

He lay as still as death as heavy shuffling footsteps

exited the room. Then all was silent and he succumbed to his fever, surrounded by the lifeless bodies of the people who had tried so desperately to save his own.

A few blocks away, Matthew, Gerald and Roy stood in a room behind the auction stage. Men and women milled about and cash flew from hand to hand as the evening's business transactions concluded. Fresh stage make-up had been re-applied since Gerald had sweated off most of his during the bidding war.

The three men stood to the side as one girl after another was marched out of the room; some easily enough, others kicking and screaming. Finally, Matthew spoke out with all the haughty disdain he could muster.

"We are in a hurry and do not countenance being made to wait! Fetch our girl here now!"

A Chinese woman dipped her head and scurried away toward the back. A few moments later, she returned clutching Amelia's arm. The girl looked both hopeful and terrified. She had only met her scandalous grandpapa a few times over the years as her parents did not want their only daughter exposed to the seedier side of entertainment. However, despite the not-so-proper road Gerald had chosen in his life, he seemed to adore his grandchildren and neither Lewis nor Muriel wanted to deprive the old man of their affections.

So when the Mideastern man had stood up and squawked, "Eighteen thousand dollars!", his voice had tickled her memory. Amelia remembered when her parents had taken her and her brother to see the play *Othello* by William Shakespeare; Gerald had starred and his voice almost exactly matched that of the caftan-wearing man who bid for her.

Amelia's heart pounded loudly in her ears. *Could it be true?* she wondered. *Have I been saved?* Glancing up with her fingers crossed behind her back, she stared at the man who had bought her. One glance was enough to affirm her suspicions and she dropped her eyes, blinking away sudden tears of relief.

Her grandpapa was a tall, thin man with a rosy-red complexion and bright brown eyes. His most prominent feature was his dark, well-defined eyebrows; like eagle's wings, they were a physical trait he had passed on to his descendants.

Amelia glanced up once more and sneaked a peek at the two men standing next to Gerald Winters. She didn't know who the smaller man was but he appeared to be in his thirties with a handlebar mustache and sharp blue eyes. The other man though...Amelia's eyes grew wide. She knew all of a sudden and without any doubt that she was staring at her auntie's husband, Matthew Wilcox. She had seen his image enough times to recognize the long, thin nose and the wide, slightly-slanted green eyes that gazed back at her. Yet Amelia also realized all three men were in disguise, that the black hair and tawny skin of her saviors would wash off with soap and water.

The Chinese woman who held her arm in a vice-like grip held her other hand out and started talking fast in her singsong voice. Gerald rolled his eyes and muttered, "I know what you want, ye damn harpy... here! Eighteen thousand dollars, as agreed."

The woman snatched the leather bag away from him and counted the coins and banknotes within. Finally, she nodded her head in satisfaction and gave Amelia a little push in their direction. "You go now," she growled.

"Gladly, Madame Harpy," Gerald mumbled with a smile and took Amelia's arm in his. He stopped and said, "Wait a minute..." He turned to Matthew. "Will you loan us your coat, please?"

"Of course," Matthew said and placed it over Amelia's scantily-clad body. The girl was weeping openly now in relief but Matthew thought those tears would easily be misconstrued as fear or sorrow to the people who might be watching their exit.

He and Roy took point with Gerald and his grand-daughter behind them and made their way out the door into the large room. The auction was technically over but dogs were fighting again in the makeshift pen and an impromptu band had started up on the other side. Although most of the men and women who had bid were leaving, many of the bystanders were preparing to carry on the festivities in their own manner.

Matthew heard a few catcalls as some of the men in the crowded room spotted their exit but no one tried to stop them, especially since Roy had decided to display his pistol in warning.

They were almost to the double doors that led upstairs when he saw the police commissioner, LeVesque, lounging against the back wall. He studied them with cold, dark eyes and the sheriff wondered uneasily just how many constables were in cahoots with the man.

Matthew thought it would be easy enough for LeVesque to simply arrest them for human trafficking and then make off with Amelia himself for more profit. Suddenly convinced that was precisely what was going to happen, he said, "Roy, you and Gerald stop just outside the doorway while I have a chat with an old friend."

Roy's eyes narrowed at Matthew's tone of voice. They had worked together far too long for the new threat in his friend's voice not to register. So he quickly hustled Gerald and Amelia out the doors and then pushed them toward a wall, standing in front of them.

A few moments later, Matthew walked out with a small fellow struggling fruitlessly by his side. "Let me go, you bastard!" the man cried.

"I will, but first you're going to listen to me," Matthew snarled. He shoved the man against the opposite wall and put his pistol to LeVesque's Adam's apple.

"I don't know—nor do I care—what kind of game you're running here, *Commissioner.*" The sheriff sneered. "What I do know is this. I could kill you here and now and no one would lift a finger."

LeVesque's eyes got big and he gagged as the pistol ground into his throat, frantically shaking his head back and forth. "No! Don't kill me, please!"

Matthew seemed to think it over. "No, I won't…not if you let us go unhindered. If you do that, I'll even keep mum about what you're up to here," he lied, silently vowing that if it was the last thing he ever did, he would bring this little weasel of a man down for using the law to cover his own illegal activities.

Pushing the pistol into LeVesque's neck a little harder, Matthew watched as the man's tongue protruded from his lips and he clutched at his belly against the gag reflex triggered by the gun's cold metal kiss. As he released some of the pressure, LeVesque squealed, "Yes! Now please stop!"

Matthew stepped back and barked, "Move forward! I'll be right behind you and if anything bad happens— anything at all—you'll be feeling what this gun is *really* meant to do!"

LeVesque nodded, wiping nervous sweat away from his forehead. With the pistol's heavy steel nose now boring into his lower back, he led the procession up the stairs through the little Chinese store and out into the street.

Then he called out, "Boys! Let these ones go!"

"You sure, boss?" another voice asked from the shadows.

Levesque yelled as the gun drilled into his kidney. "Yes, goddammit!"

A few moments later, Matthew heard Gerald's stagehand shout, "Get yer mitts off me, you filthy shite!"

A rented carriage careened around the corner and came to a stop in front them. "Get in! Those are Seattle coppers!" the stagehand warned.

Not for long, Matthew silently swore. He let his pistol fall in a heavy arc, hitting LeVesque across the temple and watched as the man slumped into a heap on the ground.

29

MATE

A<small>S</small> <small>THE</small> <small>OPULENT</small> <small>GRAY</small> <small>CARRIAGE</small> <small>SWEPT</small> <small>DOWN</small> <small>THE</small> street, Amelia wept in gratitude and clutched at her grandfather's arm.

"Thank you! Thank you so much, all of you, for saving me!"

Gerald smiled and patted her on the back. "That's all right, dearie. You are safe now, thanks to your Uncle Matthew and his deputy."

"Well, sir, I believe it was a group effort," Matthew murmured.

Blushing, Amelia moved forward on the opposite bench and took the sheriff's hand in hers. "Still, thank you so much…Uncle. I can't tell you how many times I prayed you would come to save the day." She used her grandfather's hankie to wipe the tears from her face, adding, "I was beginning to lose hope."

Matthew nodded. "Yes, I suppose you were. It hasn't been an easy thing to find you. The Donnellys have been doing this for a long time, it seems. They covered their trail effectively, too. It was only by chance that we even knew where to look!"

Sitting back with an exhausted sigh, Amelia said, "Well, you *did* find me and I thank you all from the bottom of my heart. Do my mother and father know what has happened?"

"We're heading to them now, dear," Gerald replied. "They've been scared silly and will weep in gratitude that their daughter is safely back in their arms."

"I only hope they're not too disappointed in me," she whispered and then closed her eyes and snuggled up next to her grandfather, falling into an exhausted sleep.

The first order of business was to return the frightfully expensive rented carriage to the stable and pick up their more modest transport. Then they needed to get Amelia back to her heartsick parents. More importantly, they needed to change their appearance both for comfort's sake and to keep the Mideastern prince ruse in play.

Matthew knew by now that the search for Iris's niece had become a personal vendetta between himself and Patrick Donnelly. Amelia's captor was apparently willing to do anything—including spill innocent blood —to profit from the girls he kidnapped. But he had chosen the wrong girl this time...and spilled the wrong blood.

Staring out the side window at the dark city streets, Matthew had no doubt that if Patrick knew he was the one who had taken possession of Amelia, the bastard would send his henchmen to take her back out of sheer spite.

He shook his head and tore the black wig off his head. He would deliver Amelia to the bosom of her family but, after that, he would send Iris home and renew his hunt. Now that the girl was safe, he intended to bag a few criminals. He would bring Patrick and Margaret Donnelly, Freddie Marston, LeVesque, the crooked sheriff in Wenatchee and a few others to justice.

Gerald kicked a sturdy leather valise at his feet. "In here you will find some heavy grease. That should help with make-up removal. Your regular clothes are packed in the bottom, too."

Matthew smeared the grease over his face and mustache. It stunk of pig but after rubbing a clean cloth over his face a few times, he saw Gerald nod in approval. "Looks like you're almost back to normal, son."

Roy took his turn with the grease-pot and stripped out of the caftan. He was already dressed underneath the costume, but now his pale complexion was in evidence and he grinned. "Back to the pretty boy my wife knows and loves!" he smirked.

A bit later, Gerald's coach turned the corner and started up the broad thoroughfare toward the play-house. It was well past 9:00 by now and the streets should have been empty. Instead, many people stood around the building gawking and pointing.

Matthew stared at the crowd and said, "Uh, Gerald, is it usually this busy after a show?"

The old man started from his doze and craned his head to peer out the window. "What the...?"

"Uh-oh," Roy muttered.

Matthew felt his heart sink with dismay. Now that they were closer, he could see two King County paddy wagons and an ambulance pulled up close to the alley by the theater. City constables were pacing back and forth, swinging hand-held lanterns and blowing their whistles.

"Grandpapa," Amelia whispered. "Has someone been hurt?"

"I don't know, dear," he replied. "But we shall soon see."

The carriage pulled to a stop and Gerald said, "Amelia, you stay here for the time being. Let me see what's going on."

Amelia settled back on the seat and watched as her saviors walked up to the closest constable and exchanged words. Then she saw Gerald step back and put his hand over his heart in shock.

Matthew also completely froze for a moment, then took off running down the alley, Roy hot on his heels. Amelia saw a few of the constables try to stop them but give way quickly when they saw the look in the sheriff's eyes. She felt herself grow as cold as ice.

Her grandfather was hunched over and trembling as if he had just been dealt a grievous blow. Somehow knowing that the news concerned her and her family, she disobeyed orders and jumped down from the carriage. Running up to him, Amelia cried, "Grandpapa, what's wrong? What's happened?"

Gerald stared at her with blank eyes and a tear fell when he recognized who she was. "Darling...," he choked. "Your mama...I'm so sorry, but your mama has been murdered and your pa is at death's door."

Amelia gasped, staring at her grandfather as he added, "Some ruffians hurt your ma and pa and kidnapped your auntie Iris." The old man groaned and seemed to sway on his feet.

"Sir? I think maybe you should sit down for a little while. Here..." A young constable took Gerald by the arm and led him to one of the benches in front of the theater. "Mister, if it's any comfort, I hear that Dr. Winters might be okay." He sighed, adding, "I sure hope so. He has been our family's doc since I was just a boy."

Amelia sat down next to her grandfather. Her eyes were surprisingly dry and she knew she was in shock. But too much had happened over the last couple of weeks; she felt numb and disconnected. Taking her grandpapa's hand, she closed her eyes as an older woman in a flamboyant red silk dress and heavy make-up fought her way through the line of policemen and ran to Gerald's side.

Gerald leaned into his lover's ample bosom and wept while Amelia stared into space at her mother's spirit; she saw her ma's short round body and sensed her kind touch but felt a jolt of fear when she realized she couldn't see Muriel's face. Although Amelia could also hear her mother's warm voice and smell her special fragrance, her face was only a blur.

Reaching into thin air, trying desperately to lift the veil of death over her mother's features, Amelia rose to her feet and screamed, "Mama, come back!"

The young woman's wail rose into the night, echoing eerily off the tall buildings until many of the bystanders covered their ears in superstitious dread. Some people from the "old country" believed a banshee had just come to visit and they crossed themselves before fleeing lest that spirit came to call on them as well.

By the time Matthew reached the top of the staircase, Muriel's body was on a gurney, covered by a canvas tarp. He saw her small, roughened hand sticking out from under and placed it alongside her corpse. Then he turned and noticed an unfamiliar doctor attending to his brother-in-law.

Lewis lay as still as death on a cot by the far wall. His eyes were open, though, and flicked toward Matthew as he gestured with his left hand and murmured, "Matt…"

The physician plunged a cloth into a bucket of clean water. Wringing it out, he handed the rag to Matthew and said, "Use this to wet his lips. A little water can go down but be careful because I just gave him a large dose of morphine and he might get sick with too many fluids in his belly."

Matthew gazed down at Lewis and asked, "Will he be okay, Doctor?"

The physician sighed. "I *think* so. He was hit on the back of the head by some sort of blunt object. If you're going to get clobbered on the skull, that is a pretty good place to get it, in my opinion, as the bone is quite dense. Still, there is always the risk of swelling or internal bleeding. If his condition worsens, I might have to trepan..." He sighed, adding, "I hope it doesn't come to that."

The sheriff nodded and squeezed some water onto his brother-in-law's lips.

"Can you tell me what happened? Where's Iris?" he whispered.

Lewis's lids fluttered and, when he opened his eyes, Matthew saw they were slightly crossed. Feeling a chill, he took the man's hand. "Who did this? Can you tell me that?"

It looked as though Lewis was trying to answer but the effort was too much for him. The attending physician shook his head. "I'm sorry, but the patient needs to rest right now."

Matthew paused in frustration and then heard Roy call from down the hall. He patted Lewis on the shoulder and whispered, "Get better soon, brother." Then he walked into the other room.

Roy was standing by Dicky's bed. The young man

was white as a sheet and Matthew could feel waves of heat emanating off his body from two feet away. Understanding that the young deputy might not survive his knife wound after all, Matthew took his hand.

Dicky searched the sheriff's face and whispered, "I'm s-s-sorry, boss. I c-couldn't stop 'em."

"Of course you couldn't, son. It's not your fault!"

Dicky's eyes were bright. "I know sir, b-b-but…" He shuddered, groaning in misery. Lying still for a moment, teeth clenched against the pain and fever rolling through his body, he calmed and stared up at his boss again. "I know who d-done it and where they took your wife."

30

HELL'S BELLS

EARL DICKSON GRINNED. THE REDHEAD WAS CONKED out on the bench across from where he sat in the hearse and he would earn one hundred dollars for the acquisition. Apparently, Patrick Donnelly had done his research and found out that this scorching beauty was none other than Matthew Wilcox's wife, Iris.

Fred Marston sat by his side, rubbing his hands together. "I don't see why we can't have a little taste before we bury her. That's all I'm sayin', Earl! The boss never said we couldn't."

Dickson shook his head. "Look, Freddie, I don't know how much of a head start we got. I'm not even sure if that kid got the message or if he died before the sheriff got back." He turned to the other man who was practically drooling with frustrated sexual desire. "I did what I could to lure Wilcox out here but we don't got time to mess around with the goods!

"Burying this lady alive is part of the revenge Mr.

Donnelly has planned for the sheriff. But the real objective is to put him and his deputy down after he gets to the cemetery and finds out what happened to his wife, see? I hear that Patrick will have at least ten men surrounding that grave and they're waiting for us to show up!"

"Oh, all right," Fred grumped. "Let's just get this done. It's a damn waste though, if you ask me."

Dickson eyed the woman and nodded. "Mebbe so, but we got our orders...there's Potter's Field now."

The hearse was approaching a ramshackle gate with an equally squalid hut built next to it. No one was inside. *The caretaker was probably paid a fair fee to look the other way,* Dickson thought, so they rolled right on through into the vast, overgrown graveyard. There were multiple mounds of dirt with spades and shovels sticking out of them, a large box filled with cheap wooden crosses, and pallets of flimsy pine coffins leaning haphazardly on one side of the gravel road.

Thousands of migrants had come to the Pacific Northwest's port city of Seattle to pan for gold and silver, trap for furs, fish, and log the tall trees in the last two decades. Many of those men and women had perished, leaving no home address or means of contacting their next of kin so this particular Potter's Field was almost as large as Seattle's two other public cemeteries put together. Gloomy even during the light of day, the graveyard seemed to throb with sorrow and Fred crossed himself against the haints that might be watching their progress onto their home turf.

Dickson rolled his eyes and peered out the window. Studying the road ahead, he saw the dull gleam of lantern light off to the left. Knocking a stick against the front of the buggy, he yelled to the driver, "There they are, up ahead to the left."

The men inside heard the driver say, "Whoa, whoa my beauties." Then the carriage came to a stop. Earl and Fred got out and, a few moments later, Donnelly walked out of the darkness.

"Took you long enough," he growled.

Fred stood tongue-tied as Earl answered, "Sorry, boss. We got your prize though."

"Let's give her a look." Patrick smiled.

Fred reached inside and pulled Iris out of the wagon. She was still out cold, both from the swift uppercut Earl had dealt her earlier and from the ether they had forced her to breathe.

He placed her on the ground at Patrick's feet and the older man stared at her face gleaming in the moonlight. *Well, she IS a rare beauty*, he mused and—for a moment—he thought twice about what he planned to do. Then anger filled him again and he bared his teeth.

Well, Danny was a beaut, too, he thought, and Matthew Wilcox took him away just as sure as shootin'. Let him feel the loss!

Looking up, he growled, "Take her over to that grave by the light. There's a coffin there. Dump her inside and bury it quick!"

Fred frowned at the red-haired woman but Earl stooped over, picked her up and flung her over his right shoulder. Then they moved through the burial mounds and broken crosses until they reached a newly dug hole in the ground and a pine casket.

Placing Iris's body inside, Patrick, Earl, Fred and another man Marston didn't know lowered the coffin into the hole and started shoveling dirt over it. At the last minute, Patrick called a halt and placed a long rubber tube into a hole drilled through the coffin's lid. Chances were the woman would perish long before she discovered the breathing tube or the string that sounded a tiny bell but, just in case they were able to shoot her husband and his deputy quick enough, she might come in handy.

Recently, Patrick had heard a train baron by the name of Sterling Morris say that he was desirous of a new wife—someone comely and not too green. The fact that this same man was thought to have killed off his first two wives meant nothing to Donnelly. Cash was cash and Morris was offering a lot of it.

Finally finished, the men scurried off to the furthest corners of Potter's Field where they hunkered down and prepared to wait for their quarry to arrive.

Three hours later, Sheriff Wilcox, Roy, and a young man named Tommy King rowed a small boat through the oily waters around the many piers and wharves that dotted the inland coastline of Seattle. The docks were alive with people despite the hour; Matthew could see fires burning brightly, hear the sound of late-night revelers and, occasionally, the tinkle of a piano or the keen of fiddle strings in the night.

He had spoken with Gerald earlier and learned that Potter's Field abutted against the shoreline. So the best way to get in without being seen was from the water's edge. The older man and Amelia were now sitting by Lewis's side waiting to either bid the doctor adieu or clasp him tight to their hearts if he survived the horrible blow to his head.

Gerald had sent Tommy—the same Irishman who had driven the carriage to the auction—with them to act as a guide. The young man was handsome with inky-black hair and bright blue eyes. He was also mad as hell—Gerald Winters had taken him in fresh off the boat, given him a livelihood, three meals a day and all the time he could wish for with horses, the most blessed of God's beasts in his opinion.

When he wasn't cutting and tying weight ropes, painting backdrops or helping in the production of the troupe's many performances, Tommy was downstairs in the stables caring for their horses. The success or failure of any troupe of actors was an illusion, Gerald advised. If their animals or tack looked ill-used, the troupe was seen as being unprofessional. Tommy took this as gospel and looked to Gerald as a replacement of his own father who had died so many years ago in Ireland.

He studied the shoreline carefully, looking for the small dock below the graveyard and he cleared his throat of fear. This sheriff seemed like a mean git and Tommy approved, vowing he would help the man and his deputy bring the men who had hurt his boss's children to a swift end.

"Here it is," he whispered. "Now bring us in soft..."

Roy saw a rotting dock jutting out from a patch of weeds and, standing up on the bow, he picked up a coil of rope and threw it with barely a sound. Then he stepped lightly onto the wooden structure and tied the boat fast.

Matthew and Tommy climbed quietly out of the boat and joined Roy, peering through the brush and brambles into the back acres of Potter's Field. It was as dark as ink and the air was thick with a foggy mist. As they stepped off the dock, the ground below their feet was soft with mud and the whole area stunk of moldering vegetation, fish, and...Roy shuddered...was that a whiff of human decay?

According to Gerald Winters, the first few graves dug here had been placed too close to shore and many of those interred had drifted out of their plots and into the harbor or had swum, so to speak, into neighboring graves and took up residence forevermore in the arms of total strangers. It was a poorly kept secret and the town fathers had sworn to practice better burial techniques in the future so that the likes of Seattle's Potter's Field not be repeated.

Tommy stepped up close and whispered, "I have no

way of knowing where they took your wife, Sheriff. But if they brought a wagon or a hearse in here, the main access road is over there—about two city blocks away."

Matthew regarded the cemetery and knew this was a trap. Although it was clear that Dicky was proud of himself for being able to give his boss the new intelligence, it was equally evident to Matthew and Roy that the information had been planted. The men who had taken Iris had shown no mercy when it came to Amelia's parents and if Dicky had not been necessary to their plans, they would have finished him off with no second thoughts.

Still, Matthew didn't doubt that Donnelly and his men meant to harm Iris purely out of spite so whether they also meant to lure him and Roy to their deaths was beside the point. *The trick*, he thought, *is to grab Iris as quickly as possible, get her to safety, and do it all before Donnelly even knows we're here.*

Matthew felt his heart thump hard in his chest. "But what if Iris is already dead?" a little voice in the back of his mind whispered. "What if, despite everything you do now, the love of your life has already taken her last breath?"

"Shut up," he mumbled to himself. Roy looked up at the sheriff in surprise.

"What's the plan?" he asked as he eyed his friend in sympathy. So many things had happened to Matthew during his short life, Roy marveled that he was as balanced and levelheaded as he was. Losing Iris, however, might be the one thing that tipped the scales.

Roy and his family had also grown to love Iris Imes Wilcox. They admired her strength, beauty, and determination. Maybe more than anything else, they loved how she took such good care of Matthew and had helped heal the many scars on his heart.

All things being equal, though, Roy understood that there was simply no good reason why Iris would still be alive. Donnelly's objective was to silence Matthew and anyone else he ran with so that he could continue to make money from the women he kidnapped. Roy vowed to bring the criminal and his sister to justice—and then try to keep Matthew from falling apart, if worse came to worst.

Matthew was still staring into the darkness but he turned to Roy after a moment and murmured, "We need to split up and make our way to the front of the cemetery. Use your knives, if you can, since I'm sure Donnelly has quite a few men stationed around this property and this can turn into a gunfight. But if that happens we run the risk of being arrested by the local authorities and, more importantly, not being able to find Iris in time."

Looking at Tommy, he said, "You can head on back now. I don't want you getting involved in what's about to take place here."

The young man shook his head. "Nay! I'm a good fighter, sir. Those men hurt my boss and I want to make them hurt, too."

Matthew asked, "You ever been in a fight like this before?"

Tommy nodded grimly. "Aye, sir, plenty of times. And I know how to use my blade as well as the next man."

The sheriff sighed. "Well, do what you can to avoid bloodshed, okay? I would rather arrest these men than try to explain why they are all dead. Got it?" He added, "And heaven help you, kid, if you're lying to me. This is going to get rough."

Matthew bent over and fished a knife out of each of his boots. Pointing at Roy, he gestured to the right; the deputy nodded and moved silently away into the fog. He watched as Tommy went to the left, then he moved ahead in a slight crouch...an eight-inch knife clutched in each fist and his trusty old slingshot within easy reach.

31

REDEMPTION

MARGARET SCRAMBLED OUT FROM UNDER THE DESK IN the caretaker's hut. She sneezed and shook her head in disgust. The smell under there was revolting—a mixture of sweat, dirty shoes and mice. Standing still, she listened and her eyes grew wide with fear. A bell was sounding off in the distance.

She had been lurking outside the parlor door in the warehouse earlier when she heard her brother's plans. Heart sinking, she understood then that Patrick was beyond redemption. Although Amelia Winters had fetched a huge amount of money—far more than any other girl they had ever sold at auction—Patrick was bent on revenge.

What was worse was the fact that they were going to bury a sheriff's wife alive and Margaret shuddered in shame. She knew she had done terrible things since moving to Washington with her brother but this was a mortal sin! Sitting down on the only piece of furniture in the building—a broken, straight-backed chair—she heard the bell's frantic tinkle again.

Margaret had just spent the better part of two days in the grip of withdrawals from the poppy. Actually, she'd been rudely deprived of her narcotic for almost two weeks and was only now beginning to think straight. Understanding that her addiction had implemented her compliance in Patrick's schemes, however, did nothing to alleviate her guilt.

The time to act was now. Clear-headed for the first time in years, Margaret knew that if she didn't at least try to save the young woman from suffocating to death in that coffin, she herself would suffer eternal damnation. She remembered the old stone church back home in Ireland and the priest's fierce sermons about God and the devil, and Margaret shook with fear. The anguish of withdrawal was nothing compared to the eternal fires of hell.

She crept to the door. It was so dark and there was so much fog, Margaret felt sure she wouldn't be seen if she ran to the newly dug grave. Still, she hesitated. Patrick was the only family she had left. If she were found out, Margaret had no doubt that he would either kill her or cast her out.

She heard the tiny bell once more but it seemed faint now, as if the one who pulled the string was losing the strength—or the will—to live. Throwing caution to the four winds, Margaret took off running. She had spied upon Patrick and his men earlier and had a pretty good idea where they had buried the woman. Twice, she stumbled and fell; once on a hoe that lay hidden near a pile of dirt and then again over another new grave.

The second time she fell, she placed both hands over her mouth to stifle a gasp of pain. She had twisted her ankle and spears of agony lanced up and down her leg. As she recovered her breath, Margaret heard the mournful tinkle again—this time very near to where she sat in a heap on the ground.

Peering through the misty dark, Margaret could make out a pile of soil, a number of shovels and a long white, rubber hose coiled up on the ground about eight feet away. *I found it!* She exulted even as she felt another pulse of pain from her rapidly swelling ankle.

Crawling on all fours, Margaret Donnelly made her way to the grave and peered into the opening. There was not too much dirt on the casket she noted and wondered why. Perhaps Patrick meant to let Iris Wilcox live, after all?

Lying on her belly, she seized the hose and wriggled it back and forth, not knowing whether the woman trapped inside even knew the breathing apparatus was there. Then she whispered into it. Since there was so little dirt over the casket, Margaret thought there was a possibility the sheriff's wife might be able to hear her voice.

"Hello! Grab the hose and breathe into it! Do you hear me? Breathe into the end of the tube...it should be there right next to you!"

Margaret waited as still as death and listened. The

bell was completely quiet now and, for a moment, she thought Iris had expired. Then she felt a small tug on the hose she held loosely in her hand.

"That's a good girl! Now breathe!" she crooned.

A few seconds later, she heard an exhalation of breath through the tube, then the sound of steady breathing. Knowing she had very little time to save the trapped woman, Margaret slipped down inside the grave and started scooping dirt away from the casket's lid.

Three hundred and fifty feet away from where Margaret dug, Tommy King stopped as he saw a dark form hiding behind a tree trunk in front of him. Clutching his knife tightly, he crept up on the figure and was just about to hit him on the back of the head with the hilt when the man sprang to his feet with an inarticulate shout. Unlike Matthew, Patrick had not been particularly concerned about stealth so, as soon as Fred Marston saw the threat, he brought his pistol about and shot.

He missed, though, because Tommy had stepped to his left and brought his blade down on Fred's arm. Dropping the gun, he cried out in pain. Then he cried no more when that same stinging blade swung a wide arc across his neck.

Falling to the ground, Fred Marston choked and gurgled as a slender young man picked up the pistol and disappeared silently into the fog. Wishing one last time he could have had a piece of that red-haired action, he died in the mud of Potter's Field.

Seventy-five feet away from where Fred Marston gasped his last breath, Roy was engaged in silent, hand-to hand combat with Earl Dickson. Roy was far younger and in much better shape but Dickson seemed to be all grasping hands and kicking feet. But, unbeknownst to Roy, Earl had learned as a youngster roaming the streets of New York City how to fight dirty.

The deputy knew a thing or two as well but his testicles were throbbing from being pummeled and he was bleeding steadily from a knife wound in his back. Growing weaker by the second, Roy was beginning to worry as his lower back screamed in torment. He had no way of knowing where he had been stuck but understood that, if it was in his liver, he might die before the fight ended.

He wriggled free from Dickson's clutches and was just about to jump on the man's back and bite him on the ear when he heard a gunshot. Both he and Dickson stood still for a moment, wondering who was on the receiving end of that gunfire. Then Earl stiffened, his eyes wide open and staring at nothing.

A second later, he dropped like a stone and lay still on the ground. Roy shook his head and stared as Matthew stepped out from behind a tall tree. The sheriff held his slingshot loosely in one hand and studied his quarry as he approached.

"You and that gopher-chucker," Roy mumbled.

Matthew grinned. "Well, it's gotten me out of a few jams." Then he frowned and said, "Turn around, Roy, and let me see." His fingers peeled away the wet shirt. "Oh yeah, buddy, he got you a good one."

"Is it my liver?" Roy asked.

The sheriff shook his head. "I don't think so, but you're bleeding like a stuck pig. You need to sit down now."

Roy shook his head, but Matthew glared. "That's an order, deputy!"

Roy sighed in frustration. Normally, Matthew never pulled rank but the wound must be serious enough that it scared his boss into doing so this time. Making his way slowly to a nearby tree he watched as Matthew tore a length of cloth from his sleeve.

After bundling up the material and placing it over the gash on his friend's back, he told Roy to lean back hard against the tree's trunk. "Stay right there. If you can keep pressure on that wound, it'll act as a compress until we can get you to a doctor."

Staring at Dickson's prone body, Roy asked, "Is he dead?"

Matthew knelt down and placed two fingers on the man's throat. Then he shook his head. "No, but he IS knocked out cold."

"Goddamn cheater," Roy grumbled as Matthew tied Earl's hands behind his back.

"How many did you get to before this character had his way with you?" Matthew asked.

"I was doing pretty good," Roy answered. "Got two trussed up back there and hidden in the weeds. I know how you feel about killing, Matthew, but I got to say this one here was going down the hard way or not at all."

The sheriff nodded. "I know, Roy. There was never going to be a way out of this mess without some bloodshed. Speaking of which, I've got to hurry up and find Iris. If you see Tommy, tell him to stand down and wait here with you...that is, if he is still alive."

He stood up and made to leave but Roy stopped him. "Be careful."

Matthew nodded. "I'll be right back," he whispered and moved away into the gloom.

Patrick Donnelly was bothered. First, he kept hearing something like the sound of digging and scraping... *Is the woman escaping?* he wondered. Then he heard the gunshot and cursed himself for a fool. He realized it was too late now to do anything about it, that he had not cautioned his men to be quiet. But the last thing he needed was a bunch of Seattle coppers down here snooping around.

To make matters worse, one of his city boys—a man by the name of Lanny Smith—ran up, gasping for breath.

"Boss!" he said, bending over with his hands on his knees, gulping air. "They're coming in the back way and there must be a dozen of them, if not more!"

Patrick frowned. "A dozen men? You gotta be kidding me!"

"Well, I ain't exactly seen 'em," Smith squealed. "But I know that most of the men we brung are down. I seed it with my own eyes!"

"God-dammit!" Patrick swore, "Get back out there, Smith! What are you waiting for?"

The man took off running again as Patrick heard the sound of wood being dragged across wood. Whirling around, he ground his teeth in frustration. *That godforsaken sheriff must have found his way to where his wife is buried!*

Patrick ran toward the burial site and then slowed down in caution. Creeping forward, he pulled his pistol out of its holster, expecting to see the backside of Sheriff Wilcox. Instead, he saw his sister wrenching the lid up off the coffin.

"What the hell are you doing, you stupid bitch?" he snarled.

Margaret gasped and stood up straight. "Patrick! Oh, you startled me."

"I asked what are you doing?" he snapped.

"Patrick, what *you're* doing is a sin!"

He studied Margaret's face for a moment. He didn't see the beautiful young girl that he used to adore and hold above all others...his beloved sister; the only thing he saw through the red haze of wrath filling his heart was a bony scarecrow of a woman, a wasted life...an old, scrawny whore. His face flushed purple with rage and frustration, and he flinched when she uttered his name—a name he had not heard in decades..."Paddy!"

Margaret stared at her twin brother as he lifted his gun. She didn't see the twisted, bitter old man he had become but the fine, black-haired boyo who had once brought her the finest apples from the orchards and the prettiest seashells from their Irish homeland...the youngster who had risked life and limb to present her with an almost priceless heirloom in order to make her feel better.

Remembering the beautiful ballerina that had once swooped and spun to its own music made her smile and she whispered his name before he shot her dead.

32

THE KISS

PATRICK HEARD A MILLION MOSQUITOES HUMMING ABOUT his head and ears, and he swatted them away with a shout of fright. Then they were gone and a heavy silence ensued. Looking around and blinking in confusion, he realized that his temper had gotten the better of him again.

Trying to recall the last few moments, Patrick stared into the fog and then down at his feet. *What is that?* he wondered.

His sister was lying on top of the coffin, her eyes open wide and staring into eternity. His heart skipped a beat and his own eyes filled with tears.

"Sis, what happened? Who did this to you?" he whispered and sat down heavily on the edge of the plot. The hole wasn't too deep and Patrick was able to straddle the casket easily and pick his sister's limp body up in his arms.

He placed Margaret on the ground and scrambled

back out of the hole. Picking her up again, Patrick stumbled a few feet away, singing an Irish lullaby in her ear and shaking her lightly in frustration.

"Why did you come here, Maggie?" he wept. "See what happens when ye disobey me, colleen?"

Many of Patrick's closest friends knew about his occasional fugue states—those dangerous red moods that swept him up, unknowing, into acts that he would usually not countenance in a man. None of those men or women, however, possessed the nerve to point them out to him lest those tidal urges surge in their direction.

Most times, Patrick would not remember what he'd done during one of his spells and this was no exception. As he rocked back and forth, wailing over the body of his murdered sibling, a tiny portion of his brain was already assigning blame to the deed...a deed that his heart and soul could and would not embrace as his own.

"It was that goddamned sheriff, wasn't it?" he muttered. "Yes! He snuck up here and killed you just for the spite of it...YES!" By now, he was screeching in rage and his fury rose up into the night and echoed madly through the cold, gray fog.

Lanny Smith, the last of Donnelly's hired goons, heard that inarticulate scream and he ran even faster down the street and away from the foul things taking place in the graveyard. Tommy King heard it, too, and turned to Matthew.

"Did ya hear that, sir? Sounds pretty broke up, he does," he muttered.

Matthew nodded. "Yup, I heard it. We have to be really careful now. When a man sounds off like a wounded beast you know that he is at his most dangerous." He paused. "Anyway, I want you to stay here while I go ahead. I don't know how many of Donnelly's men are left now but I need you to cover my back, okay?"

Tommy frowned but, after some thought, finally agreed. "I don't like you going out there on yer own, Mr. Wilcox, but I can see how you might need some eyes behind you."

"Thank you, Tommy," the sheriff replied.

Moving as slowly and quietly as possible, Matthew saw a figure hunched over a dead body on the ground. The man was muttering and moaning, tearing at his face and hair, and telling the prone figure he would get revenge.

Matthew sat down on his heels and listened for a moment. "It was that goddamn sheriff, wasn't it? Well, you just wait, Maggie. I'll get him, you'll see. I'll make him pay for what he done to you."

So, Margaret Donnelly is dead, he thought. No problem as far as he was concerned but he sure hadn't done the deed. Gazing past the hysterical man, Matthew saw a large mound of dirt.

Standing up, he crept around Patrick and stared into the hole. His heart skipped a beat as his eyes studied the casket and the breathing tube sticking out from the lid. *My God... Iris!* He gasped and Patrick looked up.

"Ha! There you are, ya murderous prick!" Without another word, he took a running leap and jumped into the hole in the ground. Laughing maniacally, Patrick stood up with the white rubber tube in his hand.

"See how you like losing someone you love!" he screamed and did a little jig on the coffin.

Matthew heard a slight thumping sound coming from inside the casket and his heart almost stopped. The tube Donnelly held in his wildly waving hand had been a source of air for his wife and now she was asphyxiating! He had to decide—and quickly—whether to talk the madman off the lid of the casket or to just shoot him and haul him out by hand. What would take more time? Sweat popped up on the sheriff's brow as he stood frozen and undecided. Then Patrick made it easy.

An unconscious part of his mind, one that Matthew knew lurked hidden away from view, took over when he saw Donnelly raise his pistol and three shots rang out.

The smell of gunpowder and the sting of smoke filled his nostrils as Matthew jumped into the grave and stared down at Patrick's dead body. Three holes marched horizontally across Donnelly's forehead, each one welling up with blood and trickling slowly down his face to fill the man's open eyes with red tears.

Panicking now that his ears had stopped ringing, Matthew called out, "Iris! Honey, hold on!"

He seized Donnelly by the arms and pulled, grimacing as he saw the blood and brain matter that covered the lid of Iris's coffin. Groaning with the effort, the sheriff could feel a muscle twinge in his lower back as he grunted against the strain.

Then he heard Tommy say, "Holy Jesus, sir! Here, let me give you a hand."

Together he and Matthew pulled the bigger man's lifeless body off the casket and let him fall, wedged between the dug dirt wall and the pine slats of the cheap coffin.

With a cry of fear, Matthew grabbed the front of the lid and tugged with all his might. There was still a lot of soil on the top but it fell away with a hiss as the sheriff heaved and let the wooden plank fall to one side.

Peering inside, Matthew saw his wife covered with streaks of dirt and mud. Her eyes were closed and her face was as pale as a cold, artic moon. One of her hands clutched a thin string that attached to a tiny bell; the other seemed to be frozen in place like a curled claw frantically trying to escape.

Iris was not breathing and Matthew threw his head back, howling in grief.

Matthew lifted his wife out of the casket and placed her on the ground by the head of the burial plot. His eyes were red and dry, the tiny part of what was left of his heart dying along with his beloved Iris. Then he crawled out of the hole and sat by her side.

"Sir, I'm so sorry!" Tommy moaned, then yelled, "Hey, Roy! Mr. Wilcox needs you!"

Matthew glanced up as his deputy came out from the tree line, limping heavily on a makeshift crutch. His best friend stared down at Iris's body and a sorrow Matthew had never seen before filled Roy's eyes as his lips drew down in grief.

"Oh, Mattie," he murmured.

"We have to get her home, Roy." Matthew heard his own voice and felt a chill; he did not sound like himself, as if an utter stranger spoke through his lips. But he was past caring. "Tommy, please head back to the playhouse and have a wagon brought around."

The young man was wringing his cap in his hands, but he nodded. "Yes, sir! Be right back!"

He took off running toward the main entrance but stopped short when a buggy careened around the corner and almost ran him down. The road proper ended about fifty feet away but the carriage kept coming until it was forced to a stop by a line of gravestones and crosses.

Matthew stared as first Amelia, then Gerald—and finally—Lewis Winters stepped down out of the conveyance. Lewis moved as quickly as possible to where he sat by Iris's side. Falling to his knees, he groaned and held his head. Then he looked at Matthew and asked, "How long has she been like this?"

The sheriff bowed his head. "I don't know. I found her this way a couple of minutes ago." A tear escaped from the corner of his eye although he was so numb he didn't feel it.

Lewis frowned and bent over Iris's chest, placing his head down and listening. Then he picked up her wrist and rubbed it against his cheek. His eyes grew wide and he said, "She's still warm, Mattie! I think we can save her."

He stared at his brother-in-law in disbelief but Lewis reached out and gave him a light slap.

"Matthew, wake up, dammit! You have to breathe for her. It's something the Orientals do—I've seen it and it works. But you have to do it now before it's too late!"

Reaching down, Matthew lifted his wife's mouth to his as the people around him gazed in fearful fascination. He breathed into her and watched as his air filled her lungs. Then he did it again…and again and again until he grew dizzy and stars filled his eyes.

"That's right, that's how it's done," Lewis murmured and smiled when Iris shook her head and gasped for air on her own. She flailed her arms and sat up with a little screech of fear, then stared about in a daze until her eyes landed on Matthew.

"Oh, Mattie!" She lunged forward and he enfolded her in his arms, weeping openly in relief.

They rocked together for a moment and those who

watched shook their heads. It had been a long, long night and they all needed sleep; especially Lewis, whose head felt like it might explode. But he was happy, knowing that he had saved his sister and paid the sheriff back a life for a life.

A little while later, the bedraggled procession made their way home.

EPILOGUE

Six weeks later, Matthew sat at his desk looking out the window at the first of the season's snowflakes drifting down from the heavy-laden sky. A fire crackled in the woodstove and he could smell the aroma of bread wafting upstairs from the kitchen. Hearing a squeal of laughter, he moved forward a bit and gazed down at his son Chance and his new deputy, Dicky McNulty. They were building a snowman.

Dicky had moved to Granville a week ago, about a month after recovering from the infection that had almost killed him. He still moved a little slow as the ripped muscles and tendons in his neck and shoulder pained him sometimes. But his was a bright and sunny disposition, one able to overcome and learn from adversity.

Roy was fond of the kid and called him a "game little rooster"—high praise indeed from the sometimes over-critical deputy. Roy also approved of the positive influence little Sarah was having on the once painfully shy Abner. Since she had come to stay, Abner's eyes were brighter, his smile quicker, and his confidence was growing by leaps and bounds.

Iris had even heard talk of marriage bells ringing for the young couple as soon as spring and the thought of it made her flush with pleasure. Glancing over his shoulder, Matthew studied her still form huddled under the quilt on their bed with Bandit curled up at her feet, his long gray muzzle resting on her ankles. He shook his head slightly and looked again at the letter in his hand.

Dear Auntie Iris and Uncle Matthew,

I hope this letter finds you well. I am fine and so is Papa, although he tires easily and sometimes experiences bouts of dizziness. He assures me, however, that he is on the mend.

I hope you do not mind too much, but I think I will stay home with him for now. He misses Mama terribly —as do I—and I think my place is by his side. He is teaching me everything Mama knew and thinks I will do fine as his surgical assistant without formal education. And I, for one, have had enough excitement so am happy to stay here and do my duty as a loving daughter should.

Please, if you decide to come back to Seattle for a visit, know that you and your family are always welcome to stay with us.

I can never repay you for what you did to save me.

Just know that you will always abide deeply in my heart...

   With love and gratitude,
   Amelia Winters

Matthew frowned knowing he did have to go back to Seattle sometime next spring. He had been called in to testify against Sheriff Winslow, a number of Donnelly's henchmen and the crooked police commissioner LeVesque. He had also been asked to stand witness as young Davey Humphries was sworn in as sheriff for the town of Goldbar. Although Matthew relished the idea of all the men getting their just desserts, he was in no hurry to head back to that damp, dark city.

He still couldn't believe they'd gotten away clean that awful night from Potter's Field. After he and the others had arrived back at the playhouse and recovered a bit from the harrowing events, they had boarded the train and fled for home. Once there, Matthew had written a number of letters implicating the wrongdoers in the whole sorry affair, safe in the assumption he and his deputies could—and would—remain free of guilt.

Matthew sighed. He and his family had suffered enough and sacrificed too much to let the law itself trouble them any more than necessary. Folding the letter carefully, he put it where Iris would find it. She would be happy to read her niece's words and know the girl was recovering from her ordeal.

He jumped slightly as the windowpane darkened

with a thump; looking up, he saw snow melting on the glass and realized his son had thrown a snowball at his papa's silhouette.

Standing up with the intention of running downstairs and engaging his son in battle, he stopped when Bandit whined. Iris was tossing and turning in her sleep, crying out in panic; he saw that she was covered in sweat and her hands were like claws, ripping and tearing at the covers.

Matthew ran to her side and gathered her in his arms. Rocking back and forth, he whispered, "Iris, honey...you're okay. You're here with me, safe and sound at home. Shh," he crooned until his wife awoke, sobbing. Bandit had moved to the head of the bed and stared at her with wise, golden eyes. Finally she stopped weeping and stroked the old wolf's head.

Taking a shuddering breath, Iris whispered, "I wish..." She sniffed and wiped her arm across her face. "I just wish these dreams would stop."

Matthew sighed again. He did not know if the memories of being buried alive would ever really go away but he hoped and prayed that—one day—they would fade. Meanwhile, he would love her and keep her until time stopped for both of them.

A LOOK AT DEADMAN'S REVENGE
(THE DEADMAN BOOK III)

In this third book in the Dead Man series, Marshal Matthew Wilcox heads out alone to find and capture one of the worst villains he will ever face.

Heartsick, he traces a convoluted trail of murder, mayhem and deceit... from the high gates of the Walla Walla State penitentiary, to Seattle and on into Billings, Montana.

Although Matthew feels that he must bear the burden of a "deadman's revenge" by himself, he will find help and succor in his travels from his friends, Sheriff Roy Smithers, Deputy Dicky McNulty, Calamity Jane, Liver Eating Johnson... and his son Chance.

Deadman's Revenge- Book three of the best-selling, award-winning series of novels, Deadman's Fury and Deadman's Lament

AVAILABLE NOW ON AMAZON

ABOUT THE AUTHOR

Linell Jeppsen is a writer of science fiction and fantasy. Her vampire novel, *Detour to Dusk*, has received over 44- four and five star reviews. Her novel *Story Time*, with over 130 4-and 5-star reviews, is a science fiction post-apocalyptic novel, and has been touted by the Paranormal Romance Guild, Sandy's Blog Spot, Coffee time Romance, Bitten by Books and 64 top reviewers as a five-star read, filled with terror, love, loss, and the indomitable beauty and strength of the human spirit. *Story Time* was also nominated as the best new read of 2011 by the PRG. Her dark fantasy novel, *Onio* (a story about a half-human Sasquatch who falls in love with a human girl), was released in December 2012 and won 3rd place as the best fantasy romance of 2012 by the PRG reviewers guild. Her novel, *The War of Odds*, won the IBD award for fantasy fiction and boasts 18 5-star reviews since its release in February of 2013. It also placed 2nd, as the best YA paranormal book of 2013 by the PRG.

CPSIA information can be obtained
at www.ICGtesting.com
Printed in the USA
FSHW011524280521
81775FS